# TERI WOODS

PRESENTS

# PREDATORS

...listic tale set in Detroit amidst the late eighties and earl...
...grip you from the opening chapters, and take you on an...
...aked journey.  Set amidst the decline of the tradition...
...ooth hustlers, and the emerging times of the drug lord...
...ologies, the streets of Mowtown finds itself thrust into...
...een the old ways and t...
...liances are made and br...
...y.  Masochism and sadis...
...ig, and pray that your su...
...only two things; Predat...

## STORY BY ACE

*Teri Woods Publishing Presents, Predators*

**Note:**

*This novel is a work of fiction. Any resemblance to real people, living or dead, actual events, establishments, organizations, and/or locales are intended to give the fiction a sense of reality and authenticity. Other names, characters, places and incidents are either products of the author's imagination or are used fictitiously, as are those fictionalized events & incidents that involve real persons and did not occur or are set in the future.*

Published by:
**TERI WOODS PUBLISHING**
P.O. Box 20069
New York, NY  10001-0005
www.teriwoodspublishing.com

Library of Congress Catalog Card No: 2006902431
ISBN:  0-9773234-0-4
Copyright:  TXu1-234-165

**Predators Credits**

Story by Ace for TWP
Edited by Teri Woods
Text formation by Teri Woods
Cover concept by Lucas Riggins

Printed by Teri Woods Publishing

Printed in the USA

# TERI WOODS

PRESENTS

# PREDATORS

STORY BY ACE

# PREDATORS

JULY 2000.

Sitting alone inside the plush, *LaPlaya's Lounge*, Larry Westin glanced quickly around at his surroundings, then at the front door. Outside, he could see the summer sun fading fast beyond a reddish orange horizon.

The few people inside the bar were in a jovial mood as they kicked the game around and waited for the regulars to fill up the room so the games could begin.

Larry tried to relax, but something about the entire setup just didn't sit right with him.

He couldn't explain it; he just had a strong feeling that made him uneasy. He knew he should have never left his piece at the crib, regardless of Angela's warning. It went totally against his principles as a pretty-pimping gangsta.

*Maybe*, he told himself for the second time since entering the bar, *I should just get right up and split.* He could hit Thad and BJ up later on and explain why he decided to leave instead of hanging around for them like planned. Knowing them, they would probably be high right now anyway.

Not that he didn't respect the two men or value their opinion; the fact remained, that he alone had the final say-so, and whether they agreed with his decisions or not, he

1

was calling the shots. If they didn't like it, it was too bad as there was nothing they could do about it.

Leaders in their own right, both Thad and BJ had crews of their own, but they decided to play subservient roles to Larry out of respect. He was the undisputed boss even though there had never been any kind of formal vote designating him as such. It was more or less an unwritten, unspoken, mutual agreement.

Although the three men had known each other prior to being sent to Jackson State Prison, they bonded while serving time there. They hung out together, ate together, and planned and schemed together. They had big plans for the day they got out of the joint. By the time their sentences were up, they hooked back up and began to set the wheels in motion. They took over the city of Detroit, the city where they had been born and raised. 'Don't stop until you reach the top' became their official slogan and they had no plans of doing nothing less than reaching the top.

Detroit was a high-rolling town known for its fast pace automobile industry and black population. Sitting just across from Canada, only the Detroit River separates the two. During the hey-days of Prohibition, Jewish and Italian mobsters used the river to transport tons of illegal bootleg liquor back into the United States. On occasion, it was used as a burial ground to dump the bullet-riddled bodies of slain rivals.

Detroit also had a reputation for being the launching pad for several prominent black movements and powerful black politicians like Coleman Young, a visionary who, as its controversial mayor; once ruled the city with an iron fist.

In recent years, however, the Motor City had gained the dubious distinction of being one of the nation's foremost murder capitals, a phenomenon, that can best be attributed to a wide range of social and economic factors. It was also because it no longer had a strong mayor who controlled the criminal underworld.

When the trio hit the bricks, they wasted little time

2

putting their plans into motion. They started out by squeezing small-time drug dealers, eventually working their way up to the real shot callers. Any and all resistance was met with deadly and overwhelming force. Their victims were kidnapped and tortured. They were even photographed being raped or performing sex acts with animals. Most of these men who had been ruthless killers left town in shame and disgrace; never to return. They would simply disappear if they still refused to cooperate.

Glancing down at his diamond-covered Patek Phillippe, Larry saw that it was approaching 8:00. Soon, the spot would be coming alive with the sights and sounds of Detroit's colorful black underworld.

Gangstas and playas draped in designer threads and flashy jewelry would be pulling up in expensive cars, ready to spend money and talk shit. These symbols of success gave them status and power. As to be expected, many people lost their lives – and took the lives of others – in the pursuit of this wealth.

He was so caught up in his thoughts, that Larry never saw the two men enter the bar carrying 9 millimeter pistols. The people nearest the exit saw what was about to go down and almost ran each other over, trying to get out of the way.

As the gunmen closed in, Larry was sorry he didn't leave when he had the chance. *Only God can save me now*, he thought wildly.

But God didn't save him and neither did anyone else. As the first shots rang out, those left inside the bar scattered like cockroaches. Amid the yelling and confusion, the shooters took care of their business and made good on their escape. Not a single soul attempted to help Larry. He was left lying on the cold, marble floor, his life and bodily fluids slowly leaking out, forming a huge pool of thick, dark red blood beneath him.

Lying there helpless, Larry thought about the good life

and asked himself if the ride had been worth it. In his wildest imagination; he never thought he would live like a king only to be shot down like a dog and left to die among strangers. His plan had been to go out in style.

He could hear approaching footsteps and wondered if his assassins were coming back to deliver the coup de grâce. If so, it would be an act of mercy on their part to spare him the final indignity of suffering before he died.

Out of nowhere, greedy hands appeared, snatching and grabbing. He could feel his jewelry being removed from his fingers, wrists, and from around his neck. But the last thing he remembered before the darkness took over, was his pants pockets being ripped off, as the crowd of human vultures robbed him without remorse or shame.

Outside, cruising slowly by, was a steel gray Cadillac. Behind the steering wheel was BJ. Sitting right next to him was his right-hand man, Thad. They had been sent to make sure all went according to plan.

# CHAPTER ONE

## THE EAST SIDE OF DETROIT, 1988

A crowd of young boys gathered on the grimey street corner and were busy rapping along with the latest hit by Rakim.

Their gear consisted of Kangols, Adidas tracksuits, white leather Adidas sneakers, and thick ass gold ropes that they wore proudly around their necks as a testament to their up-and-coming playa status.

A bright yellow Mustang, full of white youths, pulled up to the curb. They were making one of their daily excursions from the lily-white suburbs, to the almost exclusively black ghetto to purchase crack cocaine and heroin.

"Who goin' serve them white boys?" asked one of the older boys in the group. His name was Bobby Jackson, BJ for short. By the tone and authority in his voice, it was obvious he called the shots.

"I got 'em," volunteered this short stocky youth who sported cornrows under his Kangol. His name was Thaddeus Jones, but everyone called him Thad.

Making his way cautiously to the car, Thad glanced around, checking for five-o. The rest of his boys got in position in case they had to bust their gats. They had been jacked before.

"Yo, what up? You fellows got those big ass boulders

ya'll had earlier?" asked a chubby white guy.

Thad inched up to the car and peeped inside. "What the fuck you talkin' 'bout, Fat Boy?"

Fat Boy looked like he was about to shit in his pants. "Yo man, we don't want any static," he groveled.

"What's up with this 'yo' shit?" Thad asked. "You stupid motherfuckas ain't in New York. Y'all is in the big motherfuckin' D which means you better watch yo' pink ass. How many stones y'all want?"

Another white youth in the car quickly spoke up. He wanted to get the hell out of there. He recognized the deadly gleam in Thad's eyes and knew what that meant. "Give us ten; twenty-dollar pieces. We'll be back if this shit is tight."

Glancing around once more, Thad took out a small brown pouch. Inside it were tiny plastic vials filled with a yellowish white rock substance that had been broken down into smaller, individual pieces.

"Set the dough out," Thad said with authority.

The money was handed through the car window. After counting it to make sure it was all there, Thad handed over the drugs then beat a hasty retreat. He never liked dealing with white people from the suburbs; although he loved taking their money. He didn't trust them. Plus, he knew that if a bust went down, all the weight would fall on him, a black selling dope to whites. Shit, he'd be lucky if he ever saw day light.

As the Mustang pulled off, Thad remarked to BJ, "Man, I hate those stankin' ass crackers."

"Whadda ya trippin' 'bout nigga? We got the money. Listen, I got a run to make."

Thad, a couple of years younger than his idol, looked up to BJ, seeing in him the big brother he never had. All his life he had to take care of himself. There was nobody he could trust. At school when other kids capped on him about his looks; he wasn't the best-looking kid in school; he didn't have a big brother to run to. He had to handle it on his own. But it made him stronger and more independent, giving credence to the age-old adage that what didn't kill you, made you stronger. Even so, Thad was filled with bitterness. It really hurt to be picked on.

After telling his crew he'd check back with them, BJ walked around the corner and got behind the steering wheel of a mint green Benz. This was his pride and joy. Whenever he sat behind the control panel, he felt like he was about to take off in a spacecraft. The ride was smooth as silk, like floating on a cloud up in heaven. There wasn't anything like riding in a Mercedes Benz.

Turning right on Townsend Street, BJ pulled the car up in front of a rundown two-family building sitting in the middle of the block. He blew the car horn twice. Minutes later, a small-framed, brown-skinned girl came bouncing down the steps and ran straight up to the car.

"It's about time your ass got here," she said with a big smile. "What took you so long?"

He smiled back. "Get your lil' ass in and quit talkin' shit. I got places to go and people to see."

He watched her climb in beside him and liked what he saw. Even though her clothes weren't new or the latest fashion, BJ didn't care. *By the time I'm through moldin' her,* he thought, *she'll be a dime piece for real!*

"So, what's up?" she asked. Her name was Chaquita Williams, but everyone called her Chi Chi. She was certainly a dime piece; she was pretty, but not breathtaking, and she had a tomboyish, gangsta kind of attitude. Most men were intimidated by that. But she was just BJ's type. Her attitude impressed the hell out of him.

"Whadda you want to be up?" he asked.

"It depends," she said.

"You don't really wanna fuck wit' me baby," he joked.

"Why not?"

"Cause I'm a gangsta and a thug."

"And?"

"I'll kick your lil' ass and take your money."

She smiled mischievously. "What if I ain't got none for

you to take?  Whatchu goin' do then, Mr. Gangsta?"

He couldn't help but smile.  "So you wanna be a comedian, eh?  Is that it?"

Staring directly at him she said, "I can be whatever you want me to be."

Pulling up to a red light, he returned her stare and ran his eyes over her body, allowing his gaze to rest between her legs. He was still staring when the light suddenly switched to green.

"I thought you said you had places to go?" she asked. "Or maybe you just wanna sit here starin' between my legs?"

He grinned then eased the Benz across the busy intersection, his mind filled with lewd images of the girl beside him naked and spread-eagled on his king-sized bed.

Turning to glance out the window, Chi Chi stared at the little kids playing on the broken glass and discarded hypodermic needles scattered on the sidewalks and wondered how it felt to be a child without a care in the world. Her own childhood had been full of so much unhappiness. Since she could remember her mother had struggled to make ends meet. As a result; she was forced to grow up faster than most children.

She also saw the shabbily dressed wineose and crack heads wandering aimlessly through the city streets, searching for their next high. Their entire lives were reduced to getting high, having sex, and taking care of their body functions. At that precise moment, Chi Chi made up her mind that she would never end up like that.

She knew she was taking a hell of a chance messing around with a guy like BJ. Although he was still young himself, he nevertheless was a major baller in Detroit's violent and unpredictable dope game, and he handled a big bankroll.  To a girl like Chi Chi, who had grown up poor in the ghetto, BJ was just what she was looking for. So she was willing to take a chance. The way she saw it, she had everything to gain and nothing to lose, except the chains of poverty that kept her imprisoned in the ghetto.

As for BJ, he kept his eyes on the road and his mind on all the kinky things he planned on doing to the young girl sitting beside him, just as soon as he could get her to his apartment.

# CHAPTER TWO

"Girl, come outta that shit! You act like you're ashamed of what yo' mama gave you."

Chi Chi smiled seductively. "I ain't ashamed. I just don't wanna be one of your fly-by-night cum catchers."

"What do you want, Chi Chi?"

"I want the same thing you want, money and power. And I'm willin' to do whatever it takes to get it."

For a moment BJ fell silent as though he was in deep thought. The more he learned about the young girl in the room with him, the more he liked her. She was ambitious and game for anything, which could be a plus or a minus; depending on how you played her. Finally he spoke.

"I'll tell you what. I'll give you Glenda's clientele. You should be able to handle that. It's nothin' but a bunch of squares tryin' to be hip, postal workers, secretaries, hairdressers, entertainers, that kind of shit. I'll pay you ten gees a week."

All Chi Chi heard was, 'ten gees'. "Everything else BJ said might as well had been said in Chinese. Barely able to contain her excitement, the wheels inside her scheming little mind were busy spinning like a Las Vegas roulette wheel.

*In no time at all,* she told herself happily, *I'll be able to leave the crib and get as far away from Billy's pussy-eatin' ass as I can. And to think he has the nerve to call himself my step-daddy.*

*Betty Jean must be a god damn fool to trust that freak*

10

*ass nigga around me*, she thought grimly. *What the hell is wrong with my momma? Ain't no way she don't know what he be doin' to me.* Each and every time Betty Jean left the house, Billy made a beeline to Chi Chi's bedroom to bow down before the awesome power of her young, tight pussy.

"You don't have to give me your answer right away," BJ said, interrupting her train of thought. "Take some time and think about it."

"I already did," Chi Chi said hurriedly then began seductively unbuttoning her blouse. BJ watched her through eyes full of pent up lust. "I only got one question."

"What is it?"

"What about Glenda? Whadda ya gon' do wit' her?"

"Fuck Glenda! I'll put her in charge of the beauty salon. Maybe her fake ass can handle that."

Smiling coquettishly, Chi Chi removed her blouse, revealing a perfect set of twin breasts, topped by erect nipples that were begging to be sucked and licked. BJ's eyes devoured the sight before him.

Next, came her black miniskirt, sliding down her soft hips, followed by black lace panties. Finally she was naked, a painting come to life to be admired and loved.

BJ was mesmerized. Chi Chi had a natural beauty that seemed to glow with a heavenly brightness. She realized what she had, and was unafraid to use it to her advantage.

"Turn around and let me see that ass, baby."

All her bashfulness gone, Chi Chi turned around slowly, allowing BJ to get a good look at what she was bringing to the table. But, BJ wanted to do much more than simply look. And he did. All-night long.

■■■■■■■■■■■■■■■■■■■■■■■■■■■■■■■■■■■■■■■■■■■■■■■■■■■■■■

"Thad, I'm tellin' you man, this cat, Busta, got mo' nerve than a brass-ass monkey. He sent some of his boys down here talkin' that shit about they can sell rocks wherever they wanna, and ain't no nigga gon' tell them different," said the voice on the other end of the line.

That's all Thad needed to hear. "Okay, I'll be through in a few. Tell the fellas I said to just be cool 'til I get there. Them niggas must got a death wish or something."

Punching in a new set of digits on his cell phone, Thad entered a phone booth on the corner and stood inside, reflecting over the current events. He wondered if it might lead to murder. He hoped it wouldn't, but if that's the way it went down, so be it.

A few minutes later the phone rang. Picking up the receiver he heard BJ's voice. "Wassup, Thad?"

"Dig this, dawg. That chump, Busta, must be trippin'. He sent Raymond and a few other punks down here tryin' to lay somethin' down. Can you believe that shit?"

BJ wasn't impressed. He had other things on his mind. He spoke in a calm, measured voice.

"Handle it. Right now I gotta check somethin' else out. I think I got a handle on a new line. If it checks out, we can say fuck the Mexicans. We'll be rollin' like Escobar."

Listening closely, Thad's ears perked up. "Is that right?"

"It is indeed. Hit me back after you take care of that."

"Don't worry, it's a done deal," Thad assured him.

Jumping into his black jeep; Thad took a shortcut, and navigated the car through the hood and headed for their spot. As soon as he arrived, he noticed all the new faces. He assumed they were Busta's people.

Up and down the avenue his own guys lay in a deadly ambush waiting on his order. All he had to do was give the word and bodies would start dropping.

Double-parking his jeep right next to Raymond's blue Lexus, Thad got out and began walking in his direction. He looked like an enraged pit bull. Raymond was dressed in blue with a white straw hat and a blue band. He watched as Thad approached and tried not to panic.

"What's up nigga?" Thad asked, his eyes red like fire. He was hoping he wouldn't have to commit murder in front

12

of so many people. You never know who's going to squeal to the cops.

"How's it goin', Thad?"

Deep down inside, Raymond was scared to death. He had seen Thad's work on several occasions and didn't want any part of it. Yet, he couldn't afford to show any fear. He was Busta's top lieutenant with a crew of young and crazy gunslingers under him. If he ever lost their respect, they would chew his ass up alive and spit out the pieces.

"You must be outta yo' rabbid ass mind!" Thad shouted. His entire body was trembling with rage. "Don't you know who you fuckin' wit'?"

"Take it easy man," Raymond muttered. "Busta sent us. It's enough money down here for all of us." As soon as the words left his mouth, he knew he said the wrong thing. Thad wasn't the type you could reason with.

The open-handed slap came out of nowhere. It was so loud and unexpected, it sounded like a gunshot going off. Raymond's hat flew off his head as he stumbled backward into a clump of bushes, rubbing the side of his jaw.

Before any of Raymond's men had a chance to react or come to their boss's rescue, the sound of automatic weapons being cocked could be heard up and down the street as Thad's people came from out of their hiding places. Up on the rooftop of several adjacent buildings, a few guys on Thad's team pointed rifles down at the scene below.

Looking around, Raymond realized he had led his boys into a death trap. His head was in the lion's jaw; now he had to find a way to ease it out gently before the lion decided to snap it off.

"Dig, Thad," he said, his voice beginning to crack. "Man, we go back a long way. You know I would never do anythin' to disrespect you. I was just followin' orders. Busta said it was cool to get down over here. He said y'all wouldn't mind 'cause all of us are supposed to be cool with one another."

"That pussy ass nigga! Busta sent you fools on a

suicide mission. I should kill you, but I respect that you too damn dumb to recognize game. Get your punk ass outta here before I change my mind. And take those lil' pissy tail niggas wit' you."

Spinning on the balls of his feet, Thad marched back to his jeep, climbed in, and drove off leaving behind a cloud of dust and exhaust fumes.

The next night Raymond struck back, catching Thad off guard as he came out of his baby's mama's house over in the Brewster Projects. As he walked down the sidewalk to his car all that could be heard was the thunderous sound of gun fire targeted at Thad. A bullet struck him in the chest piercing the bullet proof vest he was wearing. Even still, he felt the pain of the thud as he fell to the ground. He breathed deeply and rolled next to a park car for safety. Seconds later, the gun fire ceased and all was silent. *Damn, these niggas tried to kill me for real. Is they fuckin' crazy? They must not know no better,* he thought to himself.

His jeep was not so lucky. It was shot full of holes.

# CHAPTER THREE

In the dead of the night, Thad woke up from a deep sleep. He was drenched in sweat. His entire body was wringing wet. After a six-month grace period, the dreams were back. Just when he thought they'd gone away, they had returned in full funky bloom.

Forcing himself out of the bed and into the bedroom, he splashed cold water on his face, then squeezed some toothpaste on his toothbrush and ran it around the inside of his dry mouth, brushing away last night's taste of gin and stale cigarettes. Standing in front of the mirror, he gazed at his reflection and couldn't help but notice the 'nobody home' look in his vacant eyes.

*Maybe I am crazy,* he thought as he remembered what the doctor told his mother. Wasn't long after that doctor's visit she was found dead in an alley, a deep gash in her throat. *"No please! Thad!"* Thad slit her throat in a moment of rage; but it was unintentional. He thought about the catholic school where he had been raped by his priest. *Father God will bless you my child, come here.* Oh, how he blamed his mother. It was all her fault, everything that happened to him there was all her fault. *She should have never left me there,* he reasoned. Perhaps that's why he never felt any remorse or guilt whenever he ordered a hit or murdered someone. All of these thoughts and much more, ran slowly through his mind as he stood there staring in the

15

mirror lost in deep contemplation.

He was pulled back into reality by the ringing of the phone in his bedroom. Walking back into the room, he picked up the receiver and was greeted by his sister's voice.

"Thad, why you didn't get back in touch with me like you promised? Did you forget something?"

Annoyed, Thad said sharply, "Don't start with your bullshit, Brenda. It's too fuckin' early. You ain't even asked a nigga how he's doin'."

"Well, excu-u-use me!" Brenda said with an attitude.

Sighing deeply, Thad sat down on the bed. His day wasn't starting out so good. "Whadda you need, Brenda?"

"Personally? I'm straight. But Shanette and Kamal need new clothes for the summer. They've outgrown their old clothes. These kids are sproutin' up like beans."

"Where's your fuckin' man? When's that coward gon' step up and take care of his responsibilities?"

"Thad, you don't have to go there," Brenda said, not wanting to argue. "You got everybody on the East-side scared of you and you wanna know why I can't keep no man? You must've forgot how you pistol-whipped Kamal's father."

"But damn," Thad protested, "The nigga needed it."

"Yeah, accordin' to you, but whadda 'bout me? Did you ever stop to think that I might have loved him?"

"Fuck him. I take good care of y'all," Thad reasoned.

"I know and I really appreciate it," Brenda said.

"How much do you need?"

"A couple of grand would be cool."

"Fine. I'll drop it off soon as I get through makin' my rounds. By the way, how's my niece and nephew?"

Brenda made a clucking sound with her tongue. "Child, those two muhfuckers is driving me crazy! They so fuckin' hard headed. I can't get them to listen. Mr. Spanky makes 'em listen though."

Thad laughed. "Girl, don't be hittin' on my babies. Little kids are supposed to be bad. That's normal."

Suddenly Brenda's voice took on a new flavor as she

16

turned serious. "You know Thad, it's all over the city about what went down last night. You could have gotten killed"

"You mean what almost went down," Thad corrected her. "A nigga's got to get up early in the mornin' to catch me slippin'."

"Thad, your birthday's next month. You'll be nineteen. Boy, you haven't even begun to live yet."

"You act like I'm getting' ready to die."

"Niggas was trying to kill you just last night, hello! By the way; me and BJ are plannin' on rentin' a yacht for your birthday. We'll go cruisin' along the riverfront. We'll make it a private affair."

"Y'all ain't gotta do all that," Thad protested, but Brenda wasn't buying it.

Pausing to reflect over his sister's words, Thad realized that he was only eighteen with a hundred grand in his stash. Not bad for a young man not yet out of his teens, he reasoned. By the time he was twenty-one; he planned to retire with a couple of million to play with. Maybe he would start promoting concerts. Suddenly he thought about his mother.

"You know, if mama was still here, she'd be so proud of you," Brenda said, as though she was reading her brother's mind. "Especially, for how you look out for me."

"You must be psychic. I was just thinkin' about her. As for lookin' out, what other choice do I got? You're blood."

"Thad, please take care of yourself. We need you."

"I keep tellin' you I'm straight!" He barked more confident than he really felt. "Ain't nothin' gon' happen to me."

"Lil' brotha, you know I love you."

"Yeah sis, I love you too. Relax, it's all good."

∎∎∎∎∎∎∎∎∎∎∎∎∎∎∎∎∎∎∎∎∎∎∎∎∎∎∎∎∎∎∎∎∎∎∎∎∎∎∎∎∎∎∎∎∎∎∎∎∎∎∎∎

Around 6:00 o'clock that evening, Thad caught up with BJ and a few of the homies at a restaurant on the corner of Gratiot and McDougal. They were sitting inside a parked van in the restaurant's parking lot.

Pulling up in a black Audi, Thad parked next to the van and got out. He walked around the front of his car and tapped softly on the side of the van.

Sitting in the passenger seat was this dude named Winky. Under the steering wheel was Bay Bay. Bay Bay's real name was Lonnie Taylor. Thad had attended Kettering High with both of them but still didn't trust them, not when it came to the murder game.

"Get in, my nigga," Winky said, trying to be cool.

Peeping inside, Thad saw BJ sitting in the backseat next to the door on the far side. On the seat beside him was a large cardboard box.

As soon as Thad climbed in the van, his nostrils were immediately assaulted by the raw stench of fresh blood. He glanced down at the box.

"Open it," BJ said casually.

Thad lifted the top. Inside the box was a pair of bloody hands and feet that had obviously been severed from a body.

Glancing at BJ, Thad put the lid back down on the box. "Where's the rest of the body?" he asked.

BJ grinned. "The head's in a sewer somewhere on the West-side. We're going to scatter the rest of this shit around the city. Hopefully, the rats will eat it up."

Glancing over his shoulder, Bay Bay cracked, "Don't you wanna know the dead man's identity?"

"For what?" Thad asked. "I ain't trippin', ya'll niggas the ones ridin' around with dead feet and hands. You need to be tryin' to get rid of this stinkin' ass shit before five-o pull us over on GP and we end the fuck up in jail. You know how they play a nigga, especially the 7th Precinct."

BJ nodded at the driver, who immediately started the van's engine then pulled off, making a sharp right on Gratiot Avenue.

"Take the backstreets," BJ ordered. "What remains of your man, Busta, is in that box. The nigga that pulled the

18

trigger on you last night also took a little trip by way of Sandusky."

The two men up front snickered. They were beginning to annoy Thad. "What's so fuckin' funny?" he asked sharply, knowing that if they got caught, they more than likely would be the fisrt to snitch.

"By the way," said BJ, "Raymond works for us now. He seen the light and decided to ride with the strength instead of tryin' to go against it."

"It's the smart thing to do if you love breathin'. But I don't trust his traitor ass. Any man that'll cross a former friend will do the same to us."

"No doubt about it," BJ agreed. "Don't worry; first time the nigga even look wrong, he'll be joinin' his former boss in La La Land."

As the four men drove down the backstreets discarding their grisly cargo, neither one of them could have possibly foreseen the terrible price they would soon pay.

# CHAPTER FOUR

Chaquita Williams was born in Detroit's Receiving Hospital at 1:00 a.m. in the spring of 1971. Her mother nicknamed her Chi Chi.

She never knew her real father, just a steady steam of black men who told her it was okay to call them Daddy. Not all of them molested her, but of those who did, Billy Jameson was perhaps the worst of the bunch.

He started abusing her when she was 12. It continued until she met BJ and moved out of her mother's house. At the time, Chi Chi was 17 and BJ was almost 22.

A gang leader at the age of 15, BJ was already a legend at 22 and well on his way to becoming one of the youngest millionaires in Detroit. All he had to do was stay alive to enjoy it.

Growing up on Detroit's East-Side, BJ's life revolved around shoot-outs, hustling for dollars, and hanging out on the street corners with his homies rapping.

But all that changed the summer BJ went off to New York to stay with his mother until school started. When he returned to Detroit, he had a brand-new attitude.

While in New York, he had been impressed by the fact that kids nine and eleven were walking around with fat bankrolls they got from selling drugs on the streets. BJ realized that the court system–at least, at that particular time-was far more lenient on juvenile offenders than it was on adults. So as a result; dudes decided to hide behind

20

young boys, putting a dope sack in their hands, then sending them out onto the streets. That's how BJ got the idea for YGS, a catchy euphemism for the Young Gangsta's Society.

It was a simple conversion process to turn the members of his gang into a full-fledged drug enterprise. Almost overnight, they went from cracking heads for fun, to selling crack for profit, and the money rolled in real fast.

BJ had never handled that kind of paper in his life, and neither had any of the other kids down on his team. They spent the money like water going down the drain.

The nickel slick jewelers down at the Greenfield Shopping Plaza loved to see them coming through the front door, anticipating huge commissions. BJ personally never spent less than a hundred grand buying watches and gold chains for his crew members and for the various little cutie pies he was freaking with. That's how he met Larry Westin, one of the smoothest OGs in the city.

Larry took him under his wing and showed him how to invest the money he was raking in, using relatives and people he could trust to set up and run legitimate enterprises. His only request was that these silent partners be squeaky-clean without criminal records.

But the most valuable lesson that Larry taught BJ was how to manage people effectively. In a few short years BJ was able to tighten up and organize his group into one of the most efficient, deadliest organizations to ever grace the city of Detroit.

"Look bitch!" Chi Chi screamed at the frightened young woman standing in front of her. "I done already told you I ain't acceptin' no shorts. Now you can either go get the rest of the money or do like I told you. And you ain't got no long time to make up your rabbid ass mind either."

The girl Chi Chi was screaming on was pretty, light-skinned, with jet black wavy hair that hung halfway down her back. They called her Lisa, but her name was Mona. Lisa was added on because of her exotic beauty.

Chi Chi hated Lisa's guts. Not only was she pretty, she walked the earth thinking she was better than somebody all because she grew up in Sherwood Forest, an exclusive Detroit suburb. Failing in private school, her parents decided to send her the local public school and that's where Chi Chi first met Lisa.

Lisa's first week at Southeastern High ended in two catfights complete with hair pulling, screaming, and name-calling. Throughout most of their time in high school, Chi Chi went out of her way to make life miserable for Lisa, who in turn bent over backwards to find acceptance, even to the point of becoming promiscuous. A few years later, came the crack explosion, and in the vicious circle they traveled in, you either used the drug or sold it. Chi Chi tried it once, but she got sick to her stomach. Not only that, but she was too ambitious to get caught up on crack. Lisa's will wasn't that strong; plus she wanted people to accept her. So, it was relatively easy to trick her into hitting the pipe and once she did, it was all over. She went from sugar to shit overnight.

Her hair, once her pride and joy, suffered from months of neglect. She could care less about her appearance or her hygiene. The drug she consumed daily had become a part of her digestive system, embedding itself in the pores of her skin. Although Chi Chi enjoyed witnessing Lisa's fall from grace, it still wasn't enough. Her diabolical mind reflected back to when they were still in high school. There had been this boy named Wilbur Reed whom Chi Chi was desperately in love with, but Wilbur had his sights set on Lisa. But the more he pursued her, the more Lisa rejected him.

Then one night at a house party where everyone was falling down drunk, Wilbur asked Lisa if she wanted him to take her home. To his surprise, Lisa said, yes. Even before they left the party, she had already made up her mind to give him her pussy.

After that night wild horses couldn't have held Wilbur back. He had consummated his fondest dream by having sex with 'Mona Lisa' his goddess of love. His nose was open so wide, a Mack truck could have driven right through to his brain. But Lisa didn't want anything else to do with him. She only let him fuck her because she was drunk. Plus, she was sick and tired of him following her around like a lovesick puppy. It turned out to be one of the biggest mistakes she had ever made. Now there was no getting rid of him.

He called her every hour on the hour professing his undying love for her. He swore that he would do anything she asked of him; all she had to do was say the word. When that didn't work, he threatened to kill himself. One particular night he called and as usual, he began his conversation with his wild declaration of love. Lisa was so fed up with him; that she told him to get lost. As to be expected, Wilbur threatened to kill himself.

"Well, kill yourself, damn it! Go jump off a fucking bridge why don't you? Just leave me the hell alone. I don't want you, not now or ever. I can't stand you and I wish you'd leave me alone."

There was a long silence and then there was the sound of a single gunshot. In shock, Lisa called a 911 operator who dispatched an ambulance to Wilbur's residence and a half-hour later the police where at her door. Poor, love-stricken, Wilbur Reed had been found on the floor of his apartment, dead from a self-inflicted gunshot to the head.

For weeks, Lisa was overwhelmed with guilt. She had no feelings for him; but yet she blamed herself for Wilbur's suicide even though the psychiatrist her parents paid to counsel her tried his best to convince Lisa otherwise. He claimed that Wilbur was a weak, unstable boy who more than likely would have taken his own life under some other pretense sooner or later. But, when Chi Chi learned the details of what had happened to her beloved Wilbur, her hatred for Lisa took on even greater dimensions. She was

23

hoping that maybe Wilbur would loose interest in Lisa and she would have a chance. Now that he had killed himself it would never happen.

"Well, Miss Thang, whatchu gon' do? I ain't got all night." Chi Chi stood there with her tiny hands on her hips, her mind bent on revenge.

Desperate, Lisa pleaded with her. "Chi Chi, why are you doing me like this? You know I'll pay you back as soon as I get my allowance."

"That's not the point. Now, I'm gon' ask you one last time. Do you wanna freak for some of this shit or do you still think your pussy is made outta gold?"

Blinded by the hot, stinging tears rolling down her face, Lisa reluctantly threw away her last ounce of pride and self-respect. Her craving for the drug outweighed her so-called morals.

"What do you want me to do?"

Chi Chi's brown eyes darted around the room. She was in a dangerous mood. Glenda had already been instructed to close the Style-A-Rama Beauty Salon earlier than usual, so a meeting could be held in the back room. Since becoming BJ's lover, Chi Chi had moved up in the ranks, earning her respect in bed and on the streets. In her own unique way she had convinced BJ that she could hold her own.

Just as they were about to lock up for the night, Lisa had come running up to the door demanding to speak to Chi Chi. She was fiening and didn't have any money. Chi Chi gave her a choice, come up with the money or trade sex for drugs.

"Who wanna fuck this bitch?" Chi Chi asked, searching the faces of the four men in the room with her.

Melvin, a kid of about sixteen, smiled and said, "Not me, Chi Chi. I don't like high yella women." He knew just what to say to stay on Chi Chi's good side. Everyone was afraid of Chi Chi, especially his little young ass.

While she was being offered around the room, Lisa

24

stood there in disbelief. She felt like a slave standing on the auction block about to be sold to the highest bidder. It was hard for her to stand there as she looked at the men's faces eyeing her around the room.

"How 'bout you, Lil' Greg?" Chi Chi asked some boy who didn't look a day over thirteen. He wore a Kangol backward and a pair of dark shades. He looked Lisa up and down, admiring the lingering traces of beauty being destroyed by the ravaging effects of drug abuse.

"Well," questioned Chi Chi, "Do you wanna hit the bitch or what? You act like the cat got your tongue."

Lil' Greg stood there staring at Chi Chi. She was simply too gangsterish for his taste. He never liked women who thought they were just as much a gangsta as a man.

"Nah, I think I'll pass," he said quietly not trying to play Chi Chi's game.

Chi Chi's eyes burned with hatred, mad at the fact no one bit at her offer. She wanted Lisa to be humiliated, used and fucked over so she could be discarded as nothing but a whore.

"Go get Champ," Chi Chi instructed.

Melvin left the room and returned with a large German shepherd. "How 'bout you, boy?" Chi Chi asked the dog as though it could understand. "Do you wanna do this slut?"

As if in answer, the dog happily wagged its tail, stuck out a long red tongue dripping in saliva, then barked loudly. Lisa felt the hairs on the back of her neck stand up. She told herself that this couldn't be happening.

Lil' Greg was thoroughly convinced that Chi Chi was insane when he heard her tell Lisa, "Well, whadda ya waitin' on ho? Come on outta them drawers and entertain us. When you get through, I might throw you an eight ball."

*Damn, that's a lot of coke,* Lisa contemplated.

"Come on, whatchu gonna do?" Lisa asked as if her offer was the greatest thing since sliced bread.

Slowly Lisa began removing her clothes. Chi Chi and the other's in the room watched as the dog began to sniff at Lisa's naked body, nudging his nose between her naked legs and licking at her pussy. One would have thought the sight of beastiality would have been too much, but no one left the room and no one stopped the dog and no one felt a thing for Lisa, except for Chi Chi who grinned on the inside. *No one will ever want this whore, I made sure of that. Don't worry Wilbur, I got her back baby, I got her back.*

# CHAPTER FIVE

Larry Westin had always been popular among his peers, but his popularity among the women who idolized him as though he was a black celebrity, was nothing less than extraordinary. They literally swooned over him.

Standing around five feet; eleven inches; with a thirty inch waistline, Larry had long eyelashes, thick black hair, and a flawless skin complexion that made him appear feminine. To counter any suspicions that he was soft, he had long ago mastered the technique of knocking a man out cold with one punch. If that wasn't enough to prove his masculinity, he was more than willing to take it to another, more deadlier level.

He couldn't say exactly how he learned to do hair; all he knew is that growing up he had spent hours watching his mom do his sister's hair. Out of ten siblings, eight of them were girls. Larry and his younger brother, Bobby, were the only males in the family. He was the eldest and Bobby was the baby. Their old man had been slain long ago. Technically speaking, this made Larry the man of the house, a responsibility he took very seriously.

His first barbershop was in the basement of his mother's home. Luckily for him, two of his partners broke into the Barber College up on Gratiot Avenue late one Sunday night and made off with two barber chairs, hair clippers, and tons of other accessories. Everything was loaded onto a stolen truck and carted off into the night. Thanks to his friends, he had everything he needed to open Club Clippers; in his momma's basement.

Although every day was a good day for Larry and his newly established business, things really boomed on the weekend when the eagle was flying high and everybody had a little money in their pockets. Not to mention, we are talking about back in the day, in the fabulous sixteies when Cadillacs and hair processes were the rage. Everybody and their brother it seemed, had their hair fried, dyed, and laid to the side. And Larry was making a small fortune.

Back then, some of the popular hairstyles were named after famous white men. For example, a 'JFK' was a style in which the hair was straightened with conk, dyed jet-black, then slicked down with Wild Root hair crème. The hair on one side of the head would be combed to the back then wrapped around the back to the front. The top would be waved to the side. Next, you would be placed under a hair dryer until it dried, then it would be sprayed with a fragrant hair spray to hold it firmly in place.

Another popular style was the 'Tony Curtis'. The hair would be cut low on the sides and in the back and styled in finger waves. The hair on top would be tightly curled, then combed out and teased. There were other styles like the 'New Yorker' and the 'Straight Back' just to name a few.

All of this was back during the days of ignorance, long before the concept of Black Power and Afro hairstyles came into prominence. But, while it lasted, Larry rode the crest and stacked his paper by doing hair all over the city. His name rang wherever he went.

In a little over a year after opening the shop in his mother's basement, Larry had saved up enough money to buy himself a brand-new Cadillac, which at the time was a poor man's dream. Owning a Cadillac back then, put you instantly in the major baller bracket. You had hit the big time when you could afford a 'hog' as the caddy would be nicknamed.

When Larry met Minnie, a heavy-set sister with big pretty titties and a sassy mouth, his future was secured. Minnie had big bank and big connections. She owned the restaurant on Gratiot between Chene and Grandy, right next door to a pawn shop. Cootie Brown, her boyfriend before Larry came along, was a living legend in his own right. Cootie was a big-time gambler and a gangsta, known from the East to the West. Not only was he well respected throughout the underworld, but Cootie was a killer, cold-blooded, too. But one thing about Cootie Brown, he wasn't living and dying for no ho. That's how his papa had raised him.

"A woman can always be replaced son, don't ever show any signs of weakness for no broad out here, you understand?"

And he always tried to live by that rule, so when Minnie chose Larry, Cootie respected the game and let her go. In his heart, he was ready to pop a cap in her ass and and that hair doin' nigga, Larry Westin, but he didn't. Didn't mean his ego wasn't bruised, but as time past, his wounds faded.

For Larry, his relationship with Minnie was the best thing that ever happened to him. Minnie's paper game was strong and she came to the table openly and gave Larry the down payment for a building on the East-Side that Larry converted into Club Paradise, a luxurious hair salon fit for a King and Queen.

Seeking out the best hairstylists in Detroit, Larry persuaded them to come work their magic for him, offering a bright future and lots of money. Soon, the spot blew up and was the toast of the town. Playas from all over the city got their wigs blasted at Club Paradise. It was a hot spot for the stylish and for men like Larry, the sixties and seventies would be called the golden years. Because as time moved forward, it brought the coming of the eighties and a major dramatic shift in the game. Gone were the days of smoothness and finesse. That would all be replaced with automatic weapons and crack cocaine. Pimps and playas still got their props, but they had to take a backseat to the flamboyant, boisterous drug dealers who didn't mind unleashing the murder game to gain a toehold in the city.

This new generation of hustlers were in a class all by themselves. Everything had changed and it could be seen, heard and felt in the shift from the soul-stirring vibe of R&B, to the hard-driving 'I don't give a fuck' attitude of Gangsta Rap. It was a brand-new era and those who couldn't fit in were phased out.

Only a few OGs like Larry Westin would make the transition from the old to the new. They understood that for every dream shattered, a new one was born.

■■■■■■■■■■■■■■■■■■■■■■■■■■■■■■■■■■■■■■■■■■■■■■■■■■■■■■■■■■■

**A** beige Rolls pulled up in front of the Democratic Club on John R. and Erskine. A few casual observers walking by, slowed their step to get a better look at whoever was about to emerge from the expensive car. As Larry climbed from behind the steering wheel and stepped fully into view, the people standing around assumed he was some type of big celebrity.

Dressed in a beige, silk, two-piece Armani suit and beige alligator shoes, Larry's jewelry sparkled brightly on his wrist and fingers like pieces of the sun. Any other time he would have been amused by the admiring expressions on the faces of the people gawking at him, but today his mind was preoccupied. Business was on the floor. Important people from New York were waiting for him inside the club, and he wanted to make a good impression.

The owner of the building was waiting for him at the door.

"What's happenin', Larry?"

Rayfil Blue was a dangerous and violent man. He was short and bald with bulging pop-eyes that made him look like a frog.

"C'mon in, pal," he said, ushering Larry further inside

the large open room that featured hardwood floors that had been polished until they shined like glass.

A pool table that would convert into a crap table after dark sat in the center of the room and over in the corner was a small bar that seated six. Around the walls were leather furniture and lamps with zebra-striped lampshades.

Sitting on the black leather sofa were two sharply dressed Italians in pin-striped exquisitely tailored suits.

"So, this is the young man you spoke so highly of, eh?" asked Tony as he stood up to be introduced.

"Yeah, this is Larry, Larry this is Tony and Lil' Luchi."

Everyone made the introduction and then they all sat at the bar, except for Larry who was still standing. Larry watched as Rayfil crossed his legs, and smiled politely.

"Yeah, this is King Larry. Check his threads out and you'll understand why we call him King. Shit, he's even got a Rolls Royce parked outside." Larry didn't dig being the center of attention, and he knew Rayfil was a hater, so he changed the subject. "I'm sure these gentlemen didn't come all the way from New York to talk about me."

Tony grinned, like a cobra. He was a cold and callous man who played all the angles. He didn't miss much.

"Larry's right, but if he did plan on survivin' in the business we're in, the flash and front will definitely have to be toned down. All the way down. You have to become part of the shadows and move like a cat on the prowl, my friend. Otherwise you'll stand out like a sore thumb."

"The business you refer to, I assume," Larry said, "is the drug game."

The suave gangsta from New York knitted his eyebrows together and stared directly at Larry. "That's another thing you're going to have to learn. This ain't a game we're involved in son. It's a business, and if you ever forget that and treat it like anything less, you'll go down fast."

His interest fully aroused, Larry took a seat next to Rayfil and keyed in on Tony and his partner, Lil' Luchi a small, wiry man sitting on Tony's right.

31

Larry relaxed a bit then decided to probe further.

"Say that I do decide to do business with you, what guarantee do I have you fellas from the Big Apple play fair? I don't even know if I can trust ya'll?"

"Listen, Larry, the only way the cross comes into play is if you initiate it on your end. Other than that, it'll be smooth sailin'. Another thing, you come onboard with us; and your enemies become ours, and believe me kid, up in New York or the Apple as you call it, we know how to deal with an enemy. By the same token, we know how to treat a friend. In fact, we can be the best friend you could ever want or we can be your worst nightmare."

Larry just sat there silent, taking in every word Tony had to say. *If Tony thinks he is impressing me with his city slicker talk,* Larry thought sullenly, *he is in for a big surprise.* Larry had grown up among violence and mayhem.

Rayfil decided to put his two cents in. After all, he had a big stake in all of this. If he could convince Larry to put up the front money to get things off the ground, he stood to earn a huge commission on both ends, and that was how he got down, playing two ends against the middle.

"Dig Larry, you know damn well I ain't gon' put you down with nobody that ain't right. When I say Tony can be trusted, you can take it to the bank."

"I believe that, big daddy," Larry said, "I'm just tryin' to convince myself that getting off into the drug game I mean business," he corrected himself, "is the proper thing for me to do."

"Things done changed out here," Rayfil said quickly. "And it's gonna get worse. That crack shit is the next big thing to hit this city and if you know like I know, you'll wanna get in on it from the top so you can get established."

Tony smiled at Rayfil in appreciation. "Thanks for the vote of confidence, Ray, but I don't believe it's necessary. Larry looks like a smart young man with a good head on his shoulders. I think he knows a good business proposition when he hears one.

Larry laughed. "You're right. Only thing about it is, I ain't heard one, at least, not yet. Now tell me what it is you're sellin', and I'll tell you if I'm buyin'."

Tony grinned like the crook he was.

"Okay, sport coat," he said with a sly smile. "Let's talk price and profit margin."

# CHAPTER SIX

It rained all night, a violent thunderstorm that knocked down power lines and sent angry flashes of lightning dancing across the blackened sky.

In the bedroom of his spacious Southfield apartment, BJ was busy making sparks fly of his own, as he plunged in and out of Chi Chi's tight vagina in time to the ravaging storm raging outside his window. After making her climb the walls half the night, BJ finally fell asleep, oblivious to everything except the sound of the rain and Chi Chi's voice moaning softly in his ear. By the time he reopened his eyes, the sun had chased the clouds and the storm far away, clearing the path for what appeared to be the makings of a beautiful day.

Refocusing his senses, BJ could hear Chi Chi moving about downstairs in the kitchen preparing breakfast. After being fucked half the night, she was in a good mood. He could hear her humming along with Whitney Houston's *Saving All My Love for You*, which was playing softly on one of Detroit's popular black radio stations.

The aroma of bacon and eggs drifted up the stairs, causing BJ to twitch up his nostrils in disgust. He told himself that he would have to remind Chi Chi not to cook any swine in his house. She must have gone shopping early that morning, because he certainly didn't keep any type of pork product in his refrigerator.

34

Even though he wasn't a Muslim, he still didn't eat swine. The pig was a filthy animal; he knew that; growing up around the Eastern Market where pigs were slaughtered daily for human consumption. The stink of a pig was a smell one could not easily forget. *Anything that smelled that bad, could not have been meant for the human body,* he told himself firmly. *I hope she don't think I'm eating that.*

Padding barefoot across the carpeted floor, BJ stepped into the shower, enjoying the feel of the warm water hitting his heavily muscled body. He scrubbed himself vigorously with a scented bar of soap that smelled faintly of mint, making sure he eliminated all traces of last night's funk.

As he was rinsing off, he thought back to the day he met Larry Westin in the Greenfield Shopping Plaza.

"**S**ay, blood," Larry had said good naturedly. "Don't you think you'd better save some of that hard-earned bread for a rainy day?"

BJ was about to go off when he saw that the man speaking was none other than Larry Westin. Larry was a living legend. Every young boy growing up in Detroit; knew who he was.

"How ya doin', Larry?" he asked with the utmost respect.

"You know who I am, blood?"

"Who don't know the King?"

Larry smiled, displaying perfect capped teeth that were white as snow. "I see you're a young man who knows how to respect the game," Larry said.

"Game respects game," BJ answered, a bit more sure of himself.

For a moment Larry just stood there giving BJ the once-over, then he said, "You know, blood, I dig your style. I was right to set my sights on you. You see, I've been followin' you for the past several weeks."

"Why would you be followin' me around?" BJ asked surprised.

35

Larry smiled again. "You know, my niece is graduating high school soon. I think I'll get her somethin' nice," he said eyeing a $15,000 platinum bracelet inside the glass showcase of an upscale jewelry store.

BJ saw that Larry was sidestepping his question. "Why do I get the feeling that you're ignoring me?" BJ asked with a half smile.

Larry laughed easily. "It ain't like that blood. Let's just say that anytime a young brotha like your self starts takin' down major paper, he's bound to attract the eyes and attention of somebody like me."

"Why is that?"

"Well, I'm a businessman, and businessmen are always on the lookout for a good deal."

"I feel that, but what does it got to do with me?"

"Everythin'. For example, I know all about that deal you got goin' with the Mexicans over on the South-West side. I also know you'd be willin' to consider changin' horses if the price is right. Am I right so far?"

Intrigued, BJ let his silence serve as his answer. In his mind he was thinking that Larry had obviously spent considerable time checking him out. He needed to know how much he knew and what his angle was.

"Why not have lunch with me?" Larry asked, breaking BJ's train of thought. "Don't worry, I'm sportin'."

BJ smiled and glanced at his Rolex.

"Why not?" he said, then headed for the door with Larry right behind him.

The two men left the Plaza in separate cars, headed for the Flaming Embers, one of Detroit's better-known restaurants that specialized in serving quality meals.

Over an order of steak smothered in mushroom gravy with a side dish of wild rice seasoned in garlic, the two men discussed business. During the course of their conversation, BJ found himself even more amazed.

"Don't be shocked," Larry coolly announced. "Knowledge and information is how I stay alive, baby. Out here in these mean streets where a thousand and one crosses go down every day, knowing when, where, and how is essential to increasin' your bankroll and staying one step ahead of the cops and stick-up boys. For example, I know the Mexicans charge you seventeen a brick, which is cool. But I'll give them to you for fifteen and a half. How does that grab you?"

Flagging a passing waiter, BJ ordered a bottle of champagne then turned back to Larry.

"For starters, I say it sounds damn good. But of course, I have to hear more."

When it was all said and done a deal was made, and on the day BJ was to pick up the first shipment, Thad called with the Busta situation, which was dealt swiftly and brutally just in case anyone else got any smart ideas about encroaching on their territory. Busta had been killed and chopped up into body parts and scattered around the city. A foot here, a hand over there, a half of leg, a thigh, it was crazy. Now, they would know the price they'd have to pay.

"BJ!" Chi Chi called from the kitchen. "C'mon down sweetheart and eat your food before it gets cold."

The sound of her voice roused BJ from his reverie. "All right lil' mama," he called back. "Give me a minute to get this soap off my ass and I'll be right down."

He stepped out of the shower and began toweling off, reminding himself to say something to Chi Chi about preparing swine with his cooking utensils. Now, he would have to throw them out. They had been contaminated.

■■■■■■■■■■■■■■■■■■■■■■■■■■■■■■■■■■■■■■■■■■■■■■■■■■■■■■■■■■

Brenda strolled through the North Land Mall with her children in tow and close behind. The last time she went to the mall her son, Kamal, managed to wander off. When Brenda couldn't find him, she'd thought she'd have a heart attack, thoughts of him lost, led to kidnapped or in the hands of a stranger. Thank god by the time her brother, Thad showed up at the mall, a white lady returned him to a clerk in the Merchandise Return section.

"Kamal, you make sure you keep your little ass close by. You hear me boy?" Brenda admonished her only son.

Frowning, the boy turned up his little face and opened his mouth, "Aw, mama. I'm a big boy! I ain't gon' get lost. I know my way back home."

Brenda rolled her eyes at him. "Sure, that's what your mouth say. If it wasn't for that white lady..." her words fell silent as she saw them rack the slides of their weapons. It all happened so fast and the two young men seemed to have come out of nowhere, wearing hoodies and jeans, carrying 9 mm semi-automatic weapons.

"No, not my babies, not my babies, she screamed as she attempted to pull Kamal and Shanetta out of harm's way as the first bullets entered Brenda's body and spun her around in a circle. The next volley of shots hit her in the face and neck, driving her violently back across the marble floor and slamming her against the wall. She was dead before her body slid to the floor.

Terrified, her daughter Shanetta went into hysterics, screaming to the top of her lungs as she ran over to her mother side. Brenda's son Kamal stood still as a scare crow unable to move. He watched in horror as the second shooter took deadly aim at him.

"Ohmigod," a bystander screamed as she saw the gunmen targeting the child. Everyone in the crowded shopping mall had heard the gunfire and that's when the shit hit the fan; total fucking pandemonium erupted.

Amid the yelling and the screaming, innocent people were trampled by the stampeding crowd. They just couldn't get out the way quick enough. Even an elderly security guard ducked behind a counter, realizing that his .38 revolver was no match for the gunmens' automatic weapons.

Grinning like he was insane, the hooded assassin squeezed the trigger. The first bullet struck little Kamal in the left shoulder. The second one grazed his right eye as the impact knocked him to the floor. His sister tried to run, but the first shooter refocused his sights and fired, hitting her twice in the back. She went down.

The gunman then calmly walked over to where she lay helplessly on the ground and pointed his weapon at her fallen form. At point-blank range, he executed her. Then he and his partner made their escape. As they reached the mall exit one of them spun and yelled, "Busta sends his greetings from the grave!"

# CHAPTER SEVEN

The old dilapidated single-family flat on Mt. Elliot and Ardnt had been taken over by members of YGS. They were using it to sell crack and as a motel for all the girls who were willing to have sex with them in exchange for crack.

Lisa was buck naked inside the house surrounded by Lil' Greg, Melvin, and Winky. She was crawling around the bare wooden floor searching for granules of crack. So high, she didn't know if she was coming or going.

Watching her, with eyes full of scorn, the trio stared disbelievingly at the spectacle. It was hard for them to believe some of the things women would do for a hit of crack, especially Lisa and especially after the incident with the German shepherd. There was no limit to what she would do. Crossing the line and engaging in bestiality had virtually destroyed her sense of morality.

Rising to his feet, Winky swaggered over to Lisa and dropped his pants to his knees. His penis stood straight out like a flagpole, angry and menacing. Positioning himself behind her, he grabbed her roughly by her ass cheeks and pulled her to him.

Already down on all fours like a dog, Lisa felt a sharp pain shoot through her rectum and realized she was being penetrated anally by Winky.

"Ahh!! Take it out. You're hurting me! Stop! Stop!" she

40

cried out.

Ignoring her pleas, Winky grunted, pushing himself further inside her as he gripped her hips so she couldn't pull away from him.

He wanted to hurt her and hear her scream and beg for mercy. He used to really like her, having the biggest crush ever on a girl, but she treated him like a scrub back in high school because of his droopy eye. He had gotten cut with a knife in a gang fight and the nerve in his right eye was severely damaged. It made his eye droop and blink constantly; which is how he got his nickname, Winky.

Back then, before she started smoking cocaine, Lisa acted like she was big shit. Now, the bitch was nothing but a crack whore and he was the one with the crack, so he was in control.

"Shut up, fuckin' whore."

In overwhelming agony, Lisa winced in excruciating pain as she felt her inflamed bowels explode. There was a foul stench in the air as Lil' Greg gagged in revulsion throwing up the McDonald's quarter pounder he had just eaten.

"Damn, what the fuck is that?" Melvin asked, glancing around the sparsely furnished room and sniffing the air.

Winky glanced down realizing his entire crotch area was covered in human feces.

"You nasty bitch! Yo, this bitch done shit all over me; you fuckin' whore."

Melvin and Lil' Greg couldn't help but to laugh at him.

"Damn, nigga you literally fucked the shit outta that bitch! Ooh wee!"

"I don't see what the fuck is so fucking funny," Winky said angrily, withdrawing his shriveled, feces-covered penis from between Lisa's butt cheeks.

Fearing Winky's retaliation, Lisa crawled over to the corner and curled up in a fetal position. Too ashamed to look up into the faces of her tormentors, she kept her head down, staring blankly at the floor. In the back of her mind she thought of her staunch, conservative parents. *If they saw me like this, they would drop dead.*

Despite what anyone said about Lisa, Lil' Greg felt bad for her. He had sisters and if a bastard ever made one of his sisters do a dog, he'd burn their ass up alive, crack head or not. Although Lil' Greg wasn't a saint, he simply didn't condone doggin' a broad out because she was smokin'.

Lil' Greg came from a deeply religious family. In fact, religion is what drove him out of his parent's home. His mother was a religious fanatic who forced him and his sisters to attend church every day of the week. As far as he was concerned, the church was full of hypocrisy. Preachers who talked the word of God, yet were fucking all the sisters in the church. And they had to be the stupidest, spreading their legs for a man of the cloth; eternal damnation indeed! The preacher would use that to instill fear and keep the members tithing.

Reverend McNeal drove a brand-new Cadillac every year, while the average poor person who belonged to his church, scuffled and scrounged like hell, just to make ends meet. Lil' Greg witnessed his mother on numerous occasions dropping her last dollar in the collection plate.

One day, he asked his mother why she gave her last to a man who appeared to be nothing more than a slick-talking, playa-preacher. His mother's answer was a hard slap upside his head. Still, he loved his mother and did whatever she asked of him, including helping his sisters get through college. Lil' Greg, however, had dropped out of junior high and had started hustling, but was determined his sisters would get their college educations. That, more than anything, was what his mother prayed for and eventhough God got all the glory; that was okay. Lil' Greg continued to hustle crack rocks for the sake of his family.

Scrounging through the house, Winky was frantically searching for something to clean himself with. Lil' Greg kept his eyes on Lisa, watching her in the corner she still sat in.

"Here, Lisa," he said, holding out several large-size

pieces of crack. "Go 'head, take it. Put your clothes on and get outta here. Ain't nobody gon' hurt you."

Winky stared at Lil' Greg like he had lost his mind.

"Nigga, I know you ain't givin' that bitch shit. After what she did to me, you got some nerve offerin' her a god damn thing? What the fuck is you thinking?"

"She couldn't help what she did. Plus, we don't need her runnin' to the cops cryin' rape."

Lisa was about to say something, but the look Lil' Greg shot her way, let her know she should keep quiet and let him handle the situation.

"He's right, Wink. Let that ho have that shit so she can get the fuck outta here. Besides you need to be focused on one thing, a bath. You got a shitty deal my man," said Melvin laughing at his own joke.

Winky glanced around the nearly empty, abandoned house. He looked at Lisa with disgust, then at his crotch.

"Why the fuck does the water got to be cut off in this rat-trap. I should burn this muthafucka down, with her punk ass in it. "Damn! I gotta get home.""

Lisa was temporarily forgotten as the trio made preparations to leave.

Just then, Winky's pager went off.

"It's Thad," he said looking at the number flashing across his beeper screen.

"Hit him back," Lil' Greg told him as Lisa quietly slipped into her clothes and headed for the door. On her way out, she turned to Lil' Greg and smiled.

"Thanks, Lil' Greg. I'll pay you back one day."

"Forget it, it ain't about nothin'," he said feeling sorry for her.

"Man, fuck that bitch! I hope she get hit by a fucking bus, fuckin' crack monkey," Winky shouted, punching in Thad's number on his cell phone. "Bitch, gonna shit all over my black ass and still get high."

Lisa glared at him, then disappeared into the black night. For some reason, Lil' Greg had a strange feeling.

Although he didn't consider himself religious, some of his mother's religious convictions had rubbed off on him and he firmly believed that what went down, came back around, sooner or later.

Winky dialed Thad's number and waited for his answer. With no hello, Thad answered sounding out of sorts and for a loss of breath.

"Have you seen the news?" Thad asked

"Nah, I been out in the field with some of the crew takin' care of business. Why?"

"They killed Brenda and Shanette. Lil Kamal's in the hospital. They shot his eye out."

"Who, who the fuck is they?"

Thad was momentarily silent, his mind lost in thoughts of murder. He couldn't believe his sister was dead, not his sister, not his niece, and certainly not his nephew. Moving on his family was a violation of the unwritten code of the streets. Family members who weren't involved in the game were supposed to be off-limits. Now, the door had been opened for any and everything and he was about to walk right through it.

■■■■■■■■■■■■■■■■■■■■■■■■■■■■■■■■■■■■■■■■■■■■■■■■■■■■■■■■■■■■■■

The entire front section of the New Baptist Church was filled with young black men all dressed in identical black tracksuits and white sneakers. These were the frontline soldiers on BJ and Thad's crew. Today was the day Brenda and Shanetta were being laid to rest.

Sitting in the front row to Thad's right was BJ, Chi Chi, and Larry. To Thad's left was Lil' Greg, Winky, and Bay Bay all dressed in three piece suits.

The good Reverend McNeal was a short, heavyset, light-complexioned fellow with a double chin and a head full of wavy salt-and-pepper hair, which he wore long and permed. In his early forties, he was known as a notorious womanizer with a penchant for silk suits and alligator shoes.

Today, he was at his best. With a standing room only

44

crowd of reporters and black people dressed in their Sunday suits, he was prepared to preach a sermon they would remember for years to come.

"Brothers and sisters," he began in a powerful voice reminiscent of the late Dr. Martin Luther King, Jr., "Today we are gathered here to honor and celebrate the lives of our dearly departed sister, Brenda Jones and her beloved young daughter, Shanetta Jones. They were both tragically slain at the hands of young black men gone out of control."

He paused dramatically, allowing his initial statement to sink in for the added effect. When he was sure that every eye in the room was on him he continued.

"With a never-ending supply of automatic weapons and drugs at their disposal, there's no limit to the evil that will be done. Instead of being the protectors of their communities, our young black brothers have become terrorizors of our community!"

"Amen, Reverend!" shouted a fat, dark-skinned woman who was busy fanning herself with a large cardboard fan. She had recently been robbed by two crack heads so she had a bone to pick anyway.

"At the rate we're going, there ain't gonna be nobody left when the good Lord comes back in his full glory!"

The crowd went wild, shouting Amen and hallelujah.

Knowing he had them under his spell, Reverend McNeal decided to turn up the heat.

"Something in our society is dreadfully wrong when our own children grow up to become murderers and a menace to society instead of a comfort to us in our old age. Children whom we cherished and beseeched God to bless and protect, have lost their sense of morality. Yes, brothers and sisters, we sacrificed our own dreams and ambitions for those same children and this is how they repay us; with Bullets, insults and a heaping heavy load of regret, pain and sorrow and now right here in front of us is the senseless slaying of a young mother and her little daughter? We are being forced to build bars across our own homes just to find a small measure of security. Our homes are supposed to be our castles where no harm can get to us, where we should be safe. Instead we are prisoners in our homes to unsafe streets. We have to buy guns and keep them fully loaded just in case some young fool decides he wants to kick in our door and take over!"

The fat lady got busy again. "Speak on it Reverend!" She was shouting at the top of her lungs, her voice booming throughout the hallowed walls of the old sanctified church, bringing chills down the spines of her fellow mourners.

Not to be outdone, a group of women sitting nearby decided it was time to put their two cents in. "Good Lord, have mercy! Save us sweet Jesus!" they screamed.

"Years ago," Reverend McNeal sang, "It was the white man and his racism we had to worry about. Now it's our own devilish children!"

Fully geeked up now, Reverend McNeal got up on the tip of his toes and began bouncing up and down speaking in tongues. The gibberish he was spitting out of his mouth made no sense at all, but it evidently was contagious, because the next thing you know, more people jumped up out of their seats and began speaking in tongues too. One woman got so excited, she made her way to the aisle where she promptly fell to the floor and began kicking and shaking her legs like she was having an epileptic seizure.

Thad sat there steaming. He had known it was a mistake to let Reverend McNeal eulogize his sister and niece. The crazy fool liked to grandstand too much. He should have been an entertainer instead of a preacher. But, then again, the two were practically inseparable.

Thad made a mental note to check the flamboyant preacher when the time was right. His only thoughts were revenge. Right now, he had to keep the peace for Brenda and Shanetta's sake. But, after they were in the ground and he had said his final good-byes, he would turn the streets of Detroit into an ocean of blood.

# CHAPTER EIGHT

Rayfil was filled with amazement at the sight of all the yellow taxicabs zooming through the crowded New York streets. They reminded him of a swarm of hungry bumblebees. Every time he came through the city, the scene had the same type of effect on him. The sights and smells of New York reflected the different ethnic groups from around the globe, all gathered together in one large, centralized area to produce a multinational atmosphere and culture of its own.

Throughout the day, the air was filled with a plurality of languages and music, each a reflection of its respective culture. The crowded streets were filled with people dressed in colorful outfits, engaged in animated conversation and frenzied activity. At night, the city came alive with bright, flashing lights and neon signs that proudly advertised pretty, naked girls, and a wide variety of fancy nightclubs and swank restaurants where you could get your party on all the way into the wee hours of the morning.

Pimps, prostitutes, ballers, and shot callers felt free to openly mingle with the rich entertainers and crafty politicians who filled their crack pipes with top-quality cocaine supplied by savvy, Harlem drug dealers seeking to find their fame and fortune amid a sea of old and new money.

No doubt about it; there is no place on earth quite like New York, not even slick, polished, Detroit. However, there's one thing the street people living in both cities most definitely have in common, and that's a blood lust or cold hard cash and the willingness to do whatever it takes to get it.

Rayfil met up with Tony and his shadow, Lil' Luchi, downtown in the meat district, in the back room of an upscale restaurant that featured fine Italian cuisine and excellent wine imported all the way from the green hills of Sicily.

"Sit down," Tony ordered. "Welcome to New York."

"Thanks, Tony," the older gangsta from Detroit said, his bald head gleaming like a new copper penny. He was snappily dressed in a white leisure suit and white silk shirt, open at the collar. A pair of white Georgio Brutini loafers adorned his size eight feet.

Taking the seat directly across from Tony, Rayfil nodded at Lil' Luchi, who mumbled something in return and kept his hands out of sight under the table, causing Rayfil to wonder if he had a gat pointed at his belly.

"You must be wonderin' why I summoned you all the way up to New York," Tony said.

"Not really. I don't believe in askin' too many questions. People might start gettin' suspicious. Know what I mean? I figure you'll pull my coat soon enough, when you get ready."

"You're a good kid, Ray. Smart."

Before Tony could continue, Rayfil cut him off. "Excuse me, Tony, but I call you by your name. I would appreciate it if you call me by mine. I'm a man, not a kid."

Lil' Luchi glared at Rayfil. It was crystal clear that he despised him and his last remark. Tony simply smiled.

"I didn't mean anythin' negative. It's just the way we Easterners talk. I know you don't think I'm a racist."

Rayfil waved it off, flashing a huge rock on his pinkie finger. "Forget about it. Let's talk business. I'm sure you didn't summon me all the way up here to discuss the fine arts of subtle, racist remarks."

Lil' Luchi started to say something, but Tony silenced him with a look. "You're right, Ray. Listen, your guy Larry is into us for a couple of mil."

Rayfil looked at him with raised eyebrows. "What's that gotta do wit' me?" he asked.

"Well, you recommended him to us, so I thought you might want to know."

Rayfil raised his glass. "Don't worry about it; he's good for it."

"Oh, I don't doubt that," Tony said. "It's just that he started out like a giant wave in the ocean, always on time. Now, it seems like he's recedin' back to the shore like a tiny little bubble, and me and a few of the guys are just wonderin' if maybe somethin' is wrong. Is there anything we should know, Ray?"

Rayfil thought for a moment. "I guess you can say there's a slight problem. But it ain't got nothin' to do wit' Larry, at least not directly."

"You want to tell me, what's going on, Ray?"

"Well, there's a war goin' on between one of Larry's top distributors and the 30/30 boys. They're beefin'. Quite naturally product is moving slow, but things'll pick up. Larry's man got the strongest crew. You gotta have faith, Tony."

Tony absorbed what was said, then asked a rhetorical question. *Is he serious, does this guy really think faith has a fuckin' thing to do with the business of war?*

"It's what you gotta have to keep from panickin'."

"Panickin'? Who's panickin'? I just asked a simple question; that's all."

"Well, don't panic. Larry got it under control. He's supplyin' both sides, plus he's got other ducks lined up; relax."

Tony leaned back and took a sip of wine, enjoying the smooth flavor as the aged wine went down his dry pipes.

49

"Ahh! That's good," he exclaimed, smiling with contentment. During the entire conversation Lil' Luchi had not once taken his eyes off Rayfil. He didn't trust the frog-eyed little man any further than he could toss him.

"I'll tell you what I'm goin' to do," Tony said, sitting up straight in his chair. "I'm appointin' you my man in Detroit. I want you to keep an eye on Larry and my investment. If things look like they might get out of hand, give me a call and I'll send some people down that way to terminate our contract – the New York way."

Rayfil shifted nervously in his seat. "Since you want me to be a watchdog, what kind of bone do you plan on throwin' my way? I mean, it seems only right that I get some kind of fee for my services."

Tony stopped smiling. "Yeah, just like that finder's fee I gave you. I'll tell you what. Do what I asked, and I'll try to forget you're the one who introduced me to Larry. Plus, each time he flips a load, I'll throw a bone or two your way, fair enough?"

Not wanting to press his luck, Rayfil said quickly, "I can't complain about that. Now let me give you my assurances. If Larry fucks up, don't worry about sendin' nobody into my city. I'll personally take care of the matter, outta respect for you."

Without changing facial expressions, Tony replied, "I wouldn't expect anythin' less, Ray. Now drink up my friend. Tonight I'm going to show you New York like you've never seen her before. All courtesy on the house of course. And in honor of our good friendship. Where are you stayin'?"

Rayfil drained his glass. "I got a suite at the Hilton Hotel. I'm headed over there right now to catch up on some shut-eye and freshen up for tonight. I'm lookin' forward to visitin' one of those famous New York strip clubs I been hearin' so much about."

Tony grinned. "Whatever you want. The world is yours my friend."

After Rayfil left the premises, Lil' Luchi looked at his

boss with a sober expression. "Why do you let that bald-headed space monkey bullshit you? Give me the word and I'll cut his black balls off and make the rest of him dissappear in the Hudson River."

Tony eyed him shrewdly. "Louie, what's the best way to catch a rat?"

Lil' Luchi shrugged. "Hell if I know. With a rap-trap; I guess."

"No," Tony replied. "You use another rat. You see, it takes a rat to know a rat. One rat knows all the hidin' places of another rat. He knows the lifestyle, customs, and habits of rats simply because he's one himself. In the Bible, Christ says that blacks are the salt of the earth – meanin' they flavor and preserve life. But once salt loses its flavor, Louie, it becomes good for nothin' but being trampled on by the feet of other men. So you see, Louie, we all got our use. But once it's gone, we're just food for the fire."

Lil' Luchi nodded his head in understanding. "Now I see why you're the boss. I hope you accept my deepest apologies, Tony, but I just ain't smart like you."

Reaching over, Tony threw his arm around his friend's shoulder and whispered softly, "Didn't I just get through sayin' we all got our use? You don't have to be smart. Leave all the thinkin' to me. You just continue to watch my back and be my strong right arm. And don't forget what I said about salt once it loses its flavor."

Baffled, Lil' Luchi sat there with Tony's arm around his shoulder trying to figure out whether or not Tony's last statement held a hidden meaning.

■■■■■■■■■■■■■■■■■■■■■■■■■■■■■■■■■■■■■■■■■■■■■■■■■■■■

Lil' Greg watched Chi Chi enter Club Paradise and shook his head. He hated it when BJ assigned him to be her driver. But since the war had started, BJ didn't allow her to go anywhere without a personal escort. Walking two steps behind Chi Chi was Melvin, who would run through hell with gasoline drawers on before he let anything happen to her. Lil' Greg didn't know if Melvin was hitting on her on the side, but one thing he knew for sure, was that Melvin was whipped. The pair disappeared through the glass double doors of the brown brick building without looking back over their shoulders.

Lil' Greg thought to himself, *that's a murder waitin' to happen. Melvin's gon' fuck around and let that bitch get him banged out. If he thinks BJ don't know what's goin' on, he's a bigger fool than Chicken Little.*

The two stayed inside the hair salon for fifteen minutes or so, then came out carrying two large suitcases. Inside them, Lil' Greg knew, were several bricks of cocaine. Their mission was to deliver it to the cut house on East Outer Drive. There, the drugs would be converted into crack, packaged, then delivered to the lieutenants. They would make sure that it got in the hands of the street runners. They were almost to the van when Lil' Greg spotted the blue and white police car cruise around the corner.

"Damn!" he exclaimed out loud.

Both Chi Chi and Melvin spotted the squad car at the same time. From his position inside the van, Lil' Greg could see the fear and panic leap into Melvin's eyes. Chi Chi, as usual, was calm in the face of a storm. Flipping her eyes in disgust, she kept stepping toward the van. Suddenly, the cop car pulled over to the curb and sat there with its motor still running. The officers inside the car didn't say anything; neither did they exit the car; they merely sat there observing, their eyes scanning the area. Lil' Greg was in suspended animation. From out of nowhere a Daw Woo .40 caliber semi-automatic pistol appeared in Melvin's right hand. He had switched the suitcase over to his left hand and was using it to hide the gat. At the same moment Larry stepped out of the building and in one glance took in the entire scene.

"Put that away!" he shouted at Melvin. "Everythin' is under control fool."

Walking up to the police car, Larry bent over and

stuck his head inside the open window and began talking softly to the officers inside. It was obvious they knew him.

Three or four minutes later he removed a thick envelope from inside his suit jacket and handed it to the cop riding shotgun, then stood back from the car. The cop riffled his greedy fingers through the sheath of $100 bills inside the envelope and smiled at his partner.

"Everything appears to be in order, King Larry. By the way, put a harness on your trigger-happy young friend. Next time he pulls a piece on us, we're going to blow his black ass brains out."

Seconds later the squad car pulled off.

Spinning on the balls of his feet, Larry hurried over to Melvin and Chi Chi, an angry expression was on his face.

"You fool!" he exploded. "What the hell is wrong with your punk ass? You were about to turn a goddamn dope case into a double homicide on two cops! Are you crazy?"

Melvin stood there looking dumb as fuck. The whole thing seemed to be pretty amusing to Chi Chi. Opening the door to the van, she tossed the suitcase in and got in behind it, shutting the door behind her. Melvin stood there on the sidewalk trying to explain his actions to Larry who wasn't hearing it.

"Just get your ass in the van and get the fuck out of here. You might be a warrior, but you're stupid as hell. It's okay to have heart, but you still gotta be able to think. Next time you get in a tight situation, weigh the odds. If you stand to lose more than you stand to gain, go with the odds. You were about to burn down a house to kill one single fly."

Before Melvin could reply, Larry turned and walked briskly away, and headed toward his shop.

"Melvin," Chi Chi called from the van. "Bring your ass on. We ain't got all day to be fuckin' around man."

Melvin walked over to the van and climbed inside. He was mumbling under his breath. Lil' Greg heard him talking about Larry being an old ass coward. Of course he ignored him. Truth was Larry was right and Lil' Greg certainly didn't wake up planning on being no accomplice to no cop killing. Detroit police were notorious for getting revenge when one of theirs fell in the line of duty. And he understood that. Why shouldn't he? He looked over at the small arsenal of guns stashed in the back of the van. They would be used to exact the same type of revenge, deadly and calculated revenge for Brenda and her daughter.

# CHAPTER NINE

The revolving strobe light flashed violet, then blue and yellow, bouncing off the sound proof walls and ceiling of the crowded nightclub. "Ain't nuttin' but a G thang baby!" rapped Snoop Dogg and Dr. Dre, over a track laid down with a heavy bass line that was popping.

It was Saturday night at Detroit's famous Legends, and the place was off the hiz-zook! Sharply dressed couples were waving their hands in the air and moving their bodies freely to the soulful sound of West Coast G funk. Especially the big butt sisters who knew how to make their plump, juicy asses quiver like an earthquake beneath tight-fitting jeans and silk dresses.

After five days of working like Hebrew slaves at a blue-collar gig, most inner-city people felt like they owed it to themselves to let their hair down at least once a week and release the pressure that comes from taking orders from mostly white straw bosses.

At a table pressed against the wall, BJ and Chi Chi sat back chilling, enjoying the action out on the dance floor. Of course, crazy ass Winky was there to watch his boss's back, and so was Thad and his baby's mama, Jasmine. It had been Chi Chi who suggested they take Thad out on the town to get his mind off his recent tragedy. So far, it hadn't done a lick of good. Thad remained out there in the ozone somewhere. Since picking him up in the rented white limo, he hadn't said more than ten words. He was in a dark, dangerous mood and any fool could see he didn't really want to be fucked with. There was an aura of unpredictability wrapped around him that signaled danger. He was like a ticking time bomb, ready to explode.

The only reason he had agreed to go out in the first place, was because he was hoping he might run across somebody from the 30/30 crew. Four of them were not enough to satisfy his lust for vengeance. The murder of his only sister and niece gave him the perfect excuse to go on a killing spree without having to explain or justify his actions.

His nephew, Kamal, still lay in a private hospital blind in one eye and listed in critical condition. Even though there wasn't anything on Gods green earth to compensate for the tremendous loss he had suffered, Thad promised that all those involved with the death of his sister would wish they had never been born. Brenda had represented the only family he had, beside Jasmine and their son, he had no one in the world. Of course there was BJ, but that was different. BJ was his comrade in arms, the closest thing to a big brother he had ever known. Still, he wasn't really family.

For BJ, his conscience was eating him up alive. He had allowed Raymond to live after he killed Busta. For all he knew it was Raymond who silently could be the sleeper that ordered the hit on Brenda and her kids. No one knew and no one could be sure. Of course Raymond sent condolences and the whole nine, but for BJ, he'd have to be sure and the only way to do that would be to get rid of Raymond. It was the only way. Raymond would have to be dealt with and so would the rest of the 30/30 crew. In the streets, he felt that had he not allowed Raymond to live, there was a strong possibility that Brenda and her daughter might still be alive.

All this mess had the streets of Detroit on fire. A war was erupting between two rival gangs and members of YGS were ordered to lay low as the streets were hot. Of course, there were a few hard-headed guys who ignored the order and attempted to go about their normal, everyday lives, and they quickly paid the ultimate price for their arrogance when they ended up lying on a cold concrete slab in the Wayne County morgue with a DOA tag around their big toe.

Around 3:00 that morning, BJ sent for the limo and ten minutes later the limosine driver paged him back letting him know he was outside the door. Everybody made their way outside happily, merrily, somewhat drunkenly. No sooner than Thad stepped outside the club did he see a black BMW come barreling around the corner with it's headlights off.

"DRIVE BY", he shouted at the top of his lungs reaching for his gun by his waistside.

Everybody heard him, but before any one had a chance to react, gunfire erupted from the BMW sending a shower of bullets in their direction. The limosine driver overly reacted and rammed his foot on the gas pedal, crashing his limo into a parked car as he exited the parking lot. By the time Thad and BJ got their hands on a gun, their bullets were shooting at the BMW's back window as the car burned rubber down the street.

"Is everybody alright?" Thad asked, keeping his eye on the BMW as it turned the corner a block away.

"I'm hit," BJ suddenly announced. "I'm hit, fuck, I'm hit," said BJ looking at his chest.

"Nooo," screamed Chi Chi, "Noo BJ", she said as she stared at a standing BJ with a gun shot wound to his chest.

Thad had his phone in his hand calling 911 the moment he saw BJ's wound and blood drenched shirt.

"Fuck, BJ, come on, sit down or something, here get him on this bench, hold his blood, hold his blood," said Winky, instructing Chi Chi to hold her hand over his wound to stop the blood from pouring out of him so fast.

Thad and Winky helped sit BJ down on the bench next to the entrance of the club.

"My chest feel like it's on fire, get me to the hospital," said BJ pleading to his friends, his breath heavy.

"That fucking limo driver, why he leave us, why he

leave us out here?" Chi Chi screamed at Thad.

"We're at the night club Legends," said Thad into the phone giving the operator the cross streets.

"Chi Chi, calm down, BJ is gonna be alright," said Winky wishing someone had a car to take his man to a hospital.

Thad hung up his phone and then looked over at BJ, his eyes were closed and Chi Chi was rubbing his face, whispering in his ear, telling him how much she loved him and that he was going to be okay. Thad hung up the phone and thought for a few seconds.

"Okay, the ambulance and the police is going to be here any minute now. Winky, I need you to take Jaz home for me."

"But what about BJ," he asked. It was more his job to stay with his man, than take Thad's girl home.

"I got BJ," Thad said. "Just do what the fuck I ask you to do."

Winky looked at his injured comrade, not wanting to leave him injured. "It's cool, Wink. I'll be alright. Take Jasmine and split."

Trying to hold back his frustration, Thad turned his attention to Chi Chi.

"When the police get here, don't tell 'em shit about what happened. This is what we're gonna say..." He began putting together a falsified version of the events that had just transpired. There was no way he was telling the police a damn thing. He'd handle shit his way, and he'd keep it street.

"Okay, but I'm not leaving his side, Thad. I'm going to ride to the hospital with BJ."

"Good, and remember the story. Now, Wink and Jaz, go on and get outta here before the cops get here.

"**D**on't you think you could ask these questions after we get to the hospital and save my man's life! Go ahead and keep playin' and he die out here, go ahead, you been here now for 14 minutes and he still ain't in that van going to the hospital," said Chi Chi counting the mintues on her Rolex knowing how the police got down. They'd leave him out there to die if they could.

It didn't take long after Chi Chi made that statement that the officers allowed the EMS workers to strap BJ onto a metal gurney and place him in the back of the EMS van. Chi Chi climbed in right behind them.

"I'm goin' with him," she told the medical attendants.

"I guess it'll be okay, ma'am," the EMS worker said.

"It's goin' have to be."

With its red lights spinning and siren wailing, the van sped off into the night and, headed for Harper Hospital.

The next day, the shoot-out in front of Legends was all in the newspapers and the local news. Channel 7's anchor, Bill Bonds, reported that the incident was one among the series of killings that had been plaguing the city. The police chief promised to put a stop to the violence and to make the streets safe again. But, at the rate he was going, the streets and the neighborhoods were just getting worse. Crime was at an all time high and the black community was suffering.

BJ was lucky, he was real lucky. The bullet had entered just above his heart and exited through his left collarbone without striking any vital tissues or organs. When he came out of surgery, two detectives were waiting in his hospital room.

"Do you know who shot you Mr. Jackson?"

Pretending to be in more pain than he really was, BJ responded, "Some white boys pushin' a blue van."

"Your choice Mr. Jackson, next time you might not be so lucky," said the same detective as he looked at his partner. He was no nonsense and after giving BJ a chance to respond, he shot his partner a furtive glance and then both men turned around and left the room. There wasn't much more for them to say. Thad and Chi Chi had made the same statements.

"They're lying through their teeth," said the detective.

"Fuck 'em, let 'em kill each other," his partner said as the two got on the elevator.

BJ hung up the phone from Larry. He wanted him to know he was alright. His hospital room was quiet with a sense of rest and relaxation, something he really needed. And this gun shot wound was giving him exactly that. With no television and no radio, BJ sat in total silence as he listened to the quiet room. A noise from out in the hallway startled him and he reached under the pillow under his head and felt for his gun.

"How are you feeling Mr. Jackson," said Ms. Petipski, a nice looking thirty-something white lady, who had been assigned to take care of him this particular evening. She strolled into his room on cue to take his stats and update his medical chart.

"Well, I'm better now that you're here. Think you could get me some ice and water please?"

The nurse fixed BJ up with a small pitcher of ice and water, and then she checked his stats. She glanced through his medical chart, took his vitals and then made some markings on his vital records and left the room. She fluffed his pillow, straightened his blankets and handed him a remote connected to his bed.

"Buzz if you need me."

Nurse Petipski was gone after that and BJ wouldn't be seeing her for another four hours. He took the remote she had handed him and decided to turn on his television. He skipped through the channels looking for something interesting to watch.

Downstairs, a curly-haired, light-skinned guy wearing a cop's uniform entered Detroit's Harper Hospital. He was strapped with a silencer-equipped .38 revolver. Any other time this black man, might have been stopped, questioned and offered a hospital pass once confirmed he belonged. However, this black man was wearing a police uniform and fortunately for him, no one looked his way twice or even thought of stopping and questioning him.

BJ flipped through the channels a second time, still finding nothing he wanted to watch. He clicked the television off and looked at the dusty dark gray screen hanging up on the wall. Within a lightenings flash he saw the gunman in the television screen's shadow. A figure was standing tall and had a gun pointed. BJ couldn't see the person because of the curtain hanging from the ceiling that the nurse had partially closed. BJ calmly reached under his pillow and grabbed the Uzi Thad had sent him earlier.

The would-be assassin had his .38 halfway out, when BJ cut loose with the Uzi, sending the gunman scrambling for his life. BJ hopped out the bed and looked like a crazed Bruce Willis as he and the gunman battled it out in the hospital hallway. Ducking in and out of hospital rooms, BJ made it to the nurses station when the hitman fired back. BJ grabbed nurse Petipski and dove under her desk.

"Stay down," BJ ordered everyone on the floor behind the desk. He popped his head up to see the gunman headed for the stairwell, he fired at him, hitting the hitman in the upper arm. His cries could be heard through the stairwell as he made his get away. By the time, BJ got to the stairwell, the gunman seemed to disappear into thin air. BJ figured he was probably on another floor hiding in a maintenance closet. In the meantime, he had to get out of there. He was sure the hospital cops would be on his floor any second and the real deal police officers were definitely on their way by now.

Moving quickly, BJ ran back into his room, put his robe on over his pajamas, grabbed his cell phone, then raced out into the hallway. The nurses at the station had just begun to bring themselves from off the floor, but seeing BJ's wild ass running around with his Uzi out in plain view, made them panic and hide again under the desk.

*Stay under there, that's good for you,* BJ thought to himself as he hit the stairwell, made it outside the building, ran down the street into a parking lot and found a nice bench at a deserted bus stop. He picked up his phone and called Thad.

"Thad, it's me."

"What's up? How you feelin'?"

"Man, these motherfuckers tried to murk your man again."

"Get the fuck out, you alright?"

"Man, I'm sitting on a bench, looking like I'm waiting for a bus that ain't never coming."

"Where you at, I'm on my way."

BJ told Thad exactly where to find him and hung up the phone.

Just then an older homeless man with missing front teeth in his mouth approached the bench where BJ was sitting.

"This my house man, you sitting in my favorite spot," the older black man said with all seriousness. This bench was his house and it was his spot, he had nothing else in the world but that bench and how dare anyone come along and try to take it from him.

Crazily, BJ looked at him and opened his robe so the homeless man could see the Uzi he was holding.

"Well, damn, partner, mi casa, su casa, nigga. Stay as long as you like."

When Thad arrived, he found BJ and the homeless man, laughing and drinking cups of tea with one another.

"Hey, Thad, this my peoples here, Charlie. You got a couple of dollars on you, I wanna hook Charlie up."

Thad reached in his pocket and pulled out a wad of cash. He carefully passed BJ three ones he picked from the stash.

"Nigga, what is you doing? Give me that."

BJ took Thad's money right out his hand and turned over all the cash to Charlie.

"Aaaww now son, this a lot of money. Lord, I ain't had no money like this in a long time." The gleam in the old

62

man's eye, damn near brought a tear to BJ. He felt like he had just saved the world.

"Hey don't drink all this money up, Charlie man."

"I won't son, I promise, I won't. Hey come back through sometime, this right where I be, everybody knows how to find me, if you need anything, ever."

"Thanks, Charlie man."

BJ shook the homeless man's hand and got in the car with Thad.

"Why you didn't give him my car while you were at it?"

"Damn, I sure am hungry. Let's go eat."

"Eat, eat with what, you just gave all the money away!"

BJ thought about it, he should have saved himself some breakfast money. He glanced at the bench and the deserted bus stop. Charlie was gone and so was breakfast.

"Come on let's get out of here before the cops have us at the precinct all day for questioning."

In the background both Thad and BJ could hear the police sirens moving toward them. BJ felt a thousand times better knowing that Thad was there. Thad was his best trusted friend in the world. He couldn't believe his enemies had tried him again and in the hospital of all places. This was their second attempt to dust him off. It was obvious they were determined. However, BJ had made up his mind that there would be no third chance at his life. He also knew he had to do something to back them up off of him. Right now he was like a floating yellow ducky in the water being used for target practice. But, that would be no more. He was going to hit them where they would least expect it and he knew just how to do it.

Teri Woods Publishing Presents, Predators

# CHAPTER TEN

**B**roadway Men's Fashion Store located on Broadway and Randolph in downtown Detroit, was well-known for its stylish clothing and elegant fashion wear.

Owned by a jewish guy named Shlomo, Broadway Men's Fashion Store had a reputation for clothing major ballers. Broadway was top of the line if you were interested in the latest styles by the brand name designers, however, you needed top of the line dollars to shop there and the average person could never afford the extravagant prices.

Larry Westin opened the door and walked into the store. Shlomo, who watched everything on the cameras in his office saw Larry come in the store and he immediately jumped up to greet him.

"My main man, Shlomo."

Tall with an olive complexion and salt-and-pepper hair, Shlomo was smooth as silk. He smiled and stuck out his hand. "What's up Larry? What do you need today my friend?"

"It depends. Whadda ya got for me?"

"Just a minute," Shlomo said, turning his back to call one of his floor managers for a quick conference. "Let me have some things set out for you to look at. I know you will

64

like," he said as he turned and whispered in the store clerk's ear.

"Do you understand what to get? Good. Get busy. And set the bar up."

Turning back to Larry, Shlomo said, "C'mon in the back, playa. I wanna show you something."

In the back room Shlomo pulled out a cardboard box from inside of a closet. He sat the box on a chair and removed the lid. Inside the box wrapped in thin white paper was a pair of beige ostrich boots.

"City Slickers is sellin' 'em too, but I can get you the best price, don't worry. I'll take care of you," Shlomo said, holding up one of the boots.

Larry took the boot from Shlomo and examined it, checking out the stitches around the sole and running his fingers across the soft texture.

"These are slick. I need a few pairs of these. They come in different colors?

"Of course, I'll get you what ever you want," Shlomo added.

"Whadda 'bout some big block gators? Can you work me a good deal?"

"Is pig pussy pork?" Shlomo jokingly asked. "Some Mauris just came in from New York. How many pair you want?"

"Gimme ten pairs and make sure one pair is stink pink to match that pink leather suit you sold me last week. Now show me what you got new on the clothes rack."

Already tallying up the bill in his head, Shlomo rubbed his hands together, got the other store clerk and went to work on Larry. By the time he was done, the bill was $32,875.00 and that was with a major major discount.

"Shlomo, you gonna take care of the tailor bill, right?"

"Don't worry my friend. I'll take care of everything for you. Don't worry, I'll have everything delivered to you at the Towers, okay."

"See ya around Shlomo."

"My friend, see you soon."

The old train station on Rose Park and Vernor Highway had been out of commission for years, but tonight it was in full use. At least ten to fifteen cars were parked near the tracks in a semi-circle, forming a protective wall for the group of Mexican men standing in the center discussing matters crucial to their future survival as a drug-dealing cartel.

Speedy, their leader, was a tall, beady-eyed dude with a Fu Manchu mustache and a pockmarked face. He committed his first murder when he was just ten years old. The victim was his mother's drunken boyfriend. Speedy ended up in the Governor Marteen Training School for Boys. Unfortunately, it didn't help. By the time Speedy turned twenty-eight he had served time in both Jackson Prison and in the Northville State Hospital for the mentally insane. So he wasn't just playing crazy, he was a certified nut. And the men who followed him were just as nuts as he was.

Take, for example, his right-hand man, Big Luna. His birth name was Jose Ortega. As a juvenile, he had been ordered to stand trial as an adult. He was charged with raping his sister and murdering his parents. He raped his sister because he wanted to and killed his parents because they found out what he had done. They punished him and that made him mad. Instead of calling the law, taking their daughter to the hospital and putting the news on front street, they tried to hide the truth because of guilt and shame. They died instantly from gun shot wounds to the head. At the time, Jose was 14 years old and big as a baby bull. By the time he got back out of prison he was 24, 6 feet four inches tall weighing two hundred fifty pounds.

Speedy noticed him one night sitting around the neighborhood club looking like he was lost and struck up a conversation with him. After a couple of rounds of drinks, Speedy decided that he liked the big fellow and told him to go over and slap this other guy, who was just sitting there at the bar minding his own business. Without saying a word;

Jose got up, calmly walked over to the cat, and just like that, hauled off and slapped the living daylights out of him.

After realizing that Jose was missing more nuts and screws than he was, Speedy decided to make him his top enforcer and renamed him, 'Big Luna'. It was a name Jose was proud to be called.

"So, ese?" Diablo asked. "How much longer do you plan on fucking around with these Negritos?" He was a short, ugly man with a long ugly scar trailing across his face from his wide forehead to his sharp chin.

Speedy stared at him with murder in his dark brown eyes. *Who does this aardvark think he is? I should kill him right here, right now.* Diablo could feel Speedy's cold eyes cutting through him like a knife. The only reason Diablo hadn't made a move on Speedy was because he knew if he made a move Speedy, it would have to be the right one. If he slipped and missed, it would be his ass and Speedy would slaughter him like a fat pig.

What Diablo had failed to realize was that Speedy had already made up his mind to kill him. Speedy was just waiting for the right opertune time to do it. Right now the only thing saving Diablo from his date with death was the fact that he was so well liked among the fellows. No need in starting shit that really didn't need to be started, so Speedy decided he would be patient, sit back and wait for the right moment.

"You know, Diablo," he said through clenched teeth. "You're beginning to get on my last nerve. You'll do what I say, when I say. You got that homes?"

A hush fell over the other gang members.

"Who was driving the BMW last night?" Speedy asked, without taking his eyes off Diablo.

Everyone turned to stare accusingly at two youths who had taken the job as part of their initiation into the crew. Theirs was a look of pure fright on their faces. They knew the price of failure was death.

"I was driving amigo," one boy sheepishly admitted.

Speedy glanced down into the terrified face of a dark-haired Spanish youth. The boy was trembling from head to toe. The rest of the gang stood around holding their breath. Finally, the other boy confessed, "I was the shooter. But goddamn homes, I did my fuckin' best!"

Without warning, Speedy came up out of nowhere with a Mac-11, 9 mm in his hand and opened fire, sending a shower of bullets that ripped into the boy's flesh, slamming him to the ground. He lay still in the dirt, his lifeless eyes wide open.

"It don't look like your best was good enough." Speedy laughed. Then he turned the gun on the other kid.

For what seemed like an eternity, they stood there staring back at Speedy never once taking his eyes off the gun that was pointed in his face. The young kid was so scared, he thought he'd piss his pants. Speedy could smell his fear.

"I think I'm gonna let you live," Speedy announced. "Since you were honest and up front and not scared to tell the truth, there's a chance you can be redeemed. But your partner was a piece of worthless shit."

Breathing a long sigh of relief, the pardoned gang member smiled broadly. "Thanks man," he whispered.

"Now, where's the black chick who set everything up?"

Big Luna nodded at one of the other gang members who headed immediately in the direction of a souped up '67 Chevy. He returned with a pretty, African-American girl.

"What's your name bitch?" Speedy asked looking her up and down. "Speak up, I can't hear you."

"My name is Glenda, not bitch."

"Is that right, Glenda? Why'd you backstab your people?"

Glenda spat on the ground. "I'm the one who was stabbed in the back. I helped BJ get on his feet, then he had the nerve to cross me for some skinny ass chick. Fuck him. He can rot in hell for all I care."

Speedy had heard enough. In that instant, Glenda was sure she was standing in the presence of Satan himself, as the psychopathic gang leader grinned insanely, displaying a mouthful of ugly, rotten teeth as he lifted his gun and squeezed the trigger killing Glenda instantly. Her body jerked like a rag doll under the deadly hail of bullets.

"Somebody get this bitch and that other piece of shit out of my sight. They both can join BJ in hell."

*That motherfucker should be dead and after we take Larry out, the rest will be history.*

Confused, Diablo stood there staring at the two dead bodies sprawled on the ground. *Why would he kill them, for what?* Speaking to no one in particular he voiced his opinion, "You don't repay loyalty with betrayal."

Speedy's facial expression never changed. "You're right. But neither do you reward betrayal with loyalty. I don't owe that bitch shit. If she crossed her homeboys, she'd cross us or are you too dumb to understand that?"

"What if we need her again? What we gonna do now that she's dead?"

"We'll just dig the bitch up, unless you got a better idea Mr. Brains."

Automatically, all eyes turned toward Diablo, who stood there with the spotlight focused on him. He may not have been the sharpest tool in the woodshed, but neither was he the dullest by far, so he did the only thing he could do under the circumstances. He backed down.

"Forget it amigo. You're right. You're always fucking right."

Speedy glared at him with a look of pure malice.

"You bet your sweet ass I'm right. Now let me tell you something for your own good homes. You're a good man to have on the team, but there's nobody indispensable. Always remember that and you'll be alright."

Diablo was wisely silent, but in the back of his mind he was busy plotting.

*You're right amigo,* he thought sullenly. *Nobody's indispensable, not even you.*

And in that moment he made up his mind to kill

Speedy. He didn't know exactly how he was going to do it; he just knew that eventually he would kill him.

# CHAPTER ELEVEN

**W**hen Thad and BJ walked through the front door of BJ's lavishly furnished Southfield apartment, Chi Chi was lounging on the purple crushed velvet sofa in the living room watching widescreen TV. She was dressed in a black negligee that showed off her luscious body to the fullest.

Surprised at seeing BJ out of the hospital, she leaped up from the sofa and ran straight into his arms and began peppering his unshaved face with tiny, electric kisses.

"Baby, why didn't you call me and tell me that they was releasing you. Why you walking around in this hospital gown, looking crazy? I could have brought you some clothes."

Glad to see her, BJ smiled mischievously. "I wasn't released. I signed myself out."

"Signed yourself out? What the doctor say?"

"I'm straight. My chest's a little sore, but other than that, I feel like a million dollars."

Releasing her grip from around his neck, Chi Chi turned to face Thad. "Homie, wassup?" she cracked.

Thad just stared at her. He still hadn't gotten used to a woman like Chi Chi. She was aggressive just like a dude, but she still knew how to be sexy. Her attitude constantly reminded him of Da Brat.

"What's up, Chi Chi? You alright?"

"Yeah, I'm good, you know Jaz called here looking for

71

you. You better call her."

"Oh yeah? I'ma call her in a few minutes."

"Baby, would you mind fixin' me and Thad a drink?" BJ asked. "And make 'em strong."

Chi Chi nodded, then headed for the kitchen.

BJ and Thad took a seat on the sofa, glad for the temporary reprieve from the heavy drama unfolding around them. Things were getting pretty tight with gangsters running wild, taking shots at them every other day.

Only a few minutes passed before Chi Chi emerged from the kitchen carrying two glasses half filled with Seagram's gin and orange juice.

"Here ya'll go. Just what the good doctor ordered," she said jokingly handing them their drinks.

"Mmm, Miss Evers, thank you ma'am," joked BJ.

"Whatever, you want something else?" she aksed before sitting down next to him.

"Um, no Miss Evers, you've just about done enough."

"No I probably haven't," she said before sticking her wet tongue inside his ear, she gave it a quick lick, then bit down gently on his earlobe.

"You didn't give the police this address when you were down at the station, did you baby?" BJ asked suddenly.

"Do I look that crazy to you, BJ?" she asked then continued her tongue bath on his ear. She stopped for a second, looked him in the eye and said. "I'd rather die in prison before telling them dirty rotten bastards anythin'. You know how much I hate stool pigeons. I can't believe you would ask me something so crazy."

"I know, I know you know," BJ said smoothly not wanting her to start ranting and raving about trust issues in front of his man. Truth was at the end of the day, BJ didn't put anything past anybody. How could he, in the business he was in?

"Hey, what you guys think about me and Jasmine taking target practice at the range? I called Shooter's Cave and they said to come on in and sign up for classes. What do you think?" she asked putting her hand on his thigh.

BJ looked over at Thad, who was smiling. Not since his sister, neice and nephew had BJ seen him smile.

"What's so funny?" BJ asked.

"I can see them two now," he said joking as BJ laughed with him.

"See whatever you want. All the drama ya'll two got going on, you need people around you that know how to shoot and got good aim."

"Alright, we'll talk about it, okay?" BJ said not to kosher with the idea.

Finishing his drink, Thad rose to his feet.

"Dawg I'ma get on up. I need to check on those fellows to make sure everything is tight for tonight. You gon' be alright?"

"Yeah. Just remember, I don't want you directly involved. I can't afford to lose you. You're my right arm, dawg. Let Lil' Greg and Winky handle business. Bay Bay and Melvin can mop things up. I already got the bondsman standing by in case somebody gets arrested. You just play the background and make sure all the loose ends get tied."

"I feel you, but I don't like it. You know I like to pop that thang'."

"Tell me about it," BJ laughed.

For a long moment the two men simply stared at each other, each of them knowing that their destinies had pretty much been shaped by forces they themselves had set in motion. And to think, their lives could be over the minute they stepped back out in the streets. But no matter what, they had determined to go down together. 'Ride or die' became their official motto.

"Well partna', I'll be seein' you around I guess," Thad said, then turned around and walked out of the apartment without looking back. BJ watched him go. Not only did he have a strong emotional connection to Thad but he had deep respect for him as well. Thad was a man who had earned his props the hard way. Even though the two of them were partners who split everything straight down the middle, one would have thought that Thad was nothing more than an enforcer since he did most of the wet work and stayed down in the trenches with the troops. But such wasn't the case.

Thad and BJ were equals playing different roles. BJ was the smooth one, able to negotiate and finalize deals. Thad was the field general who made sure that their plans were carried out with deadly precision. Together; they made quite a team.

After Thad left, BJ allowed himself to be swept away on a cloud of pure delight, as Chi Chi's skilled tongue went to work, sliding down his body until she felt him relax.

"Chi Chi, I think it's a lil' too soon for me to be getting' busy with you on the sheets," BJ said not so convincingly. He didn't even recognize his own voice.

Licking and nibbling his burning flesh inch by inch, Chi Chi mumbled, "You don't have to do nothin' but relax. Chi Chi will do all the work." Reaching out, she peeled off his shirt and began rubbing her hands across his chest.

"Is that better?"

BJ was silent as he felt her tiny hands unzip, then reach inside his pants. When she found what she was searching for, she gently eased his penis out and began stroking it up and down until it fully came to life. "Now give me what I want." She breathed heavily, lowering her head to his lap. BJ gasped out loud when he felt her wet, warm mouth engulf him. He lost what little control he had left and let her do her thing. Chi Chi was a bona fide freak who loved giving head to her man. It made her feel close to him in a special way. Since she was the victim of sexual assault at a young age, she became promiscuous and sexually advanced beyond her years. Although she really tried her best to conceal the freak inside of her, when she was alone with BJ, it all came out and she was willing to do anything.

On one occasion she let Melvin fuck her, but that didn't have anything to do with love. It was only a move to keep Melvin under her spell and at her command. BJ was her one and true love and she loved his shitty drawers. BJ probably knew about Chi Chi and Melvin; but he had other things on his mind. Feeling himself on the verge of coming, BJ reached down and attempted to pull Chi Chi's head away from his lap. To his surprise, she resisted, sucking him even further inside her warm mouth. Unable to hold it back, BJ suddenly ejaculated, spewing his cum down Chi Chi's throat. But instead of gagging like she always did; Chi Chi sucked his penis like she was sucking a popsicle, then greedily swallowed every drop of cum until he was limp and completely drained.

■■■■■■■■■■■■■■■■■■■■■■■■■■■■■■■■■■■■■■■■■■■■■■■■■■■■■■■

Tony placed the phone receiver back into its cradle. He had heard all he needed to hear. According to his Detroit source, the Mexican mob was playing Larry's top distributor, against the 30/30 crew. Their motive was two fold.

First, they wanted to punish BJ for getting off their line after BJ decided to work with Larry instead of them. Second, they wanted to eliminate, or at the bare minimum, weaken their competition. The only thing about it was that they were unwittingly stepping on Tony's toes. As for Tony, he could understand and even sympathize with their anger, but he couldn't accept it. Not when it was costing him money. He had no choice but to get in the game and reach out with a long-handled spoon. He just prayed it wasn't too late to recoup his losses.

■■■■■■■■■■■■■■■■■■■■■■■■■■■■■■■■■■■■■■■■■■■■■■■■■■■■■■■

Lisa woke up in a fleabag motel over on the West Side of Detroit with no idea how she got there. All she knew is that she was as naked as the day she was born, lying beneath a paper thin, filthy cotton blanket.

In bits and pieces, memories from the night before began drifting in and out of her cracked out mind. What she saw made her bury her head in her hands in disgrace.

Images of three men inside her at the same time made her sick to her stomach. She could see them panting and breathing over her like wild animals. One had his penis in her mouth, while the other two sandwiched her in between them, simultaneously fucking her in the vagina and anus.

She began to cry, louder and louder. Her mind flashed in and out of every tiny detail of what they did, all taking turns on her and then doing her at the same time. She rocked back and forth and trembled feeling the pain of her ass being half ripped apart. She was in a great deal of agony and grief.

Spotting a pair of scissors lying on the beat-up dresser next to the bed, she contemplated picking them up and hurting herself with them. This was probably one of the lowest points in her life. She was ready to jam the scissors in her eyeballs so she'd never have to see herself ever again. Lisa stopped looking in the mirror a long time ago. The once beautiful and graceful facial features had long been gone. But then came the dark thoughts of revenge, rushing through her mind like a black cloud streaking through the sky before exploding violently into thunder and lightning. Revenge for every one who treated her like a piece of shit and the first image to appear in her mind was Chi Chi.

# CHAPTER TWELVE

"**Y**ou crazy brothers are runnin' 'round here callin' yourselves pimps and playas, but let me tell you who the real pimps and playas are."

The man preaching behind the microphone paused briefly to allow his words to be fully absorbed before continuing. He was a skilled speaker who knew how to play on the emotions of his listeners. His purpose was to enlighten. His name was Kaleem Omorede, but most people simply called him, Brotha Kaleem.

Average height, with a muscularly build, Kaleem had a smooth brown complexion, shoulder length dreadlocks, and a thick mustache that he kept neatly groomed. An activist and a militant, he had grown up in the streets of Detroit and was known for his fiery rhetoric and willingness to kill or be killed for his beliefs. A preacher willing to die for his beliefs is one thing; but a preacher is ordained by God not to take a life. So Brotha Kaleem was certainly in a class by himself.

Sitting in the audience spellbound, Lil' Greg was glad he let his sister talk him into attending the meeting that was held every Friday night at the Kabazz Black Jewel Cultural Center on Mt. Elliot and Mack. Reba had been going to the meetings faithfully for months.

77

Kaleem continued. "When our ancestors first got off those slave ships from Africa, they were branded, then placed on the auction blocks naked as the day they were born, both men and women, to be sold to the highest bidder. They were used for labor, and to provide sexual favors and any other deviant behavior those white devils could conjure up in their depraved minds. So, you tell me, who were the first pimps? Each and every time one of our miseducated brothas calls himself a pimp, the only thin' he's doin' is imitatin' his former slave master. When he puts one of our beautiful black sistas out there on the block to sell her precious black body, all he is doin' is placin' the cruel chains of slavery right back on her."

"Go, Kaleem!" several people in the audience roared.

"So, the question is," Kaleem pointed out, "What should we do to brothas, who, out of ignorance and a lack of respect for themselves and the sistas, insist on hookin' them on drugs and a life of prostitution?"

A few of the more belligerent men in the audience wasted no time shouting, "String their black asses up!"

"No, no," Kaleem said gently. "We educate them. Ignorance and self-hatred can be erased through education. The last thing we want to do is take on the attributes of our oppressors. America eats its young under a dogmatic philosophy that dictates that the strong survive and the weak fall by the wayside. Well, as black people, we want to take our weak and make them strong. We want to remove the stigma of psychological slavery from their minds and replace it with healthy images of sistas and brothas livin' in peace, prosperity, and harmony. It'll take a lot of hard work, but it can be done."

A brother dressed in a black Dickie uniform stood up. "Brotha Kaleem, I feel what you're sayin', but what about those brothas who refuse to be educated, and who wanna insist they have the right to pimp our women and terrorize the rest of us into silence? Whadda we do 'bout crazy fools like that?"

78

Up on the platform Kaleem smiled. "Brotha, all I can tell you is, 'what's understood don't need no explanation. Any mad dog has to be put to sleep."

The meeting broke up around 9:00 that night, with people dispersing and conversing among themselves about some of the topics that had been covered during the lecture. Lil' Greg was waiting for an opportunity to cut into Brotha Kaleem. Soon, the opportunity presented itself.

"Wassup, Brotha Kaleem?"

Kaleem looked at him. "Do I know you, lil' brotha?"

"Not really, but I wanna ask you a few questions."

"Well, go ahead."

Lil' Greg paused, searching for the right words to begin. Finally he said slowly, "Well I wanna know what you think about drugs?"

Kaleem looked puzzled. "Drugs? Whadda 'bout them?"

"I mean, what do you think 'bout people who sell them to black people?"

Kaleem appeared thoughtful, as though he was searching for the right words to express himself.

"Let me put it like this, young brotha. Cigarettes are a drug, so is alcohol. Yet they are legal. Why? Because the powers that be, got their greedy little paws in the cookie jar reapin' the benefits. On the other hand, drugs – almost any drugs can be used to the benefit or detriment of mankind. In other words, there is no such thing as medicine or poison, for the same thing you call medicine, will kill you if you take too much of it, and poison can heal you if taken in the right amount."

Lil' Greg still didn't quite understand where Kaleem was coming from, so he asked, "Are you sayin' then, that it's okay to sell drugs?"

"I'm saying that oppressed people sometimes use any resource available to them to get the beast up off their back. The sales and proceeds of drugs are used by certain so called, Third World countries to finance major revolutions. The difference between them and us sellin' drugs is this: they

79

buy weapons, food, medicine, and uniforms to benefit their people and help fight oppression. We use the money we make to buy flashy trinkets and big pretty whips, so we can ride our black asses around the hood showing off. Soon as we kill enough of our own people, the white man comes and arrests us and send us off to jail for the rest of our natural lives. Now, that's gangsta."

"So, what do you say 'bout a dude slingin' rocks to help put his family through school?" Lil' Greg asked.

Kaleem looked at him and smiled knowingly. He knew Lil' Greg was referring to himself. "Listen, young blood "Do what you gotta do and leave that shit alone. Hit it and quit it. If you stick and stay you're gonna pay, and pay dearly."

"I feel you," Lil' Greg said quickly. "I think I'm gonna take your advice, but there's somethin' I have to do first."

■■■■■■■■■■■■■■■■■■■■■■■■■■■■■■■■■■■■■■■■■■■■■■■■■■■■■■■■■■■

That night, Lil' Greg and Winky, dressed up like women and were being escorted by Bay Bay and Melvin, into the Climax II over on Detroit's East Side. The popular nightclub was a known hangout for members of the 30/30 crew. Male patrons had to be frisked for weapons before they were allowed to enter the fashionable club, but females could enter unsearched.

Inside the smoke-filled club, the lights were dimmed and the smell of weed was thick in the air. There were so many people out on the dance floor; you couldn't turn to the left or right without bumping into somebody. Egged on by the stifling heat inside the club, and the hypnotic beat of gangsta rap, the crowd grew wilder and wilder, throwing away their inhibitions and giving in to their primal instincts. Standing on the sidelines quietly observing, Lil' Greg searched through the crowd of bodies until he spotted four well-known members of the 30/30 crew. Nudging Winky on the elbow, he pointed to his left.

"Check it out. There's some of dem punk bitches over there."

Winky glanced in the direction Lil' Greg was pointing in. He saw four young black males dressed in black leather jackets and sunglasses trying to look cool and nonchalant. Not one of them had the slightest idea what was about to go down.

"I see 'em," Winky acknowledged. "Let's do these clowns and get the fuck outta here. I feel just like a bitch with this tight ass dress on under my coat."

Taking a deep breath, Lil' Greg could feel his heart pounding wildly as his blood raced through his veins full of adrenaline. It was show time. Snatching the Uzi from under his coat, his eyes bucked like he had just got through smoking a ton of crack. It was now or never.

Beside him, Winky came up with a sawed off .12 gauge pump shotgun. Bay Bay and Melvin produced identical 9 mm pistols.

When they began firing, it sounded like World War III had broken out. People began screaming and running blindly for exits. Lil' Greg was careful to shoot over the crowd, so that innocent bystanders wouldn't get hurt. His partners didn't give a damn. They fired into the crowd indiscriminately and hoped that they somehow manage to hit their intended targets. Any innocent bystanders got killed; that was their problem.

In a full panic, men and women ran over each other like frightened cattle, trampling and stomping each other into the ground. In the ensuing pandemonium, Lil' Greg and his companions were able to escape out a side door.

Later on, witnesses would tell the police that they saw the shooters climb into a black GMC truck and speed off down Jefferson Avenue. But most of them changed their stories. Being a potential witness in a city like Detroit didn't hold such a promising future.

■■■■■■■■■■■■■■■■■■■■■■■■■■■■■■■■■■■■■■■■■■■■■■■■■■■■■■■

Chi Chi straddled the naked man like she was riding a thoroughbred pony. The man's hands and wrists were handcuffed securely to the bedposts.

"Oh yeah, baby, ride that dick!" he groaned.

Looking down into Billy's contorted face, Chi Chi began bucking her hips frantically. "Is it good muthafucka?" she asked in a harsh tone of voice.

Barely able to speak, Billy grunted his reply. "You know your pussy is good bitch."

"I'm glad you're enjoyin' it." Chi Chi said, " 'Cause it'll be the last piece of pussy you ever get!"

Billy's eyes flew wide-open. He began struggling against his binds, trying his best to break free from the handcuffs he had allowed Chi Chi to place on him. Panic flooding through his mind, he demanded, "Take these muthafuckin' handcuffs offa me! Ho, have you lost yo' mind?"

She laughed loudly. She still had her bra on, but was naked from the waist down. Her black lace panties were lying on the bed beside her. The trapped man lying beneath her could have sworn he saw a demon enter Chi Chi's body, as she threw back her head and continued to laugh. Picking up her panties, she began stuffing the flimsy material inside his mouth.

"U-u-gh!" he protested, tossing his head violently from side to side as tears rolled down his face.

Chi Chi's response was to pull out the switchblade concealed inside her bra. When she popped it open, it made a loud, clicking sound. Billy moaned and broke wind. Sweat beads had broken out all over his body and were running freely down his face into his eyes. Chi Chi was enjoying every single moment of her revenge. There was a look of fear in Billy's horror-stricken eyes that made her heart leap for joy. As she slowly raised the razor sharp knife, Billy could only follow the motion with a look of resignation.

The first blow penetrated his chest, causing blood to spurt out of the wound like oil gushing out of a newly discovered oil well. Billy's eyes rolled into the back of his head until only the whites of his eyes were showing. Chi Chi stabbed him repeatedly until his body stopped jerking beneath her. Climbing off his body, she took her time and spread his legs.

Reaching down with the knife, she began drawing it back and forth across his limp penis in a sawing motion until she had sliced the organ completely off. Her mission accomplished, she held up the grisly trophy in triumph, then brutally shoved it inside the dead man's rectum.

In a zone now, she calmly walked to the bathroom and turned the cold water on running it, then she turned on the shower. The cold water hit her, like a splash in a pool and she jumped out of her sleep. She looked over on the side of her. It was BJ, not Billy. She checked his penis, it was there, right where it was suppose to be. *Oh, thank God.*

But, Billy, he wouldn't be so lucky, not when Chi Chi got a hold of him. She had every intention of making her child molesting, step father's dream a reality. *The dream has to come true, it's the only way, the only way.*

# CHAPTER THIRTEEN

Lisa entered the seventh precinct on Gratiot and Mack Avenue, and demanded to speak to the detective in charge of the investigation into the recent string of murders that were happening throughout the city. She was instantly referred to Lt. Mike McQueen.

"Come in, young lady. Have a seat."

McQueen was a clean-shaven, dark-skinned, sharply dressed African-American in his late thirties, with thick black eyebrows and a receding hairline.

Noticing Lisa's shabby attire and unkempt hair, he surmised correctly that she was a crack addict. "What can I do for you, Miss – I don't think I caught your name."

"Call me Mona," Lisa said, staring straight ahead.

McQueen recognized the dull, unfocused look in her eyes. He had seen it many times before. His suspicions were confirmed by Lisa's constant squirming. She was obviously nervous and kept biting down on her bottom lip.

McQueen repeated his question. "What can I do for you ma'am?"

"To tell you the truth sir," Lisa replied politely, "There may be something I can do for you."

McQueen took a closer look at the disheveled young woman sitting across the desk from him and this time he was able to see through the layers of dirt and stale make-up, deep into the prematurely aged face of a beautiful young woman begging to be set free from a brutal addiction. He trully felt sorry for her.

"Well then, what exactly can you do for me, Mona?" he asked.

"It's about the murders taking place throughout the city. I think I know whose behind them."

That got McQueen's full attention. "Would you like a cigarette? Maybe something to drink?" he asked.

Lisa nodded yes, then spent the next two hours spilling her guts about everything she knew about Chi Chi, BJ, Melvin, and Thad. But, she didn't mention Lil' Greg whatsoever.

■■■■■■■■■■■■■■■■■■■■■■■■■■■■■■■■■■■■■■■■■■■■■■■■■■■■■■■■■■■■

Larry arrived at the Democratic Club in a white Benz. A crowd of people were gathered in the street watching the 'pimp and ho' spectacle in front of them. Rayfil was sitting in a black Volvo in the driver's seat arguing with a thin, young, black woman who was wearing a blond wig and way too much make up. She was standing next to him on the driver's side of the car, leaning in the window. Highly animated, they both continued their heated argument.

"Nigga, I'm sick and tired of you treatin' me like I'm your rag doll or a piece of toilet paper you can wipe your ass with, then throw away!" she shouted indignantly.

Rayfil stared at her like she was crazy. "Ho, check yo' self. No bitch is gonna tell me how to lay my mack down."

Having heard enough, the woman attempted to back away from the car, but Rayfil reached out and caught her wrist in a vise-like grip, then put the car in drive and drove down the street, dragging the girl from the side of the car.

"Let me go, let me go. Stop Rayfil, stop the car!" the woman screamed.

Rayfil held on even tighter and sped up before slamming on his brakes causing the girls head to crash up against the outside rearview mirror. Instantly, a huge knot appeared above her right eye. Somewhere along the way she had lost her shoes and both her feet had lost skin from being scratched on the asphalt. Releasing her wrist, Rayfil and the crowd, watched as her body slumped motionlessly to the ground. He got out his car, stood over top of her, drew back his leg and began to kick square in her back. Bending down he yanked her to her feet, hosited her over his shoulder, and marched to the trunk of his car, opened it and hurled the barely conscious woman inside the trunk before slamming the trunk hood.

"I hope you're satisfied now, bitch," he mumbled before slamming the trunk down.

Larry had seen enough. *Is this nigga insane? He must be.* Getting out of his whip, he walked over to Rayfil who was standing there breathing like he had just got through running the one-hundred-yard dash.

"If you're through entertaining the crowd, my man, maybe we can go inside the club and kick it."

"Bout time you got here. Let's go inside. We need to talk."

"What about the girl? You ain't just gonna leave her in the trunk are you?"

"Why not? The bitch'll be alright. C'mon."

Reluctantly, Larry followed him.

"Wanna drink?" Rayfil asked, making his way around the bar and pouring himself a double shot of rum and coke.

"No thanks. I wanna know why you called me down here in the midst of all these raggedy ass dope fiends?"

Through bloodshot eyes Rayfil glared at Larry. It was hard for him to conceal his contempt.

"Hey, you don't have to be actin' so high and mighty nigga. If it don't be for them dope fiends out there, your black ass wouldn't be ridin' around in those fancy pimpmobiles. You should be more appreciative of the hands that feed you."

"Don't trip, nigga," Larry said. "Just give me the four-one-one on what's goin' down. Think you can handle that?"

Downing his drink, Rayfil wiped his mouth with the back of his hand. "Tony sent you a little present. It's in the back. C'mon," he said, walking from behind the bar and heading down a long narrow hallway.

Dumbfounded, Larry followed him to a darkened room in the back of the building. Inside the small room, lying motionless on the floor was a badly beaten man. Larry could barely make out the man's facial features.

"Damn," he commented. "You got people held captive everywhere. Who the fuck is that?"

Rayfil grinned. "That's your present. The number one source behind all your problems."

Thinking that this had to be some kind of joke, Larry grinned back. "What the fuck is that supposed to mean?"

"It's simple. That greaseball on the floor got drugged 'cause BJ got off his line and got on yours. So he sent his boys at BJ's crew, hopin' they'd think Raymond was trying to get some back. I guess he didn't appreciate you steppin' on his toes."

Larry shrugged. "Business is business. This is America, the land of free enterprise. If he didn't like it, he shoulda took his punk ass down to Mexico somewhere. Maybe then he wouldn't be lyin' down there on the floor."

"In any case," Rayfil continued, "The plan was to have you and Raymond tear each other off, then once the coast was clear, move his own people in. It was a beautiful plan; he just forgot one thing."

Larry looked up. "What's that?"

"Tony Ferrano. Tony put everythin' together and had some of his people right here in the city take care of it. They brought this piece of garbage to me last night. He's yours now."

"How'd he let them catch him with his drawers down?"

"His underboss gave him up. Some cat callin' himself Diablo, which means devil in Spanish. He set my man up so he could take over. Same story that's been going down through time; dawg eat dawg."

At the mention of Diablo's name, Speedy let out a stream of profanity. "Punta!" he cursed. "Listen to me amigo. Let me go and I'll pay you a million dollars in cash money. Whadda ya say homes?"

Greed flashed through Rayfil's mind. He and Larry could split it right down the middle. Neither Tony nor anyone else had to know anything about it.

"Where's the cash at?" he asked.

Seeing a slender ray of hope, Speedy began talking fast. "Just let me make one phone call, homes. My girl will bring it to you anywhere you say."

Seeing that Rayfil was serious, Larry spoke up.

"Don't be no fool," he cautioned, turning to stare Rayfil directly in the eyes. "It sounds good, but all money ain't good money. You ain't no stranger to the game."

"Fuck all that philosophy shit you talkin' 'bout!" Rayfil said angrily.

"Check this out," Larry tried to reason. "What good is a million dollars if you ain't alive to spend none of it? You know good and damn well this muthafucka will say anythin' to get his ass outta this sling. You think Tony ain't gonna find out about this?"

"Fuck Tony!" Rayfil shouted. "Anyway, who's gonna tell him? You?"

Tired of talking, Larry popped out his cell phone.

"Who you callin'?" Rayfil asked.

"I'm calling BJ and Thad. This muthafucka is responsible for takin' out Thad's sister and baby niece. Thad is gonna be real glad to get his hands on his ass."

Rayfil stood there full of anger, resigned to the fact he wasn't going to get the chance to play Speedy out the money. But in his mind, it added up to one more strike against Larry.

*In due time,* he told himself, *all in due time.* Rayfil would be patient, he'd wait until the right opportunity presented itself and then he'd pay Larry back for all the bullshit he had to put up over the years. *God I can't wait for the day to come,* he thought with glee. *We'll see if that nigga is acting all high and mighty then. It's bad enough he thinks he some type of black king sitting on a throne. We'll see when the lights go out though. We'll see where this nigga end up sitting then.* Yes, Rayfil had every intention of bringing Larry down so low, he would have to look up at the bottom of his own feet.

■■■■■■■■■■■■■■■■■■■■■■■■■■■■■■■■■■■■■■■■■■■■■■■■■■■■■

The stakeout crew chilled inside the black van a block away from the targets of their investigation, silently observing every single drug transaction taking place.

Through high-powered binoculars, they watched and recorded the people driving up, buying drugs from BJ and Thad's people, along with the uniformed teenaged boys selling them. They took license plate numbers, snapped photographs, and made and compared notes. When they got ready to take BJ and his little crew down, they didn't want to make any mistakes. They wanted to be able to put each and everyone of them away for the rest of their lives. For years, the city had been terrorized by vicious, cold-blooded killers trying to monopolize the drug market. BJ and his crew had been among the worst. It was time to pay the piper. And leading the charge was Lt. Mike McQueen. If things went right, this case would be the highlight of his career and the start of another. All his life he had political ambitions, and a case like this; was just what he needed to build a 'get tough on crime' platform.

He would arrest BJ and his crew, then put them away for a long time. But he first had to protect his star witness; Mona Lisa. After he put her on the witness stand and after she told her story of drug addiction and sexual depravity, there wasn't a jury on the face of the earth, who wouldn't be more than glad to convict the monsters responsible for terrorizing the streets and causing so much devastation. Still, McQueen wasn't the type of man to just leave things to chance. If by some remote stretch of the imagination, the jury didn't believe Lisa's testimony, then he had another ace up his sleeve. A kid named Bay Bay.

# CHAPTER FOURTEEN

"**C**ome here son," the heavy-built man whispered in the dark. He was wearing a long black robe and even in the darkness you could see his cold blue eyes. The little boy recoiled in fear, his wide-open eyes full of dread. Bumping into a wall, he realized that he was trapped and there was no where for him to go, like a frightened animal in a cage.

"Please, don't hurt me mister," he begged, knowing his pleas would be ignored. He had been through the same routine before and knew only too well what to expect.

"I'm not goin' to hurt you," the man said unconvincingly. "Don't you want me to be your friend?"

"No!" the boy screamed. "Leave me alone or I'ma tell my mother."

The man in the robe laughed softly. "Haven't you figured it out yet? Your mother doesn't give a damn about you. Who do you think brought you to me? I can do with you exactly as I please and there's no one you can run to. You should be a grateful boy. If not for me, then you'd be in a reformatory somewhere."

The boy began to sob. There was a look of madness in his eyes that bespoke volumes of the hidden horrors to come in the days ahead.

"Leave me alone!" the boy shouted, knowing it would do no good. The last thing he heard was the man's laughter.

"Thad, honey wake up!"

Fluttering his eyelids open, Thad awoke in a cold sweat, his eyes searching the bed beside him, as he saw a look of deep concern on Jasmine's brown face as she cradled his head in her arms. "It's alright darling," she whispered. "It's only a dream."

He came out of it realizing he was in his room and his girl was rocking him like a big baby. Inside, he felt overwhelming relief to be safe and sound, then shame and disgust. Once again a part of his past was threatening to burst into the open and destroy him. He had tried over the years to suppress it, but it never seemed to go away.

"Thad, I'm really scared. I think you should see someone."

Ignoring her suggestion, he pretended to respond, "Why, why do you say that?" Even he knew it was a stupid question, he just didn't know what else to say at that moment. He had really bad dreams in his sleep and he had them a lot. This wasn't the first time he awoke to Jasmine rocking him. But there was no way he could tell her the truth, no way, Jose. That part of his life had to be hidden.

"Why do I say that? Thad, you were screaming at someone to leave you alone before you told your mother."

Thad looked at her sideways wondering what else he might have said.

Silent, Jasmine watched him through eyes full of growing concern. Sensing her worry, Thad said, "I'm alright now. It was just a nightmare."

"Yeah," agreed Jasmine, "but one that keeps coming back. Thad, why don't you let me introduce you to this friend of the family? He's a black psychiatrist who..."

"So you think I'm crazy?" Thad asked, cutting her off in mid-sentence.

"I didn't say that," Jasmine said. "But I do feel you need help, someone to talk to."

"I said I'm alright!" Thad spat.

Angrily, he got up from the bed and stomped off in the

direction of the bathroom. Minutes later Jasmine heard the sound of water running in the shower. Thad emerged twenty minutes later re-energized. He was an entirely different person. Leaning down, he kissed Jasmine passionately on her thick juicy lips.

"Don't start nothing you can't finish," Jasmine warned, already feeling the stirrings of sexual arousal between her shapely thighs. Her beauty compared to Thad's ugliness, often made people refer to them in private as Beauty and the Beast. Who knew and most couldn't figure it out. But, it was Thad's unappealing looks that drew her to him the most.

For Jasmine, she had always went for the handsome guys, not realizing, they're the ones all the girls want too. Jaz caught more diseases and more heart break realizing the truth was that it didn't matter what a brother had on the outside, it all added up to the character and moral fiber they were built with on the inside. A good man is hard to find and it's not many that have loyalty to one woman. Jaz pretty much had that in Thad. He wasn't a womanizer, that just wasn't his thing. He didn't even like the strip clubs and since he was so ugly, the women didn't really look twice at him. With Thad, she didn't have to worry about him cheating or deceiving her with sweet lies. Thad was a man who not only appreciated her for who and what she was, but he lived to please her and didn't care who knew it. On top of that, he needed her.

Turning, he walked over to the closet and selected a denim outfit with matching Timbs. He made sure he slipped on his body armor before putting on his jacket. Jasmine sat there silently observing him. What he lacked in looks, he made up for in style. Thaddeus Jones was one of the sharpest-dressed men in the city of Detroit, a city known for its stylish fashion wear.

Once he was dressed, he walked back over to the closet and he took a shoe box from off a shelf. He sat the shoe box on the bed, took off the lid and lifted a wad of cash.

"Here, Jaz take this."

"What's this for?"

"It's for my nephew."

"How much is it? It looks like a lot of money."

"It's only fifteen grand. I wanna make sure he'll be alright in case something happens to me. I'm his only living relative."

For a moment, Jasmine just stared at the man she had fallen in love with, then said slowly, "The other night, those men were shootin' at you, weren't they?"

Thad looked at her with a dead serious expression etched across his heavily chiseled facial features. "To be honest, baby, I don't know who they were shootin' at. When you live the life of a PPG, anythin' might go down. I'm just glad they couldn't shoot straight."

Jasmine smiled. She had heard BJ use the expression PPG used many times. It meant Pretty Pimpin' Gangsta.

"By the way, sweetheart, I got somethin' for you too. You been so sweet to me, I just wanna show you a little appreciation. I know you think I don't love you like I should, and perhaps you're right. So check this out."

Reaching inside his jacket pocket, he pretended he had lost whatever it was he was searching for.

"Damn. I had somethin' for you, but I must've lost it somewhere. Oh, here it is." he said with a big grin, watching the expression on Jasmine's face.

Glancing down, Jasmine saw a small, square box made out of crushed blue velvet. In total shock she watched Thad open the box, then remove a beautiful gold and diamond engagement ring.

"Oh, Thad," she gushed. Her knees suddenly felt weak. She felt like she might faint at any moment.

Dropping down on one knee, Thad took her left hand and slid the ring over her ring finger.

"You know, I never thought that I would ever be able to love anyone. Beside my mother, my sister and her

94

children, I've never loved or cared about anyone until you Jasmine. You and my son are all that matters to me in the entire universe. I guess what I'm trying to say is, Jaz, will you marry me.

Eyes brimming with tears, Jasmine was speechless. For the first time in her life she didn't know what to say, so she reached down and grabbed Thad around the neck in a bear hug, holding on for dear life.

"Yes, I'll marry you. I've been waitin' a long time to hear you say those words."

Thad let out a long sigh of relief. Secretly he had been waiting on her rejection. He didn't want to believe that someone as fine and intelligent as Jasmine could actually consider being his wife.

"I'm gonna make you proud of me baby," he whispered.

Jasmine smiled at him, her brown eyes full of joy and hidden promise. "I'm already proud of you," she said.

"No," Thad insisted. "I'm gonna get out this vicious drug game and go completely legit. I want to promote rap concerts. I don't want our son growing up without a father around the crib, and if I don't stop, I'll either be locked up for the rest of my life, or dead in the cemetery before my time."

Jasmine listened closely to his every word. In the back of her mind she wanted to believe him when he said he was going to stop dealing drugs, but somehow she wasn't convinced. Of course, she would do whatever it took to help him turn that corner, but in her heart she knew it wasn't going to be easy. They were in too deep. And to be truthful, she herself had gotten used to living the lifestyle that came along with the territory. By agreeing to marry Thad, she couldn't help but wonder if she was making one of the biggest mistakes in her life.

■■■■■■■■■■■■■■■■■■■■■■■■■■■■■■■■■■■■■■■■■■■■■■■■■■■■■■

At 6:15, Thad pulled his black Cherokee in front of a small, wood-framed house on Charlevoix and Parker. It was owned by BJ under an assumed name.

Every Friday night they would meet up here and pay their workers. Thad paid everybody once a week just like any other employer. In fact, they ran their drug empire like a professional corporation. The only difference between them, and say, Kellogg's, were the products they sold. One sold corn-flakes, and the other sold flakes of cocaine.

Entering the house, Thad was greeted fondly by the men who worked for him. Not only did they fear him, but they respected him. Thad was a true field general who didn't mind getting his hands dirty right along with the troops. He was an enforcer as well as one of the bosses of YGS.

Lugging two Hefty garbage bags full of sensimilla, he dumped the contents in the center of the living room.

"Melvin, go look inside the jeep and bring inside those six cases of Remy."

"Now, that's the love I'm speakin' of," Bay Bay cracked. He already had a good buzz going on.

"In the mean time," Thad announced, "I got a briefcase full of cash for y'all. It's payday."

Rubbing his hands together, Winky exclaimed good-naturedly, "Now, that's what the fuck I'm talkin' about. Bullshit ain't nothin'. Gimme da fuckin' loot!"

By 8:00, the payday-party was in full swing, with a crowd of young drug dealers and a few hoochie mamas shaking their boots to music popping in the air. Marijuana and Remy Martin were passed around the room freely. All the known strippers who danced naked at the booty clubs up and down eight mile had been paid up front to perform and entertain the crew, and if one of the fellows wanted to go a little further, that was okay too. Most of the girls sold pussy on the side, anyway.

As luck would have it, Lil' Greg rolled up on the set late, pulling up in a money green Lexus. Just as he was about to get out of the car, drug agents rushed the house from all directions like a black cloud of hungry locusts descending on a field of crops ripe for harvesting. Dressed entirely in black ninja outfits and ski masks to conceal their identities, the agents moved in unison, quickly approaching their target. Using a steel battering ram device, the agents knocked the door off the hinges, but the noise and music were so loud, no one realized what was going on at first. When it dawned on everyone else that the spot was being raided, all hell broke loose. People were running and hiding downstairs in the basement, upstairs in the closet, under the bed, and anywhere else they could find to hind. Nobody wanted to go to jail. A few of them dove out of windows straight into the arms of the po po.

Thad was one of the first arrested. He was thrown up against the wall with such force, one of his teeth was jarred loose. "Goddamn!" he complained angrily.

"Shut up punk," said this one agent. "It's thugs like you who give the entire black race a bad name. That's why you're going down. You and the rest of your crew."

"Yeah, whatever," Thad muttered before being hustled off along with several others to a waiting police bus with DETROIT POLICE stenciled in white letters on the sides.

From the safety of his car, Lil' Greg silently observed everything going down so he could give BJ an accurate report. Turning the key in the ignition, he drove away slowly. The last thing he needed was to attract attention.

Driving carefully through the city streets, he thought about how lucky he had been not to arrive at the spot on time. Otherwise, he might have been among those arrested, and had that occurred, it would have definitely put a crimp in his plans and in his game. Still, he had to move quick. Time was running out.

The attempted hit coming out of Legends, the shoot-out at the Climax II, along with the assassination of Thad's sister and niece, all added up to one thing. Surely this latest incident was a sign of things to come, and Lil' Greg didn't have to be a prophet to see that. The handwriting was on the wall.

# CHAPTER FIFTEEN

**C**harged with being a drug kingpin along with suspicion of murder, Thad was denied bail. After finding Speedy's dead, mutilated body in a garbage-strewn alley on Detroit's East Side, Thad became the number one suspect.

Speedy had been beaten to death with a baseball bat and stabbed repeatedly with an ice pick. As for Melvin, Winky, and Bay Bay, bond had been set at $100,000 for each of them. In addition, an arrest warrant for BJ and Chi Chi had been issued and Detroit's finest were searching high and low for any sign of the missing pair. After the dust had settled, Lil' Greg came under suspicion.

That night, on a block inside the Wayne County Jail, Thad and the others sat around a steel gray, metal table dressed in matching prison-issued, pale-green jumpsuits. Mindful of their surroundings, they discussed their situation among themselves in low, measured tones so they wouldn't be overheard.

Up and down the block, the brothers laid back, trying to pass the time or to figure out a way to get out of the mess they were in. Some were sitting around on dirty gray blankets spread across the concrete floor, slamming dominoes down or playing spades, while others were discussing their cases with jailhouse lawyers who made a hustle out of telling desperate men what they wanted to hear.

"I wonder how come Lil' Greg didn't show up," Winky said. "He knew Friday was payday and he still didn't show up."

"Yeah, that shit don't even look right." Glancing over at Thad, he asked for his opinion. "Don't you think it's a little strange 'Lil Greg didn't show up at the house?"

Without hesitation Thad replied, "I think you niggas should shut da fuck up, and quit trippin' 'bout shit you don't know. Can't none of you make me believe my man is a rat."

"I ain't sayin' he is," Melvin said quickly. "All I'm sayin' is that the shit don't look right. Him not showin' up and all."

Before Thad could respond, Winky added his two cents.

"I understand what Melvin is saying. Especially 'cause our attorney says they got a confidential informant tellin' on us."

"That may be so, but a dime to a doughnut it ain't Lil' Greg," Thad repeated with an air of finality that indicated that conversation was over. "All three of y'all will be back on the bricks soon as Jasmine catches up with Boston."

James Boston was one of the top bail bondsmen in the city. Somewhat of a gangsta himself, he only dealt with high-profile cases where he stood to make a considerable profit from the high interest rates he charged.

"What 'bout you? Whadda they gon' do about givin' you a bond?" Melvin asked.

Thad shrugged his shoulders. "Right now they're tryin' to hit me with Murder One. Ain't no bond for first-degree murder. Eventually they'll break it down to second – at least, accordin' to my lawyer. They do that, then I'll walk."

Melvin digested this bit of information before trying another tactic. "How come you got a different attorney from the one you hired for us? How come we can't all use the same one?"

Thad stared at him, knowing what he was getting at.

"Listen, they call that a conflict of interest, but of

course, you don't know anything about that. Besides, what are you tryin' to imply? Spit it out. You ain't got to keep beatin' around the bush like a crafty politician. You act like you're afraid to say what's on your mind, like a bitch. Wassup?"

Flabbergasted, Melvin shot right back "I don't know where you gettin' your information from, but I ain't afraid of nothin' walkin', talkin', or movin'! I was just askin' a fuckin' question."

"Man, y'all cool it with that shit," Winky cautioned. "The phone's off the hook," he said, glancing around.

Just then, a blond-haired, blue-eyed deputy appeared at the front of the cell block and stood there peeping in.

"Is there a Lonnie Taylor in there? If so, step your ass to the front. There's an attorney here to see you."

Bay Bay looked puzzled. "That's me. I wonder who the fuck that could be? We already talked to our lawyer. Besides, why would he just be callin' me out?"

"Yeah, what's up with that?" Winky wondered out loud. Thad and Melvin continued giving each other the evil eye.

"Maybe your old girl hired you another mouthpiece, Winky speculated.

Bay Bay nodded. "Yeah, maybe so."

"Taylor!" the deputy yelled impatiently. "Front and center boy! I ain't got all day to be standing around while you lolligag with your crime partners. All of your black asses are going to Jackson anyway. Now get your ass up here before I break these doors and come in there and drag you out by your feet!"

"Drag on dese nuts, bitch!" someone shouted out.

"Yeah, bring your pink ass on in here, Billy Bob. I bet when you leave, that asshole will be as red as your face, you racist cracker!"

Up and down the block the prisoners laughed at the guard's expense. Thad sat there knowing damn right well they were all full of shit and wasn't doing shit to that guard at the end of the day. Lighting up a Kool, he inhaled deeply, then blew the smoke out slowly, watching it spiral toward the ceiling in a blue haze. Suddenly, an image of Jasmine, Kamal, and his little son appeared in his mind's eye.

*Damn,* he thought sullenly. *If I go to prison, who's going to take care of them?*

Through narrowed eyes he watched Bay Bay picking his way through the sea of hopeless men stretched out on the floor, as he made his way toward the front. He wondered if it was his imagination, or was Bay Bay suspect?

■■■■■■■■■■■■■■■■■■■■■■■■■■■■■■■■■■■■■■■■■■■■■■■■■■■■■■■■■

"**Y**ou heard about your man didn't ya?" Rayfil asked in a calm voice.

Turning away from the naked girl lying next to him nibbling his neck, Larry whispered, "Cool it baby. I'm tryin' to take care of something." Into the phone he said, "Nah, I ain't heard nothin'. Wassup wit' 'em?"

In the background Rayfil could hear the soft moans of a woman obviously in ecstasy. "If you keep your tender dick outta them sluts, you just might stay up on what's happening out here in these mean streets."

"Man, fuck all that," Larry said irritably. Rayfil was beginning to get on his nerves. It was obvious the older man didn't like him, just like it was obvious Rayfil was jealous of him. Larry knew that the only reason Rayfil tolerated him was because he needed his bankroll.

Rayfil continued to gripe. "It's all over the news. Thad, Winky, Bay Bay, and Melvin, have been arrested on a drug and murder indictment. They're lookin' for BJ and Chi Chi. The rollers are so thick out here can't nobody make a dollar. You know what that means?"

Startled and at full attention, Larry replied. "Nah, tell me."

"It means that these dirty ass niggas out here will be helpin' the police track your man and his woman down so they can get their groove back on. They don't give a fuck

101

about BJ, you, or me. Not when it comes to their hustle. Do you understand what I'm talkin' about?"

Fully alert now, Larry pushed the girl away from his dick and began putting on his silk boxers. With every word Rayfil spoke, Larry became less aroused. Reaching over to the desk he riffled through a huge bankroll and removed three $20 bills.

"Here you go, bitch. Take this and beat it. Holler back later."

Furious, the girl hurled the money back at him.

"Don't play me like I'm some kinda two-dollar ho;" she said angrily. "Keep your money; I thought you had more class than that."

Climbing from beneath the black silk sheets, the girl began storming around the elaborately furnished bedroom gathering her panties and dress. Butt naked, her breasts and ass cheeks were bouncing like rubber balls.

Ignoring her, Larry turned his attention back to the phone. "Sorry about the little interruption. Now where were we? Oh yeah, listen, do you think my name is gonna come up in any of this?"

Rayfil laughed contemptuously. "How the hell should I know? You better hope BJ and Thad are the thoroughbreds you think they are. Otherwise your ass is out."

The bedroom door slammed shut as the girl Larry had just recently met while clubbing, left the room in an uproar. Rayfil couldn't help from taking another stab at Larry.

"You like livin' dangerous, huh? Man, you're playin' with fire picking up every stray bitch that bats her eye, or shakes her fabulous ass at you. All you're doin' is throwing rocks at the cemetery. You ain't gone be satisfied until one of those bitches sets your ass up to be robbed and killed."

"Yeah, like you care," Larry said sarcastically. "Listen man, holler at one of your police connects and see what you can find out. I'd appreciate it."

"Yeah, I think I can do that for you. In the meantime, if I was you, I'd watch my back. You know how it goes. When the jungle catches on fire, all the animals scramble for safety."

"Yeah, you right. Holler back as soon as you find out somethin'. Don't leave me hangin' dawg."

Breaking the connection, Larry began dialing around the city checking his own sources to see what he could come up with. While Rayfil was working one end of the equation, he didn't see how it could hurt if he worked the other. Between the two of them, something was bound to come up.

Larry's motto was it's always wise to know before hand, if the house is about to fall. That way he can move the hell outta the way before it falls on top of him.

# CHAPTER SIXTEEN

**W**ednesday, morning, around 9:00 a.m., television cameras, roving reporters, and a crowd of curious onlookers jockeyed for position and crowded the entrance to 1300 Beaubian.

BJ and Chi Chi, accompanied by their high-priced attorneys, exited the black Mercedes and pushed their way through the crowd and up the steps leading into the brick building that housed police headquarters.

After much haggling and compromising with the prosecutor's office, the suspects had agreed to turn themselves in with the understanding that they and their codefendants would be released on bail, and that criminal charges would range from second-degree murder to sales and possession of narcotics. Chi Chi would face the lesser charge of money laundering. After going through the arraignment routine, a little $1,000,000.00 in cash and property was put up as collateral, and two hours later BJ and his entire crew were back out on the streets doing their thing.

McQueen watched them swagger out of the courtroom with fire in his eyes and murder on his mind. *They may laugh now,* he thought grimly, *but we'll see who's going to be laughing when all is said and done.*

A motion filed by their attorneys, revealed that Lisa was slated to be the state's star witness. Unaware of her brutal and humiliating treatment at the hands of Chi Chi and some of the crew members, BJ and Thad wondered what kind of compelling evidence she had to offer the prosecutor. The two of them both spoke on it, but the pieces to the puzzle, just didn't make sense.

That same night after making bond, BJ and Thad's drug operation was back in full swing. With so much at stake, they couldn't afford to sit still. They needed cash, and a whole lot of it. The only thing keeping them out of jail was money, and the only thing paying their attorneys was money.

In the meantime, Larry made sure he kept his distance so he wouldn't be associated with the indicted drug dealers. As a show of good faith, however, he made sure to donate a sizable amount of loot to their legal defense and made sure they were aware of his generosity. He was certain they were going to prison and didn't see any reason why he should be going with them. To get his mind off the current situation, he bought a lifetime membership card at Gold's Gym. One Saturday he decided to get a quick workout in before hitting the streets.

Dressed in black sneakers and a black Karl Kani sweatsuit, he entered the gym and glanced around. He could smell the sweat from the men and women who dedicated themselves to the upkeep of their heavenly temples. To his right were rows of leather-covered benches and state-of-the-art weight machines. In back of them were several full-length mirrors and a support rail, so the patrons could view themselves while they stretched or exercised. Along the wall sat several vending machines. To his immediate left were the pull-up and dip bars, and across the room were more benches and racks with free weights. Venturing to his right, he headed for the bench press machine to work on his chest.

Placing a hundred pounds on the machine, Larry dropped down on the bench and began pushing the bar up and down, inhaling on the way down and exhaling on the way up. He always used lighter weights to warm up before adding on more weight. He was halfway through his second set when out of the corner of his eye, he saw her. Tall, with long, red hair pulled back in a ponytail, a beautiful sister with green eyes stepped into his view.

She had on a body-fitting black leotard that showed every curve in her body, and she stepped like a woman who knew she was fine.

Grabbing a forty-five pound weight bar, she walked in front of one of the mirrors, lifted the bar behind her shoulders, and began squatting up and down. Each time she went down into the bucket then stood back up, her leotard slid in between the crack of her ass cheeks. Behind her, lying flat on his back, Larry watched her out the corner of his eye.

He got so caught up watching her ass that he barely heard her speaking.

"I hope you're enjoying yourself."

"I was just admirin' your muscles. You got real nice muscles for a broad."

To his delight, the girl smiled and the entire room seemed to light up. Her eyes were the color of sea green emeralds. "If you ask me," she said, "you were only interested in one muscle in particular, and I don't think I have to tell you which one."

Recovering his composure, Larry sat up on the bench and turned so that he was facing her. "Okay, I'm busted. I confess I was checking out the double bubble."

She smiled. "Well, at least you're honest."

"Of course. By the way, I'm Larry, what's your name?"

"Greta."

"Greta, that's a beautiful name."

"Are you always this aggressive, Larry?"

"As a matter-of-fact, no. This must be your first time here. Had you been here before, believe me, I would have noticed you and that's a fact."

"Is that right?"

"Yes, baby. That's right. After all, it's not every day a beautiful little angel like you descends to earth."

By this time he had walked up to her and was

standing only inches apart. He was so close to her he could feel her body heat and smell her apple breath. He had been in the presence of some of the most beautiful women in and around Detroit, and Greta definitely rated among them. Her beauty was extraordinary.

"Since this is your first time here, let me show you around. I won't bite you."

Greta stared at him, then said seriously, "How do you know I won't?" A mischievous little smile was playing at the corners of her wide mouth.

"I'll take my chances," Larry said. "C'mon, follow me. You're in good hands with me, so good my name should be Allstate."

He escorted her around the gym, making small talk and charming her with his wit. Passing the section where the dumb-bells and loose weights were kept.

"This is where the free weights are kept."

"Oh really? How much are the other weights?"

"So baby got jokes. You know, you are really beautiful. What's your nationality?"

"My father's African-American, and my mother's Italian. Does that turn you off?"

"Hell naw baby. I'm a city boy. Born and raised right here in the muthafuckin' Motor City. As you know, Detroit is a city with all types of different nationalities and cultures. On top of that, I can't afford to be racist in my line of work. It's bad for business."

"That's interesting. What do you do for a living?"

"I'm a hairstylist," he replied. "I'm also into real estate. What about you? What do you do besides look gorgeous."

"I'm studying law."

"Is that right? Where do you go to school?"

"Wayne State University."

"Are you a native Detroiter?"

"As a matter-of-fact, no," Greta said, toying with a thin gold bracelet on her wrist. "Originally, I'm from Boston." *At least that much is true,* she thought wryly.

"I knew it," Larry said. "You don't look like a Detroit girl."

"Oh, no?" Greta said amused. "What exactly does a Detroit girl look like?"

Larry shrugged. "It's kinda hard to explain, but chicks outta Detroit have a certain kind of attitude. Jazzy yet sophisticated. How long have you been in the big D?"

"About two years," Greta replied without offering any additional information.

"Well, what's your opinion of Detroit?"

"I love it so far. It's nothing like what I had in mind. You know, all the awful stories you hear."

Larry laughed. "Baby, don't believe nothin' you hear and only half of what you see. But there's another side to the city if you'd care to see it."

"Why should I?"

"Because it's fun and it's real and it's my way of askin' a beautiful woman out."

Showing no emotion, Greta said, "Oh, so you want to go out? Like on a date, right?"

"Yes," Larry replied.

Appearing to be undecided, Larry didn't wait for her to make up her mind. He instead moved in for the kill.

"Give me your phone number and I'll pick you up around nine. Is that cool?"

"Okay. That's cool." He liked the way she said the word cool.

Outside in the parking lot they exchanged digits and a few pleasantries, then headed for their cars. Larry stopped in front of his Benz and watched her climb into a black Corvette with gold rims. As she drove past him, she blew the horn and waved. As the Corvette faded from sight, he felt his manhood rising as he visualized her naked ass sliding up and down on top of him. *I can't wait to hit that.*

# CHAPTER SEVENTEEN

Queens, New York, Thursday, 7:00 p.m. The black Chrysler rolled down Queens Boulevard past the courthouse, across the Queens Borough Bridge, through crowded Chinatown, and finally into Little Italy. In the backseat, Tony Ferrano and Lil' Luchi leaned back against the plush leather upholstered seats and puffed on fat cigars imported straight from Cuba. A good cigar, along with the smooth, relaxing, sound of Sinatra playing in the background never failed to settle Tony's nerves when something was on his mind. Up front, Carmine Cambilini kept a sharp eye peeled on the passing sights, while the driver, "Too Fast" Turillo, kept his eyes on the road ahead. Both men had been watching Tony's back for more than a decade.

Arriving at a small, upscale restaurant, Too Fast pulled the Chrysler into a parking lot located in the back of the restaurant and cut the engine.

"How long you gonna be, boss?" Carmine asked.

"Long as it takes. I'll take Louie in wit' me. You guys sit tight. Keep your eyes out for anything out the ordinary. Capise?"

"Sure, Tony," Carmine answered, adjusting the 9 mm in his upside down shoulder holster.

Getting out of the Chrysler, Tony and Lil' Luchi walked up to a steel, reinforced door with a peephole cut into it and rapped sharply. Seconds later, an inquisitive eye appeared and stared intently. The sound of a bolt latch sliding across a metal plate made Tony step back just as the door opened to reveal a six-feet, six-inch man in a black Adidas tracksuit. Like Tony and his companions, the giant was clean shaven.

"How's it going, Tony?" the giant asked.

"Great, Sal. Where's the don?"

"In the back, c'mon, follow me."

Stepping through the door, Tony's sense of smell was blasted by the aroma of ripe tomatoes and freshly cut garlic. Gleaming copper pots of pasta simmered on two different Viking six burner stove tops spread throughout the kitchen. If it was one thing Tony truly appreciated, it was Italian cuisine. As he and Lil' Luchi followed Sal through the spick-and-span kitchen, they took the time to nod their appreciation at several white-coated chefs.

"Wait outside," Sal instructed "Lil' Luchi, stopping at a closed door. Lil' Luchi glanced at Tony.

"It's okay, Louie. I'll be alright."

Giving Tony a brief pat down, Sal knocked once, then swung the door open for Tony to enter alone.

Sitting at a mahogany table placed in the center of the room, was a solitary figure. Don Polinzo was a dignified gentleman who had come up through the ranks the hard way, fighting tooth and nail for every single thing he had in his possession. And he had plenty. From blue-chip stocks and bonds, to thoroughbred stallions, Don Polinzo had it all. And the beautiful thing about it, nothing was in his name except a few legitimate businesses he had inherited. This meant he didn't have too much to worry about where the IRS was concerned, but that didn't stop the agency and a few other special prosecutors from trying to nail him to a cross. So far, Don Polinzo had out-foxed his enemies who were just waiting for him to make that one mistake.

Growing up in the Bronx, Don Polinzo had been an eager, opportunistic youth who learned the game from older, more experienced mobsters. Men like Meyer Lansky and Carlo Gambino had been his idols, but where they had

110

failed, he made every move to avoid making the same mistakes they did. As a result, his approach to gangsterism was tailor-made for today's high-tech society. His motto was, 'violence is the ultimate weapon of persuasion, but it is best kept in the hands of the wise and not the bloodthirsty'. Don Polinzo knew that as long as he kept the body count down, he could avoid the spotlight, and thus, avoid endless criminal investigations.

Stepping into the dimly lit room, Tony greeted the old man. "Good evening, Don Polinzo. How was your trip down? Did you enjoy the sights from on high?"

Dressed in a gray silk Italian suit, the don looked like a vampire in need of a blood transfusion. His thick white hair and thin face underscored his startling blue eyes and bushy white eyebrows.

"Tony!" he exclaimed enthusiastically, a rosy twinkle glowing in his eyes. "It's so good to see ya. Come in, come in. Have a seat and a drink of wine with an old man." In semi-retirement, the Don had moved his base of operations to sunny Orlando, Florida, and only flew back east when something serious was on the floor. This is what had Tony on edge.

"My trip was uneventful. I'll never get used to flying. Hell, if God wanted us to fly he woulda given us wings for Chrissake."

Tony laughed good-naturedly.

"I did enjoy the peace and tranquility way up there in the clouds, but listen I think I enjoy seein' your ugly mug even better."

Tony smiled, "It's been a long time, Don Polinzo. As a matter-of-fact, I haven't seen you since my old man's funeral."

Don Polinzo didn't change expressions. If Tony was under the impression that the mention of his father might in some way beholden the Don to him, he was dead wrong. Even though it was a well-known fact throughout the underworld that Tony's father had died in prison after

111

receiving a life sentence for refusing to rat out Don Polinzo and several other high-ranking mobsters. Even with that being true, the old man still didn't feel obligated to Tony in any regard. The way he saw things, they lived in a dog-eat-dog world and that left little room for burdens like having a conscience.

"Ah yes, you have a good memory," Don Polinzo said with a touch of nostalgia. "Your father was a fine, upstanding man, a real man's man. And to tell you the truth, Tony, that's the only reason you ain't floatin' at the bottom of the river right now."

Trying to conceal his shock, Tony regained his composure and politely retorted, "Obviously I fucked up somewhere. What ain't so obvious is whose toes did I step on?"

Stone-faced, Don Polinzo stared at Tony who felt the blood in his veins turn to ice water. No one except the don had that kind of effect on him. Being in the man's presence was like being in the presence of death itself. Not that Tony was afraid of the don, he was more in awe of the man, who in the criminal underworld; was a living legend.

"You shouldna involved yourself in that beef between the spics and the niggers over in Detroit, Tony. It ain't our business."

"Yes, I realize that," Tony said quickly, not even bothering to deny his involvement. "But lookit, me and a coupla of our friends have a good thing going down there, and we made sure to spread the love around. Nobody is being greedy here."

"That's not the point," Don Polinzo said pointedly. "It's not a matter of everyone being able to dip their beaks. It's a matter of respect."

"Whadda ya mean, Don Polinzo?" asked Tony somewhat confused.

"I mean those spics are hooked up with some of our associates out on the West Coast. You making that move against their boss without our permission has placed all of

112

our balls in the fire. Now you gotta do the right thing."

Looking the don directly in his cold blue eyes, Tony asked, "Whadda you want me to do?"

"Back away from it, leave it, you understand."

"Back away? Are you fucking crazy? We're talkin' millions and millions of dollars here. And you want me to just walk away just like that?"

The don shrugged his bony shoulders at Tony. *You got to be kiddin' me, this one here just don't fucking get it.*

"Let me tell ya something," he said, pointing a long, crooked finger in Tony's direction. "Back in the sixties, long before drugs became such a hot item, the only thing the families were involved in was gambling, loan-sharking, and maybe a little prostitution from time to time. Then the blacks in the cities grew restless and began burnin' down the fuckin' buildings, clamorin' about equal rights. Well, one day this guy approached us. Said he was from the CIA. He made us a deal. The deal was this. His people would provide us with high-quality heroin, as much as we could move, providing we only sell it to the blacks. Now, at the time, I was young and green. I simply could not believe that our own government was willing to destroy the souls of their own citizens just to keep them from tearing everything the fuck up. This guy from the CIA figured if, you give the blacks all the heroin they want, they'd care nothing about equal rights and being impoverished from decades of being nothing but slaves and the riots would be no more, they'd be too high to think. But, just because I didn't think it was morally right, didn't stop the deal from going through. I'm telling you this because there are ways that don't seem right to a man, but he sometimes has to go along with the program just the same. That's just how it is. Orders are meant to be obeyed. Capise?"

Trapped in a catch-22 situation, Tony realized he was in a dilemma. If he bucked the old man's wishes, it would mean all-out war. If he gave in, he would show weakness in the face of strength, and it would only be a matter of time before he lost respect and eventually be crushed. So the only thing to do was play for time.

"Okay, Don Polinzo. What can I say? Of course I'll do what's necessary. You can tell the commission not to worry."

The old man smiled. He couldn't believe Tony had given in so easily. "I already did. You're just like your old man, ready to sacrifice for the good of the whole." The don started having visions of baskets of money falling out the sky, money and greed filled his mind as he thought about Detroit's lucrative drug market and it would now be under his control.

After hearing how much money Tony was pulling in from the blacks who were supplying Detroit through Tony, the don and a few of his greedy cohorts wanted in. But Tony wasn't about to allow himself to be squeezed like a lemon. Before he would let Don Polinzo or anybody else simple play him like a bitch, he would kill and keep on killing. If the don wanted war, then war it would be. But at a time and place of his own choosing. Not here, not like this, not tonight.

As Tony got up to leave, as a token of respect he kissed the old man on both cheeks, then quickly left the room. Don Polinzo thought the kiss was a sign of respect, but for Tony it represented the kiss of death. Stepping out into the hallway, Tony saw Lil' Luchi no where in sight. Automatically alarm bells started ringing in his mind like a four-alarm fire. Lil' Luchi would have never left him alone. Not unless something was dreadfully wrong.

"How'd it go wit' the old man?"

Tony spun around and saw Sal standing there looking like death on a stick, and he knew what had happened to Lil' Luchi.

"It went well, Sal. Where's Louie?"

Sal grinned at him, "Oh, yeah, he told me to let you know he'd be waiting in the car. C'mon I'll escort ya there."

Tony pretended to follow the big man, then in one smooth motion, pulled out a .38 pearl handle derringer that had been hidden up his shirtsleeve. Without any hesitation whatsoever, he fired; aiming high. Sal was hit point-blank in his huge head. The impact knocked him backward against the wall. The bullet exploded inside his head, blowing out the back of his skull. Tiny bits of bone fragments, blood, and gray brain matter flew against the wall as Sal slid to the floor.

Scampering past Sal's fallen body, Tony made his way back to the room where he had left the don. Kicking the door open with all his might, he saw the wide-open panel in the fake wall, and realized that the clever don was long gone.

Turning back around, Tony ran down a long, narrow hallway until he came to a set of dark blue curtains. He could hear voices on the other side. Exercising caution, he pulled back the curtains and peeked out. He had reached the main dining area. He saw patrons casually chatting as they ate their meals without the slightest clue of what had just taken place. Tucking the gun away, Tony walked across the room without glancing left or right. The only thing on his mind was reaching the front door. Once outside in the cool air he breathed a deep sigh of relief. He knew there was no sense in going around to the back to pick up Carmine and his driver. There was no doubt in his mind they, like Lil' Luchi, were already dead. And he was right.

Hanging from meat hooks inside the deep freezer in the back of the restaurant, all three men swung limply, the look of death frozen forever on their pale faces. They had been strangled and shot to death. Had Tony made the mistake of going back to the car, he would have come face-to-face with a second set of assassins who had been posted in case Tony somehow managed to get past Sal. But he had the good sense to follow his first instincs and instead of joining his partners in death, he found himself headed up the street, a fresh plot brewing in his mind.

# CHAPTER EIGHTEEN

**B**ack in the City of Detroit, Raymond ran into BJ at the Poker Flats, a gambling joint off 8 Mile. It had been a minute since Raymond had seen BJ, for a long time they were distant adversaries. Raymond wasn't sure if he should break the ice or chill until things blew over. But, as he looked over his shoulder, Thad was standing right there practically on top of him.

"Thad, wassup?"

"Raymond, you better be glad we ain't still beefin'."

Raymond smiled thinly knowing in his heart of hearts Thad was a total walking nut case.

"We shouldna been beefin' in the first place. We both got caught up in somebody else's bullshit. But that's how shit go. I ain't madatcha. Can I buy you a drink to show you there ain't no hard feelings?"

"Buy me a drink? You wanna buy me a drink?" Thad asked as if that was the most preposterous thing he had ever heard.

"Sure, why not? Whadda ya drinkin'?"

"Seagrams. Straight."

Raymond motioned to this light-skinned chick

116

working the floor. He watched her sashay across the room, flaunting her big, fat, ass.

"Damn, Shawty, you throwin' that thang like you know what to do wit' it."

Busy chewing on a piece of gum, the girl stood there with her hands on her wide hips like she knew she was all that.

"Y'all wanna order something?"

"Get my man a Seagrams. Make mine a Hennessey."

"Straight?"

"That's the only way," Raymond confirmed.

Spinning on stiletto heels, her big booty strutted off, making sure she put a little extra something in her walk. Raymond was drooling at the mouth.

"Damn, I bet that bitch got some good pussy!"

Thad just frowned. "It's probably worn the fuck out. C'mon, let's find a place to squat. I need to holler at ya about something."

Pushing their way through the crowd, they spotted two empty chairs near the jukebox in the corner and headed towards them. They both took a seat.

"Word on the streets is that you broke. Wassup? You ain't gotta front nigga. I ain't trying to get in your mix, but I'm curious."

Raymond decided to keep it real.

"You heard right. Ain't nothin' shakin', and I really ain't fakin'. Ever since my man Buster brought y'all that move, everythin' we touch seems to turn to shit. Talkin' 'bout bad breaks and short stakes? That ain't the word."

Thad watched him closely, searching his face for any sign of deception. He would never fully trust Raymond, but he was willing to bury the hatchet for the sake of business. It wasn't personal; Raymond was a soldier following orders.

"I know you heard about our recent run-in with the rollers?" Thad asked.

"Yeah, so what?"

"Well, accordin' to our mouthpiece, we gotta go some

time. Too much publicity involved. It won't be too steep. You know what they say, your game's long as your bankroll."

Raymond laughed. "Well, I know you and your man got big game. Y'all been getting' down for a while."

"We ain't doin' too bad," Thad admitted. "But hell, we might have walked scott-free if not for the media and that big mouth bastard, Bill Bonds. He made sure he kept us on the nightly news."

Raymond seemed confused. "Look Thad, I don't wanna seem impatient, but did you say you wanted to holler at me about somethin'. Wassup? Don't play with my head man."

Thad looked him directly in the eye. "I been thinkin' about turnin' you on to my connect so you can get back in the saddle. I'll put up the fronts, plug you, then you can take it from there."

"All that sounds good," Raymond said. "But what are you lookin' for in return? The price might be too high to pay. You ain't doin' this for nothin'."

Thad smiled. "You right. I'm lookin' for a straight split down the middle. Fifty-Fifty. I'll send Lil' Greg around at the end of each week to get mine."

Raymond considered the proposal, then leaned over so that he was only inches from Thad's face. "Look, I know we ain't always seen eye to eye, but game recognize game. Put me back in the race; you got another thoroughbred on the track. That's on everythin' I love."

Thad eyed him sharply. "I just might have to hold your feet to the fire on that," he stated. The two unlikely business partners gave each other some dap just as the sexy waitress returned with their drinks.

Chewing her gum, every now and then she blew a big bubble, then watched it explode. "Y'all guys straight for now?" she asked, biting gum off her lips.

"I wonder if you can smack on a fat dick the way you're smackin' on that gum?" Thad asked, suddenly annoyed.

118

Not fazed by his sarcasm, the girl answered, "If you really wanna know, come out your pocket. Ain't no shame in my game."

Thad stared at her. "Bitch, I wouldn't touch your funky ass wit' a ten-foot pole. My name's Thaddeus Jones."

Turning to Raymond, he held up his glass in a mock toast.

"Let's get this money man."

"I ain't got no problem wit' it dawg."

Little did he know, he had just signed his life away, Thad had sold him a dream that was doomed to fail.

■■■■■■■■■■■■■■■■■■■■■■■■■■■■■■■■■■■■■■■■■■■■■■■■■■■■■■■■■■■■■

**O**nce the trial began, things moved quickly with both sides jockeying for leverage. Neither Thad nor BJ were that surprised when Bay Bay began cooperating. He and Lisa turned out to be the states' star witnesses. As the trial went on, each day Lil' Greg showed up in the courtroom to give moral support to his comrades. For the exuberant fees they received, the defense team put on a gallant defense, but in the end, as to be expected, BJ, Thad, Winky, and Melvin all were convicted on a variety of charges from drugs to murder. Chi Chi was acquitted of money laundering charges and cut loose. BJ ended up with 7 years, Thad got 6 ½ years, and Melvin and Winky each received 5 years. All in all, they got away with murder. Lisa and Bay Bay were put in the witness protection program. On the night before they were to be transferred to Jackson Prison, Lil' Greg and Chi Chi visited Thad and BJ at Wayne County Jail. Sitting on the other side of the glass booth in the visiting section, Lil' Greg picked up the phone.

"Dig, Thad. I'ma keep this brief since Jasmine is downstairs waitin' to see ya. But what I wanna know is this. How do you want me to play Raymond?"

Thad didn't trust Raymond. And why should he? After Busta was killed Raymond was positioned as top lieutenant and abandoned ship to work for his new bosses – Thad and

BJ. Thad squinted his eyes and stared harshly through the thick plexiglas.

"Tight to the chest. I don't want you to take no active role in the distribution; just stay in touch wit' Larry and keep Raymond supplied. He can use his own crew gettin' rid of the shit. All we care about is our cut."

"Yeah, I feel that. Well, I ain't gone hold ya up. Like I said, Jasmine's downstairs. But dig man, keep ya head up. I'll be comin' through to holler at you and BJ every chance I get. And I'll made sure y'all keep a package."

"Yeah, Lil' Greg, I know you will."

"Tell BJ I'll be to see him as soon as y'all get settled in at Jackson. Be cool, man, holler."

"Yeah, holler," Thad replied before hanging up the phone.

In the next booth, Chi Chi was crying over the phone as she and BJ said their final good-byes.

"Look, boo, you act like it's over. What I tell ya about good-byes?"

"All goodbyes ain't gone."

"You damn right. And all closed eyes ain't sleep, so you better not be out there givin' my pussy away," BJ said, only half jokingly.

That brought a smile to Chi Chi's face. She wiped her blood-shot eyes with the back of her hand. "You ain't gotta worry 'bout that, baby. I ain't gonna lay up wit' another nigga. I'll be a fuckin' nun till you get out. Can't nobody stroke this pussy like you baby. These niggas out here can't even hold your jock-strap."

Trying to disguise the pride he felt behind her words of devotion, BJ said, "That's right. But if you get weak, then make sure you be discreet. I don't want no nigga writin' or comin' up to tell me you been unfaithful, because if they know about it, the whole town will know about it, and one thing I won't tolerate baby is being made the laughing stock of Detroit. Do you understand?"

"Yeah I understand. But just like I already told ya, you

ain't gotta worry 'bout that.

Staring at her man through the thick plexiglas, Chi Chi was filled with mixed emotions. She felt disrespected. Instead of speaking what was on her mind, she bit her tongue and said, "Baby, you don't havta threaten me. You know I would run through hell with gasoline drawers on if you asked me to. So why are you still trippin'?"

BJ looked at her with a strange expression. He didn't like the tone in her voice. This was the same young bitch he had schooled to the game; now she had the nerve to be talking shit to him like he was a punk. It wasn't like he was leaving her up Shit's Creek without a paddle; she had plenty to work with. Chi Chi had everything he had left saved, every dime of it, the Benz, the house on Outer Drive, all her jewelry, all his jewelry and that right there was a small fortune.

"I'm not askin' you to run through hell; I'm askin' ya to hold me down and keep the ball movin' while I'm gone. I don't know how you think that's a threat."

Their eyes met and locked, as they stared deep into each other's souls, and in that moment, a vision of the past and future merged into one and Chi Chi saw the light. Lowering her eyes, she said coyly, "If you gotta ask, there's no need for me to explain." Placing the phone in its cradle, she rose to her feet slowly, kissed the inside of her palm, and then placed it firmly against the window. "I love you," she whispered, then turned and walked away. Not once did she even look back.

# CHAPTER NINETEEN

Larry had never been faced with a problem he was unable to solve, at least not until he met Greta. He didn't know if it was her education, looks, or proper upbringing that made her such a hard nut to crack; all he knew for certain, was that her snotty ass was starting to get on his nerves. He had been so sure she would spread her legs on their first date, he had brought along a pack of his favorite condoms. But when she rejected his advances, all the air went out of his sails. With the insight of a clever psychologist and the wisdom of a philosopher, Greta let him down easy.

The next time they went out, she allowed him to kiss her, but just a quick peck on the lips; her tongue was out of the question.

"What, what's the matter, I need a breath mint or something?" he asked feeling incredibly unsure of himself.

"No, no, it's not that, it's just too soon for us to get intimate. After all, I don't really know you."

He almost lost his cool, but his ethics as a playa made him check himself. It was totally uncool to have a sucker stroke over a bitch, at least that's what he kept telling himself. And with all the pussy he had seen in his life, he damn sure wasn't taking none from nobody, bitches gave that shit to him all day and running.

Nearly a month went by before he got past first base, and that only involved a few wet kisses and a little breast fondling. But Greta was determined to keep her legs closed and her guard up. In the meantime, Larry continued the stalk game, certain that sooner or later she'd give in. And when she gave in, he was gonna tear her ass up, just for making him wait so god damn long.

■■■■■■■■■■■■■■■■■■■■■■■■■■■■■■■■■■■■■■■■■■■■■■■■■■■■■■■■■■■

The Gray Goose pulled up in front of what appeared to be an old, seventeenth-century haunted castle on a hill. Jackson State Prison was truly an ugly sight to behold. The twenty-five men inside the Michigan Department of Corrections transport bus were chained and shackled like a group of runaway slaves. They peered nervously through the barred windows on the bus, at what was to become their new home away from home. BJ, Thad, Melvin, and Winky managed to be shackled and sat next to each other during the long, dull ride from the county jail to the prison. Most of the trip was spent staring out at the window and nothing but greenery, green mountains, green hills, green trees, green land. Normally, they wouldn't have looked twice.

After hearing all the horror stories about Jackson, the stabbings, pipings, homosexuality, and male on male rape, even the most feared killers would have second thoughts, and BJ and his crew were no different. They weren't afraid of going to prison; they were more afraid of never getting out. With so many violent men in prison, there was always the possibility you might never see daylight again. Killing someone in prison wasn't the same as taking someone out on the streets. On the streets, you at least had a chance of getting away with it, but in prison you were almost certain to get busted. Everywhere you turned, either the guards were watching you, or other convicts were watching you.

Thad personally knew of several guys he had grown up with, who were sent to Jackson and either came home in

123

a box or didn't come home at all. Jackson was a prison where you fought, fucked, or washed some big muthafucker's drawers. From the first day you walked in the yard, predators were checking you out to see how you handled yourself. The first stop the newly arrived prisoners made was a quick trip to the showers where they were sprayed with disinfectant and lice spray. Next, they were outfitted with several changes of underwear, undershirts, two blue khaki uniforms, and a shaving and tobacco kit. Any property they brought with them had to be sent home, thrown away, or donated to a local charity to lessen the chances of someone smuggling contraband into the antiquated facility where corruption and widespread violence ran rampant and deep.

After a quick visit to the barbershop, they were given the standard close cut, then they were led before the warden who delivered his customary 'tough-guy' talk.

"Listen up," he said, staring at the prisoners like they were the bottom of the barrel. "I'm only goin' to say this once, so you'd better take heed. This is my prison. I run it like I wanna run it. You give my officers a hard time and I'll slam your ass so far in the hole, you'll spend your entire stay in quarantine. Obey the orders, don't try to be a smart ass, mind your own business, and you'll be okay. Don't accept gifts from nobody; they might want some ass in return. If you wanna avoid catching AIDS, sit on your ass and keep your mouth shut tight. Any questions?"

None of the men said anything. They were tough criminals, but they were all scared. The lieutenant gave each of them a bedroll, then told them to follow him. Going down a long, narrow hallway that sloped downward, the prisoners felt like they were descending down into hell. At the end of the hallway was a huge, solid steel door that opened up into block seven; which was used to quarantine all incoming convicts. Men usually spent anywhere from thirty to sixty days in quarantine being diagnosed, given their immunization shots, and being interviewed by head doctors, and counselors who then determined where the prisoner would do his time. They wanted to see if they were crazy, infected, and whatever else might ail them.

BJ would never forget his first impression upon entering the huge cell block that was as loud as a damn zoo. Men, mostly black, were crammed on top of each other inside small, cramped cells that were four stories high. BJ thought they looked like monkeys trapped inside of cages banging on their bars for food and attention.

*So, this is what we've allowed these white folks to do to us, they've reduced these niggas to nothing in this motherfucker.*

"Dawg, I'll never let 'em break me down like that."

"Yo, BJ you see these niggas. Fuck that, these white folks is crazy. What the fuck have they done to them."

Inside Thad was seething. His hatred for white people intensified and he felt his rage reach a boiling point. Melvin and Winky, however, seemed to fit right in. They couldn't wait to get into some foolishness. They were a little younger than Thad and BJ, plus they were wild. All that was on their minds was making a rep in the penitentiary to go along with their street rep.

"Suck it up, girls," Lieutenant Pollack ordered, being the ass hole that he was. "You may have been killers out there, but in here you ain't nothin' but a fuckin' number. Now get your asses in gear. Now!"

At night, a few idiots would sit up all hours of the night acting like damn fools. One dude thought he was Luther Vandross, singing at the top of his lungs to the dismay of the other prisoners who did nothing but yell at him to shut up.

"Shut the fuck up. You non singing motherfucker."

One week later Winky got into a fight in the yard with a guy. When Thad and BJ found out about it, that night at chow, they jumped on the dude and fucked him up pretty bad. When the officers finally broke it up, the guy who had been assaulted wasted no time spilling his guts. He was taken into protective custody, and Thad and BJ were taken to block five, which was the hole. Thirty days later they got out and learned that Winky and Melvin had been sent to the reformatory in Ionia. Soon after, an inmate clerk who had access to the files said that Thad and BJ had been classified to go behind the walls. As they were waiting to be transferred, they made a vow that no matter what awaited them inside Jackson, they would go down together and do whatever they had to do to survive, even if it meant taking someone out of the box.

In prison, homies stuck together, so if you went at one, you had to go at the other. And if you couldn't get your man in an isolated area, then you tore him off wherever you caught him. In front of the screws, on a visit, on the toilet stool, it made no difference just as long as you got him before he got you.

Thad was reading *The 48 Laws of Power* and BJ was watching National Geographic. It was one of his most favorite programs. He learned a lot from animals in the wild. In his personal opinion, animals and humas weren't that much different. In this particular episode, several female lions were stalking a herd of wildebeests, who suddenly took flight after realizing the great danger they were in. As the chase grew more intense, one of the younger wildebeests made the fatal mistake of breaking away from the main group, and as soon as it did, the lions rushed forward and took their target down.

BJ was mesmerized by the chase. "Check it out, Thad. Did you catch it?"

Turning sideways in his chair, Thad stared at his partner like he was going crazy. "Did I catch what?"

"That wildebeest getting' tore off. Did you check out the psychology behind the whole play?"

"Man, you're trippin,'" Thad said.

"No. That dumb wildebeest got just what it deserved," BJ explained. "Had it stayed with the group it wouldn't have ended up on the dinner plate. He should have stood strong

126

amongst his own. That's how nature works. As cruel as it sounds, the strong always survive and the weak fall by the wayside. You become prey for the predators who are out there just layin' to catch that ass alone so they can tear a mud hole in it."

Thad stared at him with a crazy expression. "So, uh, what's your point?"

"The point," BJ stated firmly. "Is that there will always be forces of nature that's gonna challenge you, especially if you get weak. That's why you and me gotta be down for each other. Some people are lions and some are cowardly hyenas. They'll lay back and watch you do all the dangerous, dirty work and then they rip you off for the rewards."

Thad tried his best to look interested in what BJ was saying, but deep down inside he didn't give a fuck about lions, hyenas, or anything else. But for the sake of making conversation, he went along with BJ.

"Okay, I see your point. The only thing I wanna know is why did you have to get so dramatic and shit?"

Exasperated, BJ just looked at his partner, then all of a sudden both of them burst out laughing.

"You need help, BJ."

"Man, you crazy, you the one need help, nigga, not me."

# CHAPTER TWENTY

"Hello, may I speak to Larry?"

Pulling up to the stoplight in his Benz, Larry spoke into his cell phone. "Yeah, what's up? Who is this?

"Nigga, chill. It's me, Chi Chi."

"Baby girl? How the fuck you doin' baby?"

Chi Chi laughed. "I'm straight. Look, when can we get together? I need to kick it wit' ya."

Larry paused. "I'll tell ya what. Why don't you drop by the crib later on tonight? We can kick it then."

"What time?"

Larry checked his watch. "Around seven, cool?"

"Yeah, that's cool. We really need to talk. I'll see ya then. Holler."

"Before you hang up," Larry said quickly, "How's my man BJ doin' up there? Does he need anythin'?"

Chi Chi didn't reply right away, and when she did, it was with a touch of arrogance and disrespect. "The nigga was straight last time I saw him," she said. "As far as him needin' somethin', he always got his hand out."

A bit taken aback, Larry asked, "Well, when's the last time you saw him?"

"Last week."

"Okay, look, all my business is taken care of. I'll be at the crib the rest of the night."

"That's cool. I'll be there," she said.

The light changed to green just as she broke the connection. Larry pulled the Benz across the busy intersection at Woodward and Mack, and headed for the West Side.

As he drove through the evening traffic, his mind was preoccupied with images of Chi Chi. He always wanted to fuck her. She knew it too. *I wonder want she wants that's so important. She is coming to the crib.* That was Larry's biggest weakness, pussy and different pussy and a lot of it. Chi Chi knew it too. Like they say, 'fair exchange ain't no robbery'.

■■■■■■■■■■■■■■■■■■■■■■■■■■■■■■■■■■■■■■■■■■■■■■■■■■■■■■■■■■

**W**ith great despair Tony Ferrano read the entire front section of the New York Times once more before deciding that the article he was searching for simply wasn't there. He read the New York Daily News before the Times and there was no mention whatsoever of any bodies being found in Upper or Lower Manhattan. It was as though Lil' Luchi and the other two guys had simply vanished from the face of the earth, and truth be told, they had. Tony would have been willing to back away from his deals with the niggas from Detroit. It was what the don had asked him to do. *Why didn't he just ask?* But instead he killed Lil' Luchi and the two other guys who accompanied Tony when he went to the fateful meeting.

Tony wished he knew what happened to his friend. Truth was sometimes a hard thing to take. To know that the don shot them execution style, hung them upside down like swine, cut their heads off, drained them like swine, then cut them up into tiny pieces of flesh and then scattered the tiny pieces into the Hudson River as if they were fish food, would just simply be too much for Tony. He was better off not knowing what happened to them.

Tony glanced a second time through the New York Post and realized how lucky he was to have gotten out of New York alive. Don Polinzo was even more treacherous than he had thought. He had been expecting the don to make a move, but not then, not that night, not so soon. It was totally out of left field. Tony had almost been caught with his pants down. But since he had survived, he intended to stay alive, and the only way to do that was to take the old man out of the game and he knew exactly how he was going to do it. Even the don himself would appreciate what he had in mind. It would be pure Machiavellian.

■■■■■■■■■■■■■■■■■■■■■■■■■■■■■■■■■■■■■■■■■■■■■■■■■■■■■■■■■■■■

"**I**'m tearing that big bitch out of the frame," Thad declared. "Simple as that."

BJ stood there staring at his partner, knowing it would be damn near impossible to talk him out of it, now that his mind was made up. And he wasn't going to try.

"Well," he said, "Sometimes a man gotta do what a man gotta do. What I need to know homie, is how far do you plan on takin' this thang? It could get kinda nasty. We might have to take his ass out."

Thad thought about it. "The lame ain't worth catchin' no murder beef over, but he's gotta be treated like the ho he is. He can talk all that killer shit, but he ain't really layin' like that. Trust me. I'ma bring all the ho outta that bitch."

BJ shrugged. "It don't make no difference if he's a killer or not. The only thing that matters is whether the nigga bleeds, come on let's ride."

The two men began stuffing hardback books under their prison-issued jackets, making sure they covered their vital areas, like the heart, lungs, and liver. In prison, this extra precaution could mean the difference between life and death, and was the closest thing to body armor they were going to come up with on such short notice. And it served the purpose.

The day before, a cat calling himself Westside, had insulted Thad in the gym in front of everybody by calling him a bitch and coward who did nothing more than hide behind his street reputation. His exact words were, "You might have been a killer on the streets, but in here you gotta come gladiator style and I ain't got you built like that. Anybody can be a killer when he's got a big ass gun in his hand and a gang of crazy ass young niggas riding wit' him. Nigga, you ain't nothing."

The whole thing had started over a silly ass basketball game and blew all the way out of control. Although neither man had anything to prove, neither was going to back down. Their reputations were on the line, and in the streets or in the penitentiary, your rep was everything. The measure of a man was determined by his character.

Now, block four was known as the War Zone. Anybody housed there was either a high-security prisoner or a known troublemaker, like Westside. His cell was way up on the fourth gallery in the middle of the rock. The last thing on his mind was somebody coming up in the most dangerous block in the penitentiary and bringing him a move. So imagine his shock when he saw Thad and BJ coming through his cell door grinning like they were insane. Thad had a rock in a dirty gray sock, and BJ had a twelve-inch shank. It was around 4:30 in the afternoon and the block had just broke out for dinner, so all the cell doors were open. Those who didn't go to chow were out on the catwalk smoking bud or drinking home made wine. Some, like Westside, were still inside their cells having a quick meal or laying back watching their small black and white televisions.

Standing in the back of his cell with a bowl of food in his hands, Westside panicked as soon as he saw Thad and BJ. Dropping the bowl, he reached for the shank stuck in his pants, but before he could get it all the way out, Thad and BJ were on his ass like black on night. Raising his weapon, Thad swung it at Westside. The blow landed on the top of his skull with a sickening thud. He dropped to the concrete floor like a sack of potatoes, knocked out cold. He didn't even have a chance to call out for help. Dark, red blood was pumping out of the open wound like a water fountain. *Oh, shit, please tell me Thad ain't kill this nigga.* BJ was suddenly afraid, the last thing they needed, was another murder case. Before BJ realized what Thad was up to, Thad had stretched the unconscious man flat on his stomach and was busy pulling his pants down around his hips.

"What the fuck you doing?" BJ asked.

Taking Westside's jar of Vaseline off his desk, Thad grinned at BJ.

"I'm getting' ready to fuck this big bitch."

A shocked expression came over BJ's face, then he too grinned, thinking that this had to be a joke.

"I know you bullshitting, come on let's get out of here."

"The hell I am. He called me a bitch in front of a gym full of niggas, now I'm going to show everybody who the real bitch is."

Before BJ could say another word of reason, Thad climbed over Westside's prone body, unzipped his pants, pulled out his penis, and then lowered himself on top of Westside's exposed buttocks. BJ heard an unconscious Westside groaning, but he said nothing. He was in shock, the horror of what Thad was doing was another parallel and BJ wasn't on that kind of time.

"Shut up bitch and take this dick," Thad said, then proceeded to penetrate his enemy.

By this time, a small crowd of prisoners had gathered in front of Westside's cell and stood there in shock and disbelief. They couldn't believe what was happening, but not one of them made a move to help the helpless man on the floor being raped. Later on that night, just before they got ready to go into their cells for lock down, BJ looked at Thad.

"That was some fucked-up shit you did earlier, what the fuck Thad, what the fuck was that shit?"

Thad stared back at his partner and looked deep into his eyes.

"I know it was, I know. But I did that shit for us to survive in this motherfucker. Now the rest of these punks will know we ain't to be fucked with, this shit ain't no game.

You understand, it's either us or them."

Turning, he walked into his cell and left BJ standing on the rock. BJ stood there for a few minutes and thought of what Thad said. *This nigga is out of his mind. This prison shit is turning him into a monster.* He thought back to the day when they first entered Jackson and looked around and said to each other, they wouldn't let them white folks turn them into animals, but truth was that shit Thad did earlier, was just that. *What the fuck am I going to do?* BJ didn't want to even be near Thad. *This nigga is gon' mad fucking Westside in the ass, damn, who'da thought.* He slowly walked into his cell and waited for the guards to come by and double lock the cells for the night. He couldn't help but wonder what tomorrow would bring. He wondered so much, that he couldn't even sleep. For him, this was serious. He just couldn't believe it. Thad really fucked the shit out of that dude, right in front of his eyes, like it meant nothing. It was 3:00 o'clock in the morning and BJ still couldn't sleep. He couldn't help but to think that right across the yard, in cell block 4, Westside was raped earlier that day by his right hand man. BJ just couldn't seem to let it go. He had always known that Thad had some issues, but he never thought in a million years his man could rape another man. Shooting or stabbing someone was one thing, but to take his manhood was a horse of another color. As he lay there on his thin mattress, he tried to imagine what was going through Thad's mind. *I wonder if he's having trouble sleeping or if he's over there sleeping like a baby.* Had he been able to get into the cell next door and climb inside Thad's mind, he would have discovered the shocking truth.

Thad was in his bunk, tossing back and forth as usual, trying his best to dismiss the shameful images from his bewildered mind. It was the same dream and the same spooky white priest forcing himself on Thad's youthful body.

"Mommy, please don't leave me, mommy please take me with you, don't leave me here, don't leave me here, please. No stop, don't," he screamed his cries unheard in his

133

twisted mind.

"It's your new school, Catholic school. You'll be okay."

From the very first day he stepped inside the old building that smelled like mildew and old people, he could sense that something was wrong. Throughout the ancient brick structure, grotesque-looking statues and paintings of white people floating through the air with wings on their backs, reminded him of something straight out of a horror movie. And when he was introduced to the priest, Father Reilly, the way the man looked at him, bespoke volumes of the nightmare to come.

He had begged his mother not to leave him there alone, but she paid him no attention. As the months went by, his only consolation was the thought that one day, both the homosexual priest and his negligent mother would pay dearly for what they had done to him.

And they did.

# CHAPTER TWENTY-ONE

Larry had been right. Chi Chi was ready to get in the wind. Turned out, she was the typical bag chaser, in your corner as long as you were rolling, but ready to break wide when the chips were down. But considering her background, who could really blame her? She had come from nothing and the only thing she knew, was taking advantage of people to get what she wanted. BJ helped make her a slave to materialism, and now he was paying the price for his oversight. As long as he was right there on the scene, making power plays to provide her with all the things she needed to be the Queen Bee, she was straight. But now that he was locked down, unable to look out for her, she wanted out of the situation and had decided that Larry was the right guy to wrap a fresh blanket of protection around her. She wasn't shit, a typical black bitch, out for self and they wonder why niggas call 'em bitches and hoes. Hello!

But Larry was hip to her. He read her like an open book. She was that obvious. It was to his advantage, however, to let her think that she was getting over on him, when in reality, it was the other way around. The old, 'over-lay for the under-play'. For a brief moment he thought about BJ, but a stiff dick has no conscience, especially his.

Weeks rolled by and Larry found himself on a roll. Not only had he started fucking Chi Chi, but Greta had come around. And he was in Seventh Heaven having his cake and

135

eating it too. It took some time, but it finally happened, him and Greta that is. One night Larry took Greta to Fox Theater on Woodard Avenue to see Luther Vandross perfoming live. After the concert, Larry took her to a hotel where he rented a suite. He had champagne on ice and a dozen red roses in a beautiful vase. It was then that he presented her with the ultimate ultimatum.

"Look, Greta, we've been seeing each other for a while now, and I think you know how I feel about you, my intentions and all. Yet still, you treat me like I got AIDS or something. I think it's time we came to some sorta understanding."

"Is this your nice way of saying shit or get off the pot?" she asked smiling sweetly.

"Call it what ya like, but it makes no damn sense for us to continue this so-called relationship if there ain't no trust and the relationship ain't going no where no way. Damn baby, you gotta admit it sex plays a big part between a man and a woman. And I'm pretty much ready to know if the fox is worth the chase. Truth be told, I ain't got much more chase left in me."

Greta smiled her bewitching smile and looked at Larry with a serious expression. "You might be right. Maybe I shouldn't fight the feeling. This thing might be bigger than both of us."

Sensing that the time was right, Larry made his move. When he kissed her, it was like a bolt of electricity shot through both of them. He stared deeply into her green eyes. This time she offered no resistance when he began to slowly undress her. When she was completely naked, he took a step backward and ran his hungry eyes up and down her body.

"Damn, you're beautiful, like a movie star, baby," he told her mesmerized by her beautiful body, meaning every single word.

Reaching behind her slender neck, he undid her perfumed hair watching it cascade down her back. It was red like the triangle of glistening pubic hair between her long

136

shapely legs.

"Baby, do you know that mascara ain't came up with nothing to paint your eyelashes longer or silkier than Mother Nature made them? And Avon can't begin to compete when it comes to painting your cheeks rosier than they were on the day you were born."

Blushing like a schoolgirl, Greta just stood there. This was a side of Larry he seldom displayed. He felt more natural in his thug persona, but he was willing to do whatever it took to get her pussy.

"If I was God the Creator," he continued, "charged with the awesome task of creatin' you all over, you know what?"

"No, tell me."

"I would create you exactly as you are. I wouldn't change one single thing. I would use the same twin emeralds to form your beautiful eyes, and I would use the same rose as a model for your perfect mouth. The truth is, you are fine from the top of your head to your pretty little feet."

"You're quite a poet. I didn't know you had it in you."

"I didn't either. I guess you brought it outta me."

"Is that so?"

"Pretty much," he responded in a slight southern draw.

When they came together, Greta melted like butter when she felt his strong arms embrace her tiny waist. When their lips met, automatically their tongues entwined and Greta felt herself go weak in the knees as he propelled her backward toward the couch.

*I'ma tear this pussy up right here,* he told himself with conviction.

Eyes closed, Greta relaxed and gave in to her desires. "Do whatever you want," she whispered.

Spinning her around so that her back was facing him, he bent her over the couch doggie style and slapped her playfully across her plump ass cheeks, watching the flesh jiggle like Jell-O.

"Ouch!" she giggled. "That stings."

With his fingertips he spread her pussy lips apart and inserted his rock hard penis. Greta gasped out loud at the size of him.

Just as he was about to push himself all the way inside her well-lubricated vagina, he felt himself about to explode and thought wildly, *Oh hell no! No, no, no!* But it was already too late. He skeeted so hard inside her womb, he thought he was going to pass out.

Embarrassed, he collapsed on top of her feeling like the biggest chump.

"I'll be damned. I'm sorry baby; I guess I just wanted you so bad, I don't know what happened."

"Don't worry about it;" she said understandingly. "The night is still young. We got a long way to go before the sun comes back up. C'mon. Let's go to the bedroom and really get to know one another."

"No," he said. "I got a better idea. Let's take a shower first."

After washing and rubbing each other's body down with coconut-scented body lotion, he led her to the king-size bed in the bedroom and stretched her out flat on her back. Climbing on top of her, he kissed her tenderly on the mouth.

When he felt her respond, he moved down to the hollow of her throat and kissed her there before sucking her hardened nipples into his greedy mouth. As he continued licking and nibbling his way down her body, he had his middle finger sliding in and out of her pussy. By the time he reached the little man in the boat, Greta had two orgasms and was panting for more.

"Oh, Larry, she moaned.

Using the tip of his tongue, he parted the fragrant, soft folds of her pussy lips, causing her body to twitch uncontrollably. Grabbing him by the back of his head, she roughly pulled his face between her satin thighs, then raising her legs, locked them firmly around his neck. Larry found himself trapped in the dark, furry pit of her bottomless love hole. After sucking and playing with her clitoris, he moved further down, kissing and sucking the inside of her soft tender thighs and the back of her knees.

Suddenly, he raised her legs, placing them over his shoulders, and took the plunge again. Only this time he was in full control. He stroked her with deep, penetrating thrusts, sliding in and out of her tunnel with the skill and expertise of an expert swordsman. Finally, he brought her to the edge of the mountaintop, then gently guided her into the promised land.

Satisfied and exhausted, the two lovers laid back content in each other's arms, whispering sweet endearments until they drifted off into a deep, sleep. Around 4:00 that morning, Larry woke up only to find himself laying flat on his back pinned to the bed. Greta was on top of him riding his erect penis like she was riding a thoroughbred pony. In the darkness of the room, he could hear her heavy breathing and see her firm titties being tossed from side to side as her long red hair flew in her face while she rocked her burning body back and forth and up and down. Reaching behind her, Larry palmed the cheeks of her ass with both hands like he was gripping two basketballs and pulled her all the way down on top of him as she began to grind and twist her hips in a fury of passion and red-hot lust. Lying there beneath her and staring up into her closed eyes, the look on Greta's face let him know she was nearing an orgasm. *She got a lot of freak in her, I would have never known.* But as he felt himself being brought nearer and nearer to a mind-blowing climax, he simply relaxed and allowed the good feeling to sweep throughout his entire body. He had no regrets, none at all.

# CHAPTER TWENTY-TWO

"**J**ackson, you got a visit!" yelled the guard down at the desk. He was dressed in the standard gray and black uniform reminiscent of Nazi Germany.

Upstairs in his cell, BJ reluctantly put down the 48 Laws of Power, a book he had been reading, and wondered who had come to see him. Between that damn, Dante Reigns and his crazy family and Robert Greene he was ready for war. Where's the enemy? Bring him to the front line.

"Hey, BJ," Thad called from the next cell, "How come you didn't tell me you have a visit coming? I could have had Jasmine and my nephew ride up."

"Shit, I didn't know myself. I wasn't expecting nobody."

Going over to the small sink in the back of his cell, BJ took a quick birdbath and splashed on a few drops of Muslim prayer oil. Next he replaced his prison blues with a slick, two-piece, gray denim outfit and matching Timberlands. Glancing at himself in the small, cracked mirror hanging over the sink, he noticed some new worry lines creasing his forehead and told himself, *I got to hurry up and get outta this motherfucker. I'm turnin' into an old man.*

Walking over to the front of his cell, he stuck his hawk between the bars and glanced down the rock. He caught a glimpse of Smitty, the old prison guard who had been around forever. Officer Portis Smith was his name; but everybody called him Smitty. He was taking his own sweet time coming down the rock, jingling his keys loudly so that the convicts locked inside their cells, would know he was coming. That way, he wouldn't have to walk up on anybody doing something they weren't supposed to be doing and then have to bust them.

"Cop on the rock!" someone yelled out, as if it was necessary.

A few minutes later the guard was standing in front of BJ's cell.

"It's about time your old slow ass got up here," BJ said jokingly.

"Fuck that shit you talking about, young blood," Officer Smith cracked. "Had it been somebody other than you waiting to go out there, Jackson, they'd still be waiting."

"Smitty, you stay on some shit, but you alright for a prison guard."

Portis Smith had been around when members of the old Detroit Purple Gang were locked down in Jackson, so he knew all the ropes and didn't take any shit. But he often turned a blind eye to minor infractions. He hated rats almost as much as the average convict did.

"Don't try to bullshit the bullshitter, Jackson," the wise old guard said, at the same time unlocking BJ's cell. "Take your ass out there and don't be sticking your finger up your girl's pussy either." Officer Smith joked figuring a woman was visiting BJ.

Stepping out of his cell, BJ watched Officer Smith continue down the rock, making his rounds and jingling his keys.

Standing at the front of his cell door, Thad waited until BJ came by. "Dig man, if that's Chi Chi out there, holler at her for me."

"No doubt."

"Oh, yeah. Tell Dirty Red to hold me a gallon of that

liquor. I'll pick it up soon as we break out for for yard."

BJ nodded. "I'll do that. But I'm tellin' ya, man, you should leave that cheap shit alone. One of these days all that yeast is gonna eat the linin' outta your stomach and fuck you up."

"We all gotta die from something. Shit a nigga need something to do this bid for the next seven years, shit. That's why so many of these niggas are going crazy around here."

*This nigga is the leader of crazy, always talking about everybody else. Thad needs counseling,* BJ thought to himself as he smiled at his partner.

"Whatever, fool. It's your life."

"You goddamn right," Thad replied in jest.

Outside in the yard, the sun was beaming down relentlessly. The white folks had cut down all the trees so the guards in the towers could have a clear shot in case of an emergency. But thanks to them wanting to shoot a nigger in the ass, there was no shade no where. Everybody gathered around the picnic tables gambling or playing chess. However, they were at the mercy of the relentless sun. But they would rather be outside; braving the weather, than being cooped up inside their tiny cells all day.

Spotting a group of men sitting on a wooden bench in front of block 4, BJ approached them cautiously. He and Thad had fucked over so many people in the streets that they had to be careful at all times. One could never tell when payback was coming.

"What up Dirty Red?" BJ asked casually. "Dig, Thad told me to tell you to hold him a gallon of that spud juice. He'll be out when block 3 breaks for the yard."

Dirty Red, a tall, skinny, light-skinned convict with gray eyes, idolized BJ and Thad for their exploits in the streets and wasted no time to suck up to them. In return they promised to let him ride with their crew once they all got back out on the streets.

"No problem," Dirty Red said in an-ass kissing tone. Noticing BJ's outfit, he added, "I see ya on your way out

142

there. Have a good visit, homie."

Across the yard on the bandstand, a group of inmate musicians had started jamming, to the delight of the others inmates. Several homosexuals in tight pants and halter tops, started shaking their asses. They had their eyebrows arched and had covered their lips with red Kool Aid. From a distance they looked and acted like real women. BJ was reminded of a conversation he had with an old convict named Bull Head, when he first hit the yard.

"Blood, I hear you know my man, Rayfil?"

"So what?" BJ asked suspiciously.

"Well, any friend of Rayfil is a friend of mine. They call me Bull Head because some fools say I'm stubborn as a bull. But it ain't that. I just stick to old school values and this is why I'm tellin' you right now, if you wanna survive this bid, stay away from these faggots around here. They start more shit than the Lord allows. Trust me, I know, behind every murder in the penitentiary, is a muthafuckin' fag. Take my word for it."

BJ thanked him for his advice and assured him that he didn't have to worry about him because he didn't fuck around with sissies. As for Thad, that was another story. He didn't like all and out homosexuals, but he sure didn't mind turning them out, especially if they were white. He saw it as a way of demeaning them. Around the yard he had become known as a notorious booty bandit. BJ didn't understand him.

When BJ entered the crowded visiting room, he caught several good-looking women giving him the eye. *Ain't ch'all hoes here to see a nigga. Flirts in skirts and good for nothing, can't trust 'em hoes.* But what had really caught their eye, was the $25,000 gold and diamond necklace hanging from his neck. Finally he spotted a familiar face.

"Lil' Greg. Wassup homie?" he exclaimed, giving his partner some dap. Finding two empty chairs, the two men copped a squat.

"I wasn't expecting you til next week. What brings ya

up this way today?"

Lil' Greg looked down at his alligator shoes, then back up at BJ. He didn't know how to say what he had come to say. But, as a friend, he knew he had to.

"It's Chi Chi."

"Chi Chi? What about her? She's alright, ain't she?"

"Oh, yeah, yeah, ain't nothing happened to her or nothing like that, it's um... Well, you see, this hard to explain."

"What, just spit it out."

"She fuckin' Larry."

"Larry, Larry Westin, our Larry?"

"Yeah," said Lil' Greg as he kept a close eye on his friend, trying to see what his mind was thinking.

BJ couldn't believe his ears. "You can't be serious. I know she not fucking no Larry."

"I wish I was. At first they were carrying it on the down low, but now they don't seem to care who knows it. Any time you see one, you see the other, unless he's with this red head he got. I don't understand, he got the red head, and I know for certain that Chi Chi know about her. I don't know why she doing what she doing, but you just give me the word and I'll pop his slimy ass."

"No, I don't want you doing nothing crazy, we don't need you up in this bitch with us. Is he still servin' you and Raymond?"

"Yeah. But now Raymond done started talking shit too."

"Whadda ya mean?"

"Well, last time I pushed up on him for Thad's cut, this lame started actin' funny. Then he said he was goin' to kick it down – this time, but as far as he was concerned, he had paid Thad enough money, more than twice what he felt he owed him. He then gave me thirty-five hundred. I gave Jasmine twenty-five and I put five a piece on your books when I signed in, so ya'll got that for commissary. Just give me the word and I'll pop his ass too."

"He said that, he said that he done given Thad more than enough. Is that nigga crazy or just plain mad."

"Man, I don't' know, all I know is the nigga act like he ain't got nothing for me. Listen, I'll take care of his black ass too."

"Oh, no, hell no, let Thad have him," BJ said smiling thinking of crazy ass Thad fucking the shit out of Raymond. "As a matter-of-fact, I want you to step back from the game all together. Go back to school or something, just lay low. I got somethin' up for later on down the line. It's called 'long-range game played on a short frame.'"

Puzzled, Lil' Greg remained silent.

"I'm glad you came up and hollered at a nigga. Be careful on the way back to the city."

Feeling as though he was being dismissed, he really wasn't ready to go, he missed his friends. He missed Winky, Melvin, BJ and Thad terribly. He was like the Lone Ranger with no Tonto out there in the streets and he knew his crew was locked down, but he was hurtin' too without them.

"How's Thad's crazy ass doin' in there?"

"I don't know, man, I don't know," said BJ staring off into space. "He's cool when he ain't trippin'."

"Trippin'? Whadda ya mean?"

"Man, I think Thad done gone crazy. I thought I knew a nigga, but fuck, I don't know who this motherfucker is no more. He's in here getting high and he's raping motherfuckers, man, especially them white boys. Lord knows he tearing them up every chance he gets. And that ain't the whole of it either. He's squeezin' damn near everybody with a sack and you know he don't need no cash."

Lil' Greg was in shock.

"How you know he's raping people."

"This nigga raped a big burly nigga right in front of me. Pulled his dick out and fucked the dude right there on the spot."

"In front of you," asked Lil' Greg in amazment as if he didn't believe one word BJ was saying.

"Man, in front of whoever, the whole block be standing around watching this nigga fuckin' these dudes. Man, this shit is crazy. I don't know what to say."

"Don't he know he can get AIDS?"

"Man, sometimes Thad acts like he don't care if he lives or dies and it's not just him, that's the menatality of most of these niggas in here. They got cats walkin' around on the yard with small spray bottles filled with acid and AIDS-contaminated blood so they can spray the shit in your eyes if y'all beefin'. Look around the visiting room. Why you think everybody wearing glasses and shades up in this chumpy."

"Get the fuck outta hear," said Lil' Greg hoping that he never got dealt the hand of incarceration.

"Yeah, real fucked up, I'm serious, I'm like real cautious with Thad right about now cause the nigga's mind ain't right."

"Shit, I feel sorry for Raymond," said Lil' Greg.

"Mmm, hmm, that's why I said let Thad at him. Don't get involved with this shit. I don't want you in here, Lil' Greg. I don't want you ever in here you understand. I want you to go do something else with yourself. Shit, sweep floors, go work in McDonalds, anything, just don't come here, you understand me?"

"Yeah, I understand," said Lil' Greg missing his friend even more. He really wanted to hug him at that moment, he loved BJ and he wished he could take him up out there.

"Dig, so listen when you get back to the city, I want you to find Chi Chi. Tell her I said I'm givin' her her walkin' papers. Take my Benz from her and tell her she's got one week to find another place to live. Tell her I said she can't stay at the crib on Outer Drive no more. If she's still there after a week, firebomb that muthafucka. And I don't care if her funky ass is in there when you do it. Hopefully, she will be. Don't worry, I got insurance on the crib, but I don't think she's got any on her black ass."

BJ gave his orders and then he stood indicating that the visit was over. Lil' Greg was still sitting in his chair, not ready to leave.

"What?" asked BJ wondering why he was still sitting.

"Nothing, it's just not the same no more for me, you know. All y'all gone. I mean I know it's hard on y'all being locked up, but damn shit's just not the same for me in them streets with out y'all. You the only family I ever had."

"Come on, Lil' Greg, shit's okay, man, I'm right here. If you need me, you just come up here anytime you want. I'm right here. Thad's here, well in body any way, and Melvin and Winky is making it. We all gonna be home soon. It'll be okay, don't worry, just get that bitch out my house and get my car for me. Everything is everything," BJ said as Lil' Greg stood up from his chair.

Lil' Greg looked like he was damn near in tears and the truth was, it should be the other way around. Hell, that nigga was going home, they were stuck in demonized crackerville hell for the next couple of years.

"Hey, it's gonna be alright. We here, I'm gonna call you and check on everything. I'ma call you later on tonight."

"Tonight?" Lil' Greg asked cool with that.

"Yeah, motherfucker and that's a long line, too," said BJ giving his friend a brotherly embrace. "I'll call you. Don't forget what I said, go to school or something till I get out."

Lil' Greg nodded, then turned around and left.

Later that day, BJ caught up with Thad who was drunk as a skunk, and gave him the rundown. As to be expected, Thad blew up like a stick of dynamite.

"Calm down, baby boy," BJ urged. "Ain't nuttin' to be upset about. A ho gon' be a ho, and a snake gon' be a snake. Neither can change their nature, just like the game don't change, right."

"True," thought Thad listening to some logic. "And just like there's the boss double cross, there's the triple cross."

BJ laughed with him. "And don't forget the cross out. Ain't no comin' back from that shit. But until then, we play it close to the chest and never let 'em see us sweat."

■■■■■■■■■■■■■■■■■■■■■■■■■■■■■■■■■■■■■■■■■■■■■■■■■■■■■■■■■■■■■■¡

Larry was living high on the hog. He got Chi Chi a brand new Mercedes and a two-story brick home in Farmington Hills. They made an agreement and Chi Chi would be the one in charge of handling his books for him. She would also be in charge of moving the cash around for him. In return for the house, the car and the new day job, she promised to stay out of his business and she even agreed to let him keep fucking Greta on the side as long as he kept the bitch out of her face.

Traveling all around the country, Larry tried his best to keep Greta in the dark while he handled his business, setting up drug deals and expanding his drug operations to different cities. Although she pretended not to know what was going down, she was fully aware of every single move he made. Larry was lucky, in the process of expanding, he met several upper level drug dealers in other cities who could supply him the large quantities he needed. He tried reaching Tony, couldn't get an answer, then the number was changed and being as though it seemed Tony was going through a little something, Larry had no choice but to find a light at the end of the tunnel and he did just that. He had his connects and he was good. The best part about it was that he thought Thad and BJ didn't have a clue. He figured them niggas was doing time. But nothing ever stays a secret too long and it was just a matter of time before everything that was done in the dark would come to light.

In the meantime he and Greta enjoyed the best life had to offer, dining on Kobe Beef steaks from Japan and shopping at exclusive boutiques in Paris. They partied in the south of France, made love in the plush One and Only in the Bahamas, and gambled in Vegas, dropping bundles of cash like it was going out of style. Before long, Larry had Greta dabbling in cocaine, snorting that shit like Ginger in Casino.

But had he known that the bottom was about to drop out of his dream castle, it's a damn good possibility he would have hopped his ass on a jet plane and never, ever, looked back. But he didn't.

# CHAPTER TWENTY-THREE

Lil' Greg had just parked his black GMC SUV in front of the Kabaz Black Jewels Cultural Center, when he saw Chi Chi go flying by in a bright red Mercedes. Headed south on Mt. Elliot, she made a sharp left on Mack and disappeared from sight, traveling east. Sure that she had seen him, Lil' Greg figured she hadn't acknowledged him because she was still pissed at him for delivering BJ's message.

"Who told BJ me and Larry was fucking around?" she asked when Lil' Greg told her that BJ wanted her out of the house.

"I did. Why?"

"Why'd you have to run and tell him? You act like he's your daddy. But it don't make no difference. He can have his whip and his crib. That shit don't make or break me. Just keep watching, you'll see."

Lil' Greg started to tell her exactly what was on his mind. *What's the use? It ain't gonna do a bit of good.*

"Whatever you say Chi Chi."

Then he turned and walked away from her while she was still standing there talking shit. He had his orders, and she had hers. He only hoped he wouldn't have to carry his out. BJ had told him to firebomb the crib if Chi Chi's not out in a week. And Lil' Greg really didn't want to hurt her.

Actually, he was tired of hurting people, especially black people.

Three days later Chi Chi called and said she was leaving the keys to the green Benz in the mailbox and vacating the premises. Lil' Greg promptly turned over everything to BJ's mother then washed his hands of the whole sordid affair. Now Ms. Chi Chi was parading through the hood in her new Mercedes, flaunting her newly discovered wealth and independence. She was determined everyone needed to know she could get by on her own without BJ. As Lil' Greg started up the steps leading to the huge, double oak doors of the cultural center, he hoped Chi Chi knew what she was getting herself into, because despite everything, he still thought of her as a friend, little crazy perhaps, but still a friend.

Ringing the doorbell, he stood back and waited.

Seconds later the door opened and there stood a huge, heavily muscled, bald-headed brother with a diamond stud in his left earlobe. He was dressed in a black Dickie uniform and gleaming black combat boots.

"Who you here to see, blood?"

"I wanna see Brother Kaleem."

"C'mon in and wait in the lobby," the man said while running a handheld metal detector up and down Lil' Greg's body, scanning for weapons.

Lil' Greg was glad he left his nine inside the SUV. Being frisked for weapons when coming to see a preacher, surprised Lil' Greg. But then, he figured, everybody had enemies, even a man of God. The man disappeared behind a closed door on the other side of the lobby and two other men who were dressed in identical black uniforms, came out of the room and stood guard at the door.

In the meantime, Lil' Greg busied himself browsing through the lobby, checking out the pictures on the walls. Several of them showed Kaleem shaking hands with well-known political activists. Lil' Greg was impressed. He hadn't realized that Kaleem was that popular.

"Welcome to the palace. What can I do for you?"

Turning, Lil' Greg found himself standing face-to-face with Kaleem. I just dropped by to talk to you about a few things that's been on my mind."

Kaleem glanced shrewdly at him.

"Alright, that's cool. C'mon, let's go upstairs to my office."

Lil' Greg followed him to the stairway leading to the second floor. A door suddenly opened, and Lil' Greg was able to catch a quick glimpse of men and women clad in black, practicing the martial arts. They formed the nucleus of Kaleem's private security team. They were known as the Paladon Force, and were highly trained to protect or kill with their hands or weapons.

Entering the soundproof office that was modestly equipped with a desk, lamp, several chairs, a computer, and home entertainment center, Kaleem motioned for Lil' Greg to take a seat. The bald-headed bodyguard stood point at the door.

"What's on your mind?" Kaleem asked. "You can talk freely around him," he said, as the huge bodyguard stood at the door with a blank, distant look on his dark brown face. Kambui had been a professional hit man before being recruited by the charismatic Kaleem.

Lil' Greg glanced at Kambui, then back at Kaleem. "I'm ready to make a move," he said. "I wanna join your organization and become a Melanic."

Kaleem smiled softly. "I knew it wouldn't be long before you stepped up and took your place in the affairs of real men. Organizations like ours are always lookin' for strong, young brothas like yourself. Once we can properly educate these brothers, they can in return educate their peers. The youth are much more apt to listen to someone who comes from their own generation. But let me ask you this. What made you finally decide to step up?"

Lil' Greg thought for a moment then said truthfully, "I'm tired of seeing black people hurt. More than that, I'm tired of hurting black people. The other day I went up to Jackson Prison to check out a friend of mine, and the entire visiting room was filled with black men and the sisters who had come up to see them. It made me realize just how many brothers are getting locked up or took out, mostly at the hands of other brothas. Plus, the guy I was visiting told me to get back in school, which really surprised me. It was like I had been hit with some kind of revelation from on high."

Kaleem smiled knowingly. "These days God works in mysterious ways. That is, if you believe in God."

"Oh, yeah, I believe in God. I just don't understand him sometimes. For example, I don't understand why white people have all the glory of power in this world, and we have nothing. People all over the world robbed, starving and in complete devastation while some where a white man is holding all the money and all the power, while people of color suffer. I don't understand the mass destruction and devastation of natural disasters and all the innocent lives that are constantly taken, while evil prevails with no justice for the minority. Why, why is it like the way it is? I don't know, but maybe you can explain."

Kaleem shrugged. "I'm not sure that I can, but I can give you my personal opinion if that's alright with you."

"Go right ahead," Lil' Greg said.

"Well first of all, it's not God who's lettin' the white people kill and oppress blacks and others. It's the people themselves. Even though blacks and people of color make up the majority of people on this planet, they allow a small minority to rule over them with an iron fist. God gave us free will. If we choose to be oppressed, oppressed we shall be."

"But white people got the military might," Lil' Greg interjected.

"That, they do. But there's all kinds of organized resistance that can be employed by a people determined to get the boot of oppression off their back. And as far as people dyin' in natural disasters, that could simply be God's way of using nature as a check and balance to reduce the population when it starts getting too far out of hand. You see, young brother, most of us view death as something final and absolute, something to be terrified of. But to God who made all life there is no such thing as death, only a constant recycling of energy."

"That's a deep way of looking at things," Lil' Greg stated. "What religion do you practice? My mother's a Christian. Been one all her life, but it don't seem to have done her a lick of good. She's given every spare dime to her church, all her life and I know she thinks she's going to get some extra blessings, but the only thing I see is the preacher living good riding through the streets in his brand new Cadillac."

"Let me tell you somethin' about religion. Men never do evil so completely and cheerfully as when they do it from religious conviction." That's a quote from this cat named Pascal. You see, son, men can delude themselves so thoroughly and completely until they can persecute and slaughter entire nations believing they're doin' God's will, when it's their own perverted will they're putting in motion. Religion is the main source of most of the wars and hatred you see taking place around the world today, and it has been going on for centuries. Not all religions, mind you, just the ones that claim to be the only correct religions, the only right religion. The followers of these types of religions are taught that they are better than everyone else, so they begin to spread dissension and confusion among the masses.

"Now, the Melanic study all religions, but they practice spirituality, and there is a world of difference between the two. Religions are man made, but spirituality comes from God."

Lil' Greg was confused. "I don't understand" he said.

"What I mean," Kaleem continued, "is that every man, woman, and child are born with a built in sense of right and wrong. It's called a conscience. We are also born with an innate sense of power higher than ourselves. Some call this power God, others something else, but I truly believe that we

154

all understand that we didn't create ourselves and that therefore, are the creation of a creator. But the Melanic's philosophy is Black Nationalism, which means that we seek to spread and preserve our own culture, just like the Arabs, Jews, or any other nationality of people with race pride. Even water seeks its own level."

Lil' Greg sat there speechless. He was trying his best to comprehend all that Kaleem had said, but it was an awful lot of information to digest at one time. Finally, he said, "Well, I still wanna join if it's okay with you."

Getting up from his seat, Kaleem walked over to him. "Let's go back downstairs. There's somebody I want you to meet."

On their way out the door, Kaleem lagged behind.

"Kambui," he said in low tones. "Take blood downstairs and run a LIEN on him. Make sure the enemy didn't send him here to gather information. You know what they say, 'an army without spies is like a man without eyes or ears' and what good is a deaf and blind man? He's no good to the enemy, and he's certainly no good to us."

∎∎∎∎∎∎∎∎∎∎∎∎∎∎∎∎∎∎∎∎∎∎∎∎∎∎∎∎∎∎∎∎∎∎∎∎∎∎∎∎∎∎∎∎∎∎∎∎∎∎∎

**L**il' Greg had been right. Chi Chi had seen him getting out of the SUV. In fact, she had been following him around, waiting on the right opportunity to flash her new Mercedes at him. She wanted him to report it to BJ, so they both would know she was doing alright despite being grounded and put out on the street. So caught up in her own vengeful thoughts, following Lil' Greg, she didn't even notice a beige van with two men inside was hot on her trail. Headed for her mother's house, she made a right on Townsend, and drove through her old neighborhood, looking at the run down slum houses and garbage-cluttered streets.

Pulling up in front of her mother's house, she parked on the street and cut the engine, she hopped out the new red Mercedes feeling like a million dollars. The next thing she knew, the beige van pulled up right beside her, boxing her in and cutting off any route of escape.

A huge, dark-skinned brother wearing dark shades, leaped out of the van and grabbed her in a full nelson. At the same time she was desperately reaching for the Glock inside her Gucci purse.

"Let me go muthafucka!" she shouted, struggling with all her might to break free from the massive arms encircling her small body.

"Shut up, bitch, and get your funky ass in the van before I choke you out right here."

Before Chi Chi could scream for help, a huge hand clamped down over her mouth, muffling all sounds. She felt herself being lifted off her feet, then she was inside the van and she could feel it speeding off down the street.

The whole thing happened so fast, Chi Chi doubted if anyone had seen what had taken place. This realization, coupled with the fact she was trapped inside a vehicle with two kidnappers, convinced her to remain calm and keep her wits. She was going to need them.

"I know BJ sent y'all. How much is it goin' to cost for y'all to let me go?" she asked, positive it was money the men were after.

While she was talking, the big guy who grabbed her, had been busy rummaging through her purse. When he found the Glock, a strange smile came over him. "Nice little pop gun you got here baby. Me and my man carry cannons," He bragged, then-upped a chrome-plated .357 magnum.

Suddenly there was a blur of motion and a flash of blinding light, then a tremendous pain unlike Chi Chi had ever felt, exploded inside her head as cold blue steel connected with flesh, sending jolts of excruciating pain throughout every part of her body. Falling back into the cushioned seat, she could feel the warm, sticky blood dripping down the side of her face, some of it going into her mouth. The taste of her own blood sent her into a state of panic. No one had to tell her that she was standing on the threshold of death.

"We might as well get somethin' straight," the big guy said. "We ask the questions; you answer them. You got the game all fucked-up."

Glancing in the rearview mirror, his partner chuckled softly. "You one cold dude," he joked.

"We don't work for no fuckin' BJ," the first man spat arrogantly. "His stank ass is rotting away in the joint. Me and my man is out here in the sunlight doing our merry little thing. So bitch, you all mixed up. When we get where we're going, you gonna call King Larry's bitch ass and have him drop off half a mil. We'll tell him when and where to drop it off. He'll have twenty-four hours to get it there, or we'll ship him your dead body."

Dazed, Chi Chi lay there in total silence, cursing her stupidity. She couldn't believe how cheap she had played herself. *If I get outta this alive,* she told herself, *no one will ever get up on me this easy, ever again.*

Her captors were serious. That much was clear. If Larry didn't come through with that money, they were going to kill her just like they said. Vainly, she tried her best to recall where she had seen the men before.

Twenty minutes later, the van was pulling up in a two-car garage. Chi Chi was transported from the van through the side door of a ranch style home where she was taken downstairs into the basement and tied to a metal-framed bed, spread-eagled on her back.

"Take her clothes off," one of the men ordered.

From somewhere upstairs in the house, Chi Chi could hear the sound of a dog barking. Then she heard heavy footsteps coming down the stairs.

Straining, she turned her head to the right and saw a pretty, light-skinned chick wearing a black, see-through robe and a long blond wig. In her right hand she held the leash to a large German shepherd that was slobbering on itself. As recognition began to set in, Chi Chi's heart sank.

"Hello, Chi Chi," Lisa said. "Looks like we've come a full funky circle right back to where we began. I guess all good-byes ain't gone after all."

Even though she was scared, Chi Chi still couldn't help responding, "Yes, bitch. And all closed eyes ain't sleep."

Lisa laughed at her. "We'll see about that."

Now that things were out in the open, Chi Chi remembered where she had seen the two men. They were the same two deputies who had escorted Lisa in and out of the courtroom during the trial. *Damn, so if Larry pays them, they're not going to let me go. Why would they, I can identify them.*

Refusing to accept her fate with death, she cleared her mind of everything except survival, nothing else mattered.

# CHAPTERTWENTY-FOUR

**T**ony couldn't believe his eyes. It was too good to be true.

On page 3A of the New York Times, was the entire story. Dominic Salvordore Polinzo had been found dead in his own bed, apparently of a heart attack. He was naked as a baby, and so was the young woman found in the apartment with him. The old don had decided to ride into the sunset lying on top of a soft young body, his tiny dick buried inside a tight, warm pussy. Tony wasn't mad at him; it saved him the trouble and expense of a long, drawn out war. Fate had stepped in and destiny had taken its course. As to be expected of a man of his stature, the don's funeral was vainglorious and spectacular, featuring a motorcade of Lincolns, Cadillacs and Mercedes and weeping widows. The don himself had been laid out like a king. Though he was freshly shaven and decked out in a $3,500 immaculately tailored suit, he was still pale, stiff, and cold. His lips, thin and wax-like, were fixed in a permanent scowl, as though he knew something, and was laughing about it all the way to the cemetary.

Perhaps he did know something. He had certainly outlived most of his contemporaries and died in bed digging into a piece of pussy, unlike the vast majority of his gangsta pals who died with their boots on, shot full of holes on a lonely street or in a crowded restaurant when they least expected it.

Immediately following the funeral, Tony was summoned to Long Island for a sitdown with the commission. The subject of the meeting was a cease-fire between Tony's men and what remained of Don Polinzo's crew. At the meeting Tony saw quite a few men who had been laying low until the smoke cleared.

From the Bronx, Joey Giavanni was representing. Don Polinzo's underboss, Sal, "the Gip" Gisseppee, was there representing Queens, and the heads from the other New York families were all there representing their individual interests. The meeting began on a sour note.

"So, old Don Polinzo decided to go out lyin' on top of a piece of pussy young enough to be his own daughter," cracked Joey. He never had a problem letting it be known that he wasn't a big fan of Don Polinzo, even though the two of them knew each other since childhood.

Sal, went on the defensive immediately.

"Hey, what's wit' the fuckin' jokes? Dominic just got put in the ground hours ago and here we are makin' fuckin' jokes for Chrissake."

"Take it easy," Joey smiled. "We're all pals here."

"Oh yeah?" Sal asked, glancing over at Tony sitting across the table. "There's at least one of us sittin' at this table who didn't lose any sleep over the don's departure."

Tony felt his anger rising. "You're fuckin' right. Why should I lose any sleep over a guy who tried to kill me? Give me one good fuckin' reason!"

"Settle down, guys."

Everyone turned toward Johnny DiAngelo, who sat there calmly lighting the end of a Cuban cigar. His face was bronzed and leathery, like a man who sat outside in the sun too long. His hair was silvery white, just like Don Polinzo's. Out of all the men present in the room, Johnny held the greatest amount of respect. He was the Boss of all Bosses without being officially declared as such.

"Sure, Johnny," Sal said, still giving Tony the evil eye. "My only concern is that the dead are shown the proper respect, especially when it's Don Polinzo."

"That's understandable," Johnny said. "But it also has to be noted that Tony has a legitimate reason to be angry. After all, it was Dominic who transgressed the rules, and all of us simply sat back to see which way the wind would blow. Well, gentlemen, the wind has blown and our good friend, Dominic has been scattered to the four winds. As it stands, there's nothing to be gained by seekin' revenge. I kill your cat, you kill my dog. What's the point? We would be wise to leave things as they are and move on to bigger things."

Assessing the entire situation, Tony spoke softly. "I agree with Don DiAngelo. I'm willin' to let bygones be bygones. It's the wise thing to do, provided all of us here are indeed that wise."

With the ball clearly in his court, Sal looked down at the table, then back up at Tony. "What the hell?" he asked rhetorically. "Let the dead bury the dead. All of us here are alive. I say we celebrate the memory of our good brother by burying the hatchet."

If looks could kill, Tony would have been dead on the spot. He knew it and so did everyone else in the room. That's why it had been decided that Sal would have to go. He was too powerful and unpredictable. Tony was a rising star with plenty earning power, which could greatly benefit the men at the table. As compensation for Tony's injuries, he would be given Sal's head on a silver platter.

Johnny learned long ago that if you were going to be a leader of men, it was best to avoid frivolous, insignificant squabbles between members. That way you couldn't be accused of showing favoritism, which would create unnecessary enemies who would plot behind your back. It was best to leave that kind of decision making to underlings.

However, when it came to a beef between two, equally powerful members, the leader had no choice but to choose whose side he was going to be on. Usually, it would be the side that was the most valuable to the party line. The opposing party would be crushed, his supporters broken

161

down and absorbed into the ranks of the victors. This way peace and harmony would be established and the continued existence of the clan would thus be assured.

■■■■■■■■■■■■■■■■■■■■■■■■■■■■■■■■■■■■■■■■■■■■■■■■■■■■■■■■■■■■

Larry was getting his dick sucked when he got the call.

"Yeah who is this?" he asked, hypnotized by Greta's head bobbing up and down on his lap.

"Listen, you punk muthafucka. We got your bitch, Chi Chi. We gon' kill this ho if you don't drop off a half a mil."

Startled, Larry pushed Greta's head away from his swipe. "Hold up, baby. They got Chi Chi."

Puzzled, Greta looked up and asked, "Who?"

"Chi Chi's been kidnapped," Larry repeated.

Into the phone Larry said, "Listen man, we can work this out. Just don't hurt her. Where do you want me to drop the ends off?"

There was silence. Finally the voice said, "I'll call you back in half an hour and let you know."

After the caller hung up, Larry leaped out of bed and began pulling his clothes on. His mind was racing like a runaway train. He had to do something real fast.

Half a million dollars wasn't exactly chump change, but he was willing to pay it to get Chi Chi back. Once that was done, he would find the man behind the kidnapping, then make an example out of him.

"You know I'm gonna have to pay, but whoever these cats are, they not gonna live long enough to spend it," he told Greta.

Forcing herself to relax, Greta closed her eyes and let her mind drift off. Things had taken an unexpected turn of events. There was one important thing she hadn't counted on, and that was falling in love with Larry. What was she going to do about Chi Chi? *Evidently, he has feelings for her. Look at him scrambling around. This black man done hopped*

162

out the bed that quick, got his clothes on and is gonna come up with that $500,000 grand for that ho.

*Teri Woods Publishing Presents, Predators*

# CHAPTER TWENTY-FIVE

From the first moment they walked through the iron gates of the Ionia Reformatory, Melvin and Winky began raising hell, violating the rules and squeezing other inmates. Finally, the prison administration had enough and decided to transfer them to Jackson so that they could be around older convicts. It was hoped that it would slow them down, or, better yet, get them killed. After spending the first week in the hole, Melvin and Winky hit the general prison population and ran into BJ and Thad, who gave them care packages to last them until they received their own property.

The next day, BJ sent Melvin out on a visit to move some balloons that were supposed to be filled with weed, but were in actuality filled with pure heroin. On BJ's instructions, the balloons were punctured with tiny pinholes so that the dope would leak out slowly. The balloons were delivered to the visiting room by this attractive young woman who used a set of fake ID to enter the prison. Even though Melvin didn't know her from a can of paint, he immediately began feeling all over her, running his grimy hands over her thighs and between her legs. The guard sitting behind the desk gave them a stern look.

"Baby, don't you think you better chill out?" the young woman asked. "That guard is scopin' us out."

Melvin bristled up like a hungry lion. "Fuck that

guard! What he gon' do, put us out the visitin' room? C'mere girl. Let daddy feel that fat monkey."

"No, Melvin," she insisted. "BJ will be mad as hell if we get busted for fuckin' around."

Forcing himself to bite his tongue, Melvin reminded himself that he wasn't strong enough just yet to take BJ on, but if things went as he planned, it wouldn't be long before he could tell BJ and Thad to kiss his ass.

"Alright bitch, you ain't nuttin' but a dumb-ass mule, anyway. Gimme the shit and get your scared ass outta here."

Fighting back her anger, the girl removed the balloons from her bra and slid them to Melvin, who immediately swallowed them. He never knew about those tiny pinholes. He was tricked. Later that night, the dope had seeped out of the balloons to flood Melvin's system with enough heroin to kill a horse. The guard found him dead in his cell the next morning while making his rounds. The prison was locked down while the prison administration conducted a half-assed investigation before notifying Melvin's next-of-kin. On the real side, the prison authorities couldn't have cared less about Melvin's death. As far as they were concerned, he was just another dead convict and one less nigger they had to feed and house.

After the lockdown was lifted, Thad showed up in front of BJ's cell.

"Homie, what's happenin'? Old Melvin went out high as a kite. Nobody else know you sent him out there, do they?"

BJ smiled. "Hell naw! I ain't no damn fool. I planned everythin' to a T. His greedy ass won't be disrespectin' me anytime soon."

Thad looked up in surprise. "Shut da fuck up!" he exclaimed. "That was fine straight Machiavellian shit."

"Goddamn right," BJ said proudly. "I wonder if that punk actually thought I was going to let him get away with talking shit to me, plus freakin' Chi Chi behind my back? He thought I didn't know. But I knew. On top of that, if his freakish ass hadn't been dogging that bitch, Lisa, we wouldn't be here now."

Thad smiled like a sissy in boot camp. "You ain't gotta explain nuttin' to me dawg. Tell you the truth, for a minute I thought you had got soft on me."

Smiling back, BJ said, "Homie, revenge is a dish best served when it's cold. Feel me?"

"Hell yeah," Thad agreed. "And before all is said and done, bitch ass Raymond will understand that too. I must've been outta my mind to trust that dude again." Lil' Greg had come up to the prison for a visit with Thad two days ago to tell him that Raymond was no longer paying him and he didn't know what Thad wanted him to do about it.

"Well," BJ said thoughtfully, "just like the old folks say, 'a hard head makes a soft ass'."

Larry pulled the rent-a-car into the vacant lot on Linwood Avenue as he had been instructed. At this time of night the street was practically deserted. A few people hurried to-and-fro, making last minute stops, but none of them paid any particular attention to Larry sitting alone in his car puffing on a Kool. In the dark, the lit end of the cigarette gave off an eerie glow as Larry thought back to the day BJ had first introduced him to Chi Chi. They were at Bobby's Millionaire Club drinking and gambling when BJ walked through the door with her. She had on this red leather pants outfit that hugged every curve on her body and also showed a fat pussy print between her legs. *Damn, let me have some of that pussy right there, baby girl.* She had a body made for sex.

After that initial meeting, BJ often sent her to Larry's Beauty Salon to pick up drugs or drop off money. In the process Chi Chi started flirting with him, but they never took things beyond the point of no return. Now, he had taken her away from BJ and someone had kidnapped her. He tried not to imagine the things her abductors may have been putting her through. If it was the last thing he did, he was going to get her back, then punish severely whoever had been behind it. He had real feelings for Chi Chi. It wasn't just sex. Maybe it was love, he wasn't sure. He just felt he had to help her. Maybe it was because she was BJ's woman and BJ was his homie, even though he was sleeping with Chi Chi. He didn't really know how to explain it.

Ten minutes went by, then a beige van pulled up and parked right next to the rent-a-car on the left-hand side. Instantly, Larry became fully alert.

The window on the passenger's side of the van slid down and a big black guy wearing dark shades peered out.

"You bring the cash?"

"Yeah I got it. Where's Chi Chi?"

"In the van. You didn't call the cops did ya?"

"I ain't cut like that. Plus, I gave you my word, which I always keep. Now, how do you wanna do this? We can do it rough or we can do it smooth."

The kidnapper glanced over at his partner sitting behind the steering wheel, then turned back to Larry. "Get out the car, slowly. Keep your hands where I can see 'em. And bring the money wit' ya," he instructed.

"Okay man," Larry said. "Don't do nothin' stupid. The money ain't worth my woman's life, and it sure ain't worth mine." After saying that, he cautiously got out of the car the bag of money in his left hand and a .50 caliber Desert Eagle in his right, resting reassuringly against his thigh.

"Drop the bag on the ground," said the kidnapper. "Then get back in your ride and pull off.

"No way," Larry said. "I ain't goin' nowhere without my woman. I acted in good faith by showing up alone with the ends. Now I ain't goin' for no more bullshit. Let my woman out of the van, or we can go out like two cowboys. It's your call."

The guy in the shades laughed. "What makes you think I won't blast you right now and take the money?"

"This," Larry said, dropping the bag on the ground and pointing the huge weapon at the kidnapper's head.

"Now, I'm gon' say this one last time. We can either take care of business or die right now. Do you want the money or not?"

Suddenly the side door of the van slid open and the kidnapper Larry had been talking to, got out. He was holding Chi Chi in front of him as a human shield. She was gagged, blindfolded, and her hands were tied behind her back. Her face was bloodied and swollen to twice its normal size. It was obvious she had been severely beaten. Larry felt his blood boil over.

"Alright, guy," said the kidnapper with a smirk on his face. "Drop your piece and back away from the bag. Once I have the money in my hands,, you and your woman can drive away from here in one piece."

Chi Chi tried to alert Larry with her body movements that she had overheard her abductors plotting to kill both of them as soon as they got the money.

Larry was about to squeeze the trigger when suddenly the entire area lit up like the Fourth of July. He heard a voice shouting through a bullhorn, "Drop your weapons! You are surrounded. This is the police! I repeat, drop your weapons and lay on the ground and no one will be hurt."

Frantic, the kidnapper in the dark shades glanced around him. All he saw were a bunch of dark shadows, but his experience and instinct told him that a trained SWAT team had their weapons cocked and pointed right at him.

With a thousand things going through his mind at the same time, the kidnapper debated whether to give up or hold court in the street. The sounds of tires screeching against the pavement made him turn around just in time to see the van backing out of the parking lot at top speed, as his partner made a desperate attempt to escape. He never got the chance. Bullet after bullet rained down upon the van until it went out of control and crashed into the front of a supermarket on the other side of the street and came to a complete halt. A police chopper circling overhead, illuminated the street with a powerful floodlight as uniformed

168

cops and plainclothes detectives appeared seemingly out of nowhere, with their guns drawn and body armor strapped in place.

"Get down on the ground!" they yelled.

The remaining kidnapper dropped his weapon immediately and did as he was told.

"You too," a detective bellowed at Larry, pointing his service revolver in Larry's direction.

Easing the Desert Eagle to the ground, Larry laid down on the ground next to the kidnapper. Their hands were instantly cuffed behind their backs.

Looking over at Larry, the kidnapper said, "Wait til I get to the joint," he taunted. "I'm going to tell everybody what a fuckin' rat bastard you turned out to be."

"I don't know what the hell you talking bout," Larry growled, turning his head to face the man laying beside him. "I didn't call the cops. I wanted your punk ass all to myself. Your partner got off lucky. Wait and see what happens to your bitch ass when you touch down in the yard in Jackson."

"Get 'em off the ground and place 'em in separate cars for the ride downtown," ordered a black detective who was obviously in charge.

As Larry hustled to his feet, he asked, "Why am I being arrested? I'm the victim."

Detective McQueen laughed. "Victim my ass! I been waiting a long time for this moment, King Larry."

Turning to a tall, light-skinned woman who had her back turned to Larry, McQueen said, "Good job, Agent Fanelli."

Larry caught the faint scent of her perfume. Something about it was familiar. When the woman turned to face him, his heart nearly stopped.

"Greta? What are you doin' here?"

Amused, Detective McQueen stepped forward. "Allow me to introduce you to Agent Angela Fanelli. You probably know her as Greta. How does it feel to be played like a

169

sucker, sucker?"

Standing there in the dark, the woman Larry had loved as Greta, was unable to look at him. She stood there with her head down, staring at the ground.

"Book him for CCW for now," McQueen said. "I'm sure more charges will come later. The feds will probably want a piece of the action."

As Larry was being led away, Angela brushed away a single tear.

"I know it's difficult," McQueen said, his voice full of understanding. "But it's part of the job. Whenever you work undercover there's always the possibility of becoming overly familiar with your subject, making it that much more difficult to make the bust when the time comes. I know; I've been there, I've done that."

Shoving her hands deep into the pockets of her black leather trench coat, Angela walked away without replying. How could she help put a man behind bars when she had fallen in love with him and was pregnant with his child? When she first volunteered for the job, the last thing on her mind was falling in love with Larry. McQueen could talk about the difficulties of undercover work all he wanted, but her heart would never understand it. Even with all that had happen, she didn't regret alerting her superiors to Chi Chi's kidnapping. Angela was glad she was with Larry when the call came in that Chi Chi was kidnapped. As Chi Chi would tell it later, those kidnappers were planning to kill them both. In a way, Angela may have fucked up Larry's life, but she also saved it, the irony.

The deputies that had escorted Lisa in and out of the courtroom were a dangerous pair who killed for the fun of it. Both of them had been under investiagion for the last year for everything from stealing drugs and money from the evidence lockers to first-degree murder. There was definitely no way these guys were going to simply walk away when they could possibly be identified. After the suspects had been read their rights and led away, the area was secured and the van searched. Two bodies were discovered inside the van. One belonged to the slain deputy, and the other belonged to Lisa. She had been shot through the head.

Chi Chi, barely conscious, was taken to the emergency room at Detroit's Receiving Hospital where she was treated. Her physical injuries would eventually heal over time, but Chi Chi's abducters had severly traumatized her. She was tortured by Lisa, repeatedly raped by her male kidnappers and burned with cigarettes, but the final act of humiliation was when she was forced to have sex with the dog. That's when something inside her head snapped.

In the hospital, she refused to talk with detectives, withdrawing into herself and staring blankly at the four walls. The only thing that kept playing in her mind over and over like a broken record was 'what goes around comes back around.'

# CHAPTER TWENTY-SIX

**W**hen Larry entered the lawyer conference room at the end of the hall in the Wayne County Jail, the last person on earth he expected to see was Angela. She was still beautiful and still desirable. Dressed professionally in a gray blazer, matching pleated skirt, and black pumps, she stood there in front of the desk, arms folded across her chest with a look of grave concern on her pretty face.

"Hello, Larry. How are you?"

"How the hell you think I am? Shit, you got to ask me a stupid question. The woman I been layin' up with turns out to be a fuckin' narc and you have the nerve to ask me how I'm doin'? You shoulda been a man baby, 'cause you got balls like a brass ass monkey. Why did you come here, Greta? Aww damn, I forgot, that ain't even your name."

Taking a deep breath, Angela sighed and exclaimed slowly, "Look, Larry, I know how you must feel, and you have every right in the world to be angry with me. After all, I deceived you."

"Deceived?" Larry shouted. "Betrayed is a much better word."

"I know, and not only do I apologize, I would like for us to start all over."

Larry couldn't help but laugh. "Start all over? Bitch, I

172

don't even know your real name! Or what the fuck to call you."

Looking down at the floor then back at Larry, Angela said softly, "It's Angela."

"Is that right? Well, Miss Angela, why did you come down here to gloat cause I really don't understand what you're here for."

"No, I came to let you know that I've fallen in love with you."

Before Larry could get over the initial shock, Angela hit him with another one, this one far more devastating.

"I'm also pregnant with your child," she said simply.

His hands manacled in front of him, Larry stood there in disbelief. He was speechless.

Not only did he feel helpless and at a loss for words, but he was at the mercy of his pent up emotions that were threatening to spill over at any moment. Fighting for self-control, he finally found his voice. "What did you say?" he asked, his mind still unable to accept what he had just heard.

"I said I'm in love with you and we're going to have a baby."

"But that's impossible!" Larry managed to say. "I'm on my way to the penitentiary and it's your testimony that's going to send me there."

"That's where you're wrong," Angela replied. "A wife cannot be compelled to testify against her lawful wedded husband."

"Whadda you talkin' 'bout? First of all, we're not married, and secondly, what's goin' to happen to the baby?"

Brushing back a lock of red hair with a slender, well-manicured finger, Angela ran her tongue over her dry lips and cleared her throat.

"You're right. We're not married, at least not yet. But I know this girl who works over at the City County Building who owes me a favor. She can have our blood tests back in a few days and we can be married before anyone gets wise to

173

what's going on. As for the baby, I plan on having it, and I don't care who doesn't like it."

Looking around, Larry spotted a chair and eased down on it. Things had taken such a strange turn of events he felt like he was on a merry-go-round.

"How are you gonna raise a child without its father being around? Have you considered that? I was brought up without a dad and it's not easy. Trust me."

Angela sat down on the edge of the desk and crossed her long, lovely legs. The motion caused her skirt to slide up her thighs, attracting Larry's immediate attention. He couldn't help but think back to the times they had spent making love and sharing their visions for the future.

"Without my testimony," Angela said, "The most they'll be able to charge you with is carrying a concealed weapon, which carries five years max. I've checked and you don't have any felony convictions on record. You'll end up doing two or three years. I can wait that long, darling, and so can the baby," she said, smiling.

"I got to give it to you. You got things all figured out, don't you? But there is still one thing you didn't add into the equation."

Angela stared at him. "And what is that?"

"Chi Chi," Larry replied, staring back at her.

"Are you trying to tell me you're in love with her?" Angela asked, her green eyes sparkling like twin jewels.

Shrugging his shoulders, Larry replied truthfully. "To be honest, I don't know. But I do know that I feel a certain obligation and responsibility toward her. I mean, I just can't..."

"Listen," Angela said, cutting him off in mid-sentence, "It's not your fault. Chi Chi knew the consequences of her actions just like you. She chose to play and now she has to pay. Besides, her being in the nuthouse might not be such a bad thing."

"Whadda ya mean?" Larry's eyebrows shot straight up.

"Chi Chi's being investigated for the murder of her step-father who was raping her when she was a child. She's the prime suspect. The police plan on making an arrest. But, she never made it out the hospital, Larry, she was admitted to psychiatrics. Whatever happened with that Lisa girl and those kidnappers, it was just too much for her."

"What?" Larry asked in shock. He never knew this or even heard of such. Chi Chi never confided in him about this shameful part of her life. Everybody thought that Chi Chi was a tough gangsta and most were afraid of her. She didn't want any of them to know her weakness—that she let her step-father rape her.

"Larry, listen, I don't want us to get off-track here, but I'm willing to give you some time to get her out of your system. After that, it's all-or-nothing. If I'm willing to give up my career in law enforcement and have your baby, then you must be willing to give up your life as a drug dealer and all the trappings that go along with it."

Getting up from the desk, she walked over to him, bent down, and kissed him on the mouth. "You need to think about it. I'll be back tomorrow. You can tell me then what you want to do."

As she walked away, Larry watched her go with a growing sense of resignation. He felt like a mouse caught in a mousetrap.

If he didn't agree to marry her and she testified against him, he'd be up Shit's Creek without a paddle. Not only would he have to deal with the state, after they got through wringing him out, but the feds would be waiting in the wings for their pound of flesh, and they would try to skin his ass to the bone. Angela had him over a barrel. She was blackmailing him as certain as the kidnappers had been. The only difference was that they wanted his money. Angela wanted his heart and a wedding band. And that was just for starters.

After she disappeared through the gate, a few minutes later a Wayne County deputy in a brown and beige uniform showed up to escort Larry back to his cell. For the rest of the night Larry laid quietly in the dark, staring at the four walls. He was contemplating being happily married and living in a modest, comfortable home surrounded by a white picket fence. Angela and he, and the baby would make three. *Wow, I can't believe I was crazy enough to fuck the police, literally.* It was then at that moment, he heard that weasel-ass nigga, Rayfil. *I told you all that strange pussy you like to pick up nigga was gonna get you no where, but a heap of trouble. Ha Ha Ha!*

■■■■■■■■■■■■■■■■■■■■■■■■■■■■■■■■■■■■■■■■■■■■■■■■■■■■■■■■■■■

In Jackson prison, Thad and BJ watched the nightly news with great anticipation. All over the prison yard the news of Larry's arrest and Chi Chi's kidnapping was on the lips of almost every black convict. Most of them had never met Larry before, but they had heard so much about him exploited in the game, he was almost like a living legend, someone to be envied and looked up to. But as far as Thad and BJ were concerned, their interest centered around an entirely different motive that was as old as time itself, plain old revenge.

Barely able to contain his excitement, Thad was starting to get on BJ's nerves.

"I can't wait til they bring King Larry's nickel slick ass through here. I got something for his dirty red ass that can't wait. I'ma squeeze that nigga's ass til it bleeds green!"

"I don't know man, I been thinkin', it might not be such a good idea to play Larry for twos and fews. The nigga's worth millions."

Thad looked at him with a strange expression on his rock hard features. "What da fuck you think I'm talkin' 'bout? I ain't talkin' 'bout squeezin' for no chump change."

"Stop drawin'," BJ replied smoothly. "All I'm tryin' to say is Larry's not only caked the fuck up, but he's got more moves around the dope circuit than Allen Iverson got on the basketball court. If we play our hand right, soon as our feet touch back down on the bricks, we can step our game all the way up. All we need is one of his outta town connects. We'll be able to dance like we wanna. Then we really won't need him up in our business."

"But what about Chi Chi?" Thad asked, trying his best to reason with his partner. "You done forgot how he crossed you for a bitch?"

"Hell naw," BJ replied. "Justice delayed ain't justice denied. What did I tell you just the other day about revenge? Have you forgot already?"

"Naw, I ain't forgot. You said revenge was best served after it got cold," Thad answered.

BJ smiled coldly. "Now you're startin' to see the picture. Not the whole picture, but enough of it to know that things are never what they first appear to be. You have to learn to look beneath the surface. Quit being so damn petty and coldhearted. In order to see the entire picture, you have to step outside the picture frame."

Spinning on his heels, BJ began walking away.

"Take it easy, greasy. And stay up," he hollered back at Thad, who was standing silent as he watched BJ walk away. In his heart, he wished he could be as smart as his partner, but he knew that wouldn't happen. He simply wasn't cut out to be an intellectual. He was a cold-blooded killer, and truth be told, he didn't aspire to much more than that.

Actually he enjoyed doing what he did. BJ was the only person on earth who could talk crazy to him. Other than his nephew and son, BJ was the only person alive who he really trusted. While it was true that he loved Jasmine, that didn't mean he trusted her. All the women he had ever known in his life had crossed him, including his own mother. He only hoped Jasmine never crossed him. It would just be like his mother all over again. But he knew in his heart if she did, he'd slit her throat, just like he had his mother's. *No Jasmine would never hurt me, never hurt me,* he told himself over and over.

# CHAPTER TWENTY-SEVEN

Lil' Greg hopped into the backseat of the black Lexus next to Kaleem. Kaleem acknowledged him then nodded to the two men up front. The car pulled away from the curb.

A little nervous, Lil' Greg glanced uncertainly at Kaleem. "My lady told me you called. She said you wanted to talk to me."

"Yeah, I wanna show you somethin' I think you need to see," the older man replied. The serious expression on his face let Lil' Greg know that it was probably best to keep quiet.

"So, how have you been?"

Lil' Greg shrugged. "I've been okay. Just thinkin' about bein' inducted. I can't wait."

Kaleem smiled at an unknowing Lil' Greg.

"Neither can I, neither can I."

The rest of the trip was spent in silence.

Arriving at a dilapidated, rundown, single-family apartment on Detroit's notorious East Side, the Lexus parked between two cars and all four men got out. One of them was Kambui.

Walking up to the front door of what was obviously a crack house, Kambui rapped sharply on the door. A few seconds later, a man dressed in a raggedy tracksuit that was falling apart, came to the door and peeped out. Recognizing Kaleem, he opened the door.

"Hey, bro! Y'all come in," he grinned, displaying missing and yellow, tobacco, stained teeth. He had a long, bushy, beard and a head full of salt-and-pepper hair.

"It's still hard for me to believe that you have allowed yourself to fall this low. You went from sugar to shit. As long as you were down with us, you shined like new money. Now look at you. You're back on the pipe and you look like death on a stick. When are you gonna get yourself back together, brotha?" said Kaleem pushing himself past the fallen soldier named Joe.

He held his head in shame, remembering when he was part of the movement. Back then, he was proud, strong, independent, and a part of something that had made him feel like life was worth living. But that was years ago before he fell off and started smoking again. Now he was running a crack den for crack heads like himself. He allowed them to use the premises to get high, as long as they gave him a few hits off their pipe.

The crack house had a funky odor that permeated the air. It smelled worse than stinky feet and was so dirty, Lil' Greg couldn't believe Kaleem had them standing inside. He glanced around the room, saw two women and a man crawling on the floor and knew what they were looking for; crack on the floor. Over in the corner, a dirty, unkept woman watched her crack-head boyfriend sucking up smoke through a glass pipe. Her eyes, yellow with hepatitis, were full of hunger as she watched the smoke twirl around inside the pipe before being drawn deep inside the lungs of her boyfriend. Her greed and anticipation of getting high got the best of her, and she broke wind. Unashamed, she casually looked around the room to see if anyone could smell her stinkin' ass.

"Damn, see what you made me do? Nigga, hurry up and pass that pipe!"

Her scarecrow-looking boyfriend wasn't hearing her.

He dragged even deeper on the pipe, his mind lost on cloud nine. Lil' Greg stood there watching them, feeling like he had lost his own soul right along with them.

He glanced at Kaleem, "I think I understand what you brought me here to see," he stated.

There was a sad expression on Kaleem's face.

"No, I don't think you have seen what I brought you here to see, or at least you haven't seen yet. Look over there by the window," he said, nodding his head in that direction. Lil' Greg looked toward the boarded up window. There, sitting serenely on a threadbare couch that had springs poking through it was his sister, Reba.

Her eyes were bulging out of her head like she had just seen a ghost. Her hair was dirty and uncombed, and her sunken jaws made her look like a living skeleton. Lil' Greg almost fell on the floor in shock.

"Reba?" he asked unbelievingly.

Rushing over to where she was sitting in a daze, he accidentally bumped into a crack head who eyed him angrily.

"Nigga, watch where da fuck you goin' before you knock my shit over!"

Ignoring him, Lil' Greg grabbed Reba by her skinny shoulders and snatched her to her feet. Her eyes were wide-open in surprise.

"What the hell are you doin' here?" he asked.

Her mind in a cocaine-induced fog, it took a few seconds for her to register that the man talking to her was her brother.

"Oh, hey, lil bro," she said, trying to pull herself together. "You got any rocks on ya?"

Lil' Greg stood there paralyzed. He couldn't answer her question because he couldn't think.

"Damn, Reba, what happened to you? C'mon, sis, I gotta get you away from here."

"I'm not goin' no where. Don't be pullin' on me. Let me go!"

Kaleem came up behind them and touched Lil' Greg

180

on the shoulder.

"It's alright," he said gently. "Sista Reba, let us help you. Ain't nobody tryin' to hurt you. We're here to help you get well."

Squinting her eyes against the faint sunlight slipping through a crack in the board over the window, Reba asked, "Is that you, Brother Kaleem?"

"Yes, it's me, Reba. C'mon, you're in good hands."

After they got her outside, on the way to the car, Kaleem pulled Kambui aside. Kaleem didn't want Lil' Greg to hear his plans.

"Dig, give everybody inside that death trap ten minutes to get their shit together, then blow it off the map."

The big man nodded, his shiny bald head dripping with perspiration.

"No problem, spiritual one," he said, then headed back toward the house thinking about the hand grenade concealed inside the pocket of his leather jacket.

# CHAPTER TWENTY EIGHT

Larry and Angela were married on the twenty-eighth day of March 1993, on the sixth floor of the Wayne County Jail. The only other person present was the jail's chaplain. There was no big crowd of well-wishers, no champagne, and afterward, no honeymoon. All that would have to wait.

"Well, baby, how does it feel to be Mr. Westin?" Larry asked, still holding her in a tight embrace.

"It feels great. Don't worry about being unable to take me on our honeymoon. It can wait until after you come home."

Pulling back, Larry looked at her, then kissed the tip of her nose. "Baby, did you talk to the prosecutor about my case?"

"Well first he tried to talk me out of marrying you. After that didn't work, he threatened to give you the max on the gun charge."

"That was to be expected. What about the feds? How did they carry you?"

"Of course they asked me to resign, but I was way ahead of them. I had my resignation papers in my pocket. The district attorney agreed to drop all charges against you, seeing that without me they had no case. He, of course, also told me I was making a terrible mistake by helping free a

182

vicious criminal like you."

Larry kissed her again. "What about you? Do you feel you're makin' a mistake?"

Angela kissed him back, enjoying the feel of his lips and the smell of his cologne.

"No, darling. If I had the opportunity to do it all over, I'd do the exact same thing. They're just mad that a black man got away from their special brand of justice."

Over in the corner of the small room a medium-height deputy glared at the newly wedded couple through reddened eyes.

"Alright, your time is about up. Wrap it up," he announced in a cold tone of voice.

Larry was about to say something sarcastic, but Angela stopped him. "Don't feed into his little game. That's what he wants you to do. We've got far too many plans to let someone like him get in our way. The game is over. We won and they lost."

As Larry and his new bride embraced for one last kiss, he thought about what she had said about the game being over. *I don't know what she's talking about, ain't no game over. Shit, I'm just getting started.*

One thing he did know for certain is that he would have to face Thad and BJ when he got to Jackson. *I wonder if BJ mad about Chi Chi. If he is, he'll get over it.* Suddenly, his mind switched and he thought about all his fallen childhood comrades. He had never failed to neglect his peoples while on lock down. He always reached back in, when they were reaching out. Now that he was on his way to join them, all that reachin' would come in handy.

**N**orthville State Hospital for the mentally and criminally insane, was located in rural Michigan; the multicomplex building had the appearance of a college campus. Sprawling, well-manicured lawns, flower beds, trees, and a small pond complete with floating ducks. It was hard to imagine the pain and horror on the other side of its brass-handled doors.

Chi Chi had been sent there after failing to respond to the medication and psychotherapy her doctors had prescribed for her. She was sitting alone in her room on the second floor gazing out the window when she saw two detectives pull up in the parking lot. Ten minutes later a kind-faced black woman in her middle fifties appeared in the doorway. She had gray hair and was dressed in a white uniform, white stockings, and white shoes.

"Good morning, Miss Williams. There are two detectives here to see you. Don't worry. I won't let them bother you with a whole lot of unnecessary questions. You get tired of 'em bothering you, just nod at me and I'll put 'em out."

Automatically, Chi Chi dummied up. She couldn't afford to trust anyone, not even the kind nurse. Too much was at stake. Going to prison for the rest of her life wasn't exactly the type of future she saw for herself. She knew the detectives were there to ask about her stepfather's murder. They could ask all the questions they wanted, she told herself, but she didn't have to answer any of them and she wasn't. Fixing her face with a blank expression, she focused on her favorite spot on the wall. She had it down pat. They would never penetrate her wall of defense. She had been through the routine before and knew just what to expect. They would ask their questions and she would pretend to be catatonic until they grew tired and decided to leave empty-handed. But she knew they would return the next day, or the next week perhaps, and each time she'd be waiting for them in her nut role. Soon it would dawn on them that they were just wasting their time; time that could have been better spent chasing down other suspects with a lot less to lose.

# CHAPTER TWENTY-NINE

**A** broken down hooptie filled with a conspicuous-looking group of men, cruised down Third Avenue.

"Hey Reba!" one of them yelled out.

On her way to the campus bookstore to purchase books for the upcoming spring semester, Reba hesitated, knowing that the men inside the car represented everything she was trying to get away from. She quickened her pace.

The men were all former crack-smoking buddies, and were on their way to a crack house. One of them, the one who called her, used to be her boyfriend, until Lil' Greg threatened to kill him if he didn't leave Reba alone.

"Reba! Baby, don't act like you don't know me. Where ya headed? C'mon, we'll give you a lift." The car slowed down and was inching its way down the street.

Reluctantly, Reba stopped and stared into the car. "Hi, Willie. I'm on my way to the bookstore. I appreciate the offer, but no thank-you. I'd rather walk."

Suddenly the car came to a complete stop and the guy she'd spoken to, got out. His name was Willie Jefferson. Tall, slender, and brown skinned, it was obvious that at one time he had been quite good-looking, but that was before the effects of crack addiction had taken its deadly toll. Now he was just a bag of skin and bones with oversized clothing hanging off his skeletal frame.

Walking up to her, he gave her his most charming smile. It was the same warm smile he had when they first met, before they started smoking and crack cocaine destroyed their relationship.

"Hey, lil' mama. Wassup?"

"Not much, Willie, just tryin' to get my life right. I'm goin' to college now. It's been three months and I'm still clean," she said proudly.

Willie felt alarm spreading through-out his body. He was smart enough to realize that the longer she stayed off the drug, the lesser his chances would be to win her back. Desperate, he searched his dope fiend mind for words that would convince her to get in the car.

"That's good Reba. I'm proud of you. I wanna get off this shit too, but I'm not strong like you. I need help. Will you help me?" he asked, trying his best to look sincere while appealing to her emotions.

"Of course, Willie. No matter what happens, you can count on me. Sweetheart, I will always be here for you. I could never turn my back on you; it's just that we're on two different paths at the moment."

"Hey Willie! Man, c'mon. Leave that funny-actin' bitch alone and let's go take care of our business!" yelled the driver of the beat-up hooptie. He and the other men were growing impatient. They wanted to get where they were going so they could smoke their rocks.

"Hold up a minute," Willie called back. Turning back to Reba, he spoke softly. "Baby, please, just come with me while I smoke these last few stones. When they're gone I swear I'm through with it. I just need you there beside me to give me strength."

Looking into his eyes, Reba felt herself growing weak. "I-I don't know, Willie," she said.

"Reba, please."

"Well, okay. But you can't take all night. I still have to pick up my schoolbooks."

"Sure, baby. I'll even go with you. Okay?" he tried to

kiss her but she quickly turned away as she smelled his bad breath and body odor.

"Willie, when's the last time you had a bath? I'ma have to clean you up."

Smiling, Willie helped her get in the car, and then climbed in beside her. As the car took off down the street he was busy scheming on a way to talk her out of her school book money.

For a brief moment, he considered Lil' Greg and his threat to kill him if he bothered his sister again. But his fear was quickly overridden by the prospect of winning Reba back. *Fuck Lil' Greg,* he thought sullenly. *I'll deal with his ass if it comes down to it. His ass bleed too.*

Two days later Lil' Greg received a call. It was his mother. "Child, have you seen your sister?" she asked, her voice full of dread.

"No. I ain't seen her. I gave her money to buy her schoolbooks two days ago, and that's the last time I seen or heard from her," he answered truthfully.

"Well, if you see her, have her call me please. Will you do that for your mama? I'm worried, Greg, honey."

"Yes. I'll have her call you. Don't worry."

When he hung up the phone he was steaming. After all he had been through to get Reba straight. What a waste of time. He was sure she had started smoking again. Someone said they had spotted Reba and Willie back together.

He called Kaleem and told him his suspicions.

"Calm down," Kaleem urged. "How can you be sure she's back on the pipe? Have you talked to anybody who has actually seen her in a crack house?"

"No. But I do know she's back with that bitch ass Willie, and as soon as I see him I'm goin' to pop a cap in his dope fiend ass! I told him to stay away from her."

"Whoa! Wait a minute now," Kaleem cautioned. "What good is it goin' to do to take a crack head out the box? There's nothin' you can do to him worse than what he's doing to himself. Besides, you must have forgotten about all

187

the times you sold that shit to your own people. Now you wanna kill some fool who ain't got a pot to piss in just because you believe he enticed your sista to get back on the pipe, that's not right my brotha. What we have to do is find Reba and make sure she's alright."

Knowing that Kaleem had spoken the truth, Lil' Greg got a grip on his emotions and spoke in a quiet voice.

"You're right. I'm just so frustrated. I don't know what to do. I love my sista. She's got so much potential. I hate to see her throwin' her life away."

"I know," Kaleem said. "Look, why don't you meet me at the center? In the meantime I'll make a few calls and see what I can come up with."

"Thanks, I appreciate that."

"Try not to worry. I'm sure she's alright," Kaleem said, trying to sound more confident than he actually felt. In the back of his mind he tried not to think of what could have happened to Reba. He could only hope and pray for the best.

# CHAPTER THIRTY

**O**ut on a half million dollar bond, Larry managed to stay free for the next six months by filing postponements. During that time, he and Angela, with the court's permission, went on their honeymoon in the Cayman Islands and really got to know each other. It had been a lot of pretending and a lot of deception, when both were pretending to be something and someone other than themselves. When they returned to the states, the first thing they did, was purchase a home in suburban Detroit and decorate it from top to bottom with expensive furniture.

They next set up a joint bank account and an ironclad insurance policy as they prepared for Larry's imminent departure. Angela was offered a job as an assistant professor in the criminal studies department at Wayne State University and after talking it over with Larry, she accepted. Meanwhile, Larry immersed himself in his work as a professional cosmetologist, but it seemed that every time he turned around, the feds were there, watching and waiting for him to make that one false move so they could send him away to a maximum security federal penitentiary until his head turned white as snow.

Marrying Angela, a former agent, had been a slap in their face, adding insult to injury, and they were determined to avenge their honor at any cost. That meant that no opportunity to harass or intimidate was overlooked nor ignored. All-out war had been unofficially declared against the newlywed couple. With the baby due in three months, Angela and Larry enjoyed their last moments together, living each day as though it was their last. Until, finally, it was time. There would be no more postponing the inevitable. Larry was sentenced to five years in state prison for carrying a concealed weapon. With good time and jail credit, he could be out in a little over three years. Angela promised to bring the baby up just as soon as it was born and she was able to travel.

When Larry reached Jackson, he found his homies waiting for him. In addition to the care package they had for him, they also slipped him a nine inch, sharpened piece of steel.

"For your personal protection," G Man said.

He and Larry had grown up together and knew each other's family.

"I hate to see you under these circumstances, but it's good to see ya."

"Same here." He was glad that Larry had acknowledged him in front of his friends. For years he had been bragging to them about how cool he and Larry were, but he knew they never really believed him and he couldn't blame them. In prison people often pretended to be something they weren't.

Because he had been convicted only of the gun charge, Larry was housed on block eight on the prison's south side. Thad and BJ were housed on the other side of the prison, the side reserved for those convicted of murder, drugs, kidnapping, or armed robbery. BJ sent word that he wanted to see Larry that evening on Cooper's Field, a hardball diamond named after the street the prison was located on. Situated at the back of the prison grounds, it had a dugout for the players and metal bleachers for the spectators. Convicts usually congregated there to watch the games, get high, discuss law, or other important matters.

Anticipating trouble, most of the convicts stayed away from the field that day. They heard that there might be trouble between BJ and Larry and didn't want to get caught in the middle of a big knife fight. Most of them had enough trouble of their own, and considered taking a man's woman an act of gross disrespect that demanded retaliation.

When Larry arrived with four of his homies, Thad and BJ were already sitting at the top of the bleachers surrounded by several men loyal to them. Unbeknownst to Larry, it had already been decided not to smash him.

"If it ain't King Larry. What's poppin' nigga?" BJ asked, his handsome features sheilding his anger.

Not knowing what to expect, Larry surveyed his surroundings, then looked up at BJ. "Long time no see."

"C'mon up," BJ said. "The air is clean up here. A nigga can breathe and think straight."

Not wanting to show any fear, Larry began walking up the aisle followed by his guys. All of them were carrying some type of hand-made weapon and were ready for anything. When he reached the top where BJ and Thad were standing, he hesitated.

"Everything's straight," BJ said with a smirk on his face. "C'mon, sit down. We need to talk."

Reluctantly, Larry sat down next to him, the shank up his sleeve, ready to slide out.

"So, was sup?"

"You tell me. You're the one who put shit in the game."

"It ain't like that," Larry said.

BJ shrugged, glancing at him out of the corner of his eye. "Oh really."

"Look man," Larry said with a serious expression. "Ain't no sense in bullshitting each other. I know what I did and I ain't gonna try to sugarcoat it. But it ain't the way it seems. Chi Chi hit on me. Like most men, I got weak when confronted with the pussy. I know that ain't no excuse, but it's the truth, for real."

BJ fought back the urge to sucker punch the older man.

191

"It is what it is. You don't have to tell me nothin' about Chi Chi. I used to fuck her too. Remember? The bitch got hot pants. How's she doin' anyway?"

Relaxing somewhat, Larry breathed deeply and said, "Last I heard she was still in the nut box. Lisa and those punk ass deputies did a good job on her, man. They messed her head up."

BJ was silent, thinking about all the times Chi Chi had professed her undying love for him, then turned around and crossed him like a car going across railroad tracks. *Just goes to show you,* he thought matter-of-factly. *You can never trust a bitch.*

"I hope we ain't gotta fall out about this," Larry said, interrupting BJ's thoughts. He was ready to bring things to a head, one way or another.

"Damn, nigga!" Thad instigated, "You strong as acid."

"It ain't about shit," BJ reassured him. "The sad thing about it, he's right. Two playas should never fall out about a bitch, no matter how bad she is. Gorilla pimps play cop, lock, and block. Real playas know the name of the game is cop and blow. I ain't never loved nobody who didn't love me. When a bitch leaves me, it's her loss and my gain."

Larry sat there feeling guilty as sin. He had always liked the two partners, and the truth of the matter was that he himself went out like a sucker when he crossed BJ for a woman. But what was done was done, and there wasn't anything he could do to change that plain and simple fact.

"Anyway," BJ continued without missing a beat. "I never did thank you for sending those ends to our attorney. Just goes to prove that you might have a tender dick, but you still got a good heart and I guess that's what really counts. So, how have you been doin', King Larry?"

The ice broken, Larry could breathe a little easier, but he still kept his guard up. He wasn't about to get rocked to sleep.

"I been alright, man, just lucky to have dodged them muthafucking feds. Them niggas play for keeps."

192

"Yeah, I know," BJ agreed. "I heard you married the fed broad they had on you. I know they ain't too happy about that."

"Tell me about it. But if I ever slip, my ass is out like Idi Amin."

"Ya know, Larry," Thad interrupted. "I ain't gon' even bullshit ya. I wanted to burn that ass for how you played my man, but BJ is right. True playas should never fall out over a piece of pussy."

"You're right," Larry admitted. "But don't worry about it. I'll make it up to you. As soon as we touch back down on the bricks, I got a plan to turn us all into instant millionaires. I got it all laid out. Fuck all that selling dope shit. The game done changed. The feds have stepped in and they're passin' out time like runnin' water, and we can't get around them. They got too many resources and too many punk ass snitches."

"What's your point?" asked BJ.

"My point is, the future lies in selling insurance."

"Insurance?" BJ asked with a puzzled expression. "Who the fuck is gonna buy insurance from us?

"Everybody selling dope in the city."

BJ looked at him like he had gone mad. "Maybe Chi Chi ain't the only one gone crazy, cause I'm not feelin' you."

"It's simple," Larry explained. "They'll buy insurance so they'll be protected."

"Protected, from who? The police?"

Larry grinned even wider. "No, from gangstas."

# CHAPTER THIRTY-ONE

Lil Greg was shocked at how much weight Reba lost since the last time he had seen her. All that energy spent trying to save her had been a complete waste of time. She appeared to be nothing more than a walking, breathing, human skeleton, an empty shell devoid of spirit. Her eyes that once burned bright with promise were now dull and lifeless. Even her mother, a devout, die-hard, born-again Christian, had given up hope on her oldest daughter. All of her prayers had gone unheeded, powerless against the temptation of the crack demon. Her pastor told her that God only helps those who help themselves.

After two weeks of searching high and low for Reba, Lil' Greg finally found her in a cheap, run-down, motel. It was hard for him to accept that his sister was nothing more than a junky crack addict looking for her next hit. He had combed the streets trying to find her and had a long speech all planned out. But now that he had found her, he knew his speech would just be a waste of air.

"Why, Reba? Why are you throwin' your life away like this?" he said holding back his tears.

"I know you wish better for me, but I am what I am baby brotha. Fuck white America and her corporate world.

194

That dream was shattered a long time ago when I realized how hypocritical and racist America really is."

"Don't give me that bullshit!" he screamed. "What does America being racist have to do with you sucking on a muthafucking crack pipe?"

"If you have to ask, there's no sense in me answering. I'm not the first victim of this fucked up society, and I won't be the last."

"Reba, listen to me," Lil' Greg pleaded. "It's still not too late. You can get your shit together! I'll help you in every way I can, and you know Brother Kaleem will be there for you. Reba, mama is going crazy worryin' about you."

"Mama? What does she know? Her and her sanctimonious bullshit! All that Christian garbage ain't nothin' but a great big con and those slick-talkin' nigga preachers ain't nothing but con men. And you know it!"

"We're not talking 'bout no slick-talkin' preacher or Christianity. We're talking about your black ass! Girl, you can be anything you want to be. You're smart, pretty, and you got good people standing behind you."

"You forgot one thing," Reba said solemnly.

"What's that?" Lil' Greg asked.

"I'm a crack head," she said simply.

"But you don't have to be," Lil' Greg insisted. "Reba, please, just give it one more try. Please. Do that for me and if it don't work out I swear, I'll never bother you again. But, I can't leave you here like this, Reba, I just can't," he said his eyes filled with water.

"Greg, you're not still sellin' are you?"

"No," he said quickly wondering if she was hoping he had some rocks to give to her. "I gave it up. I got a job working downtown in the Renaissance Shopping Mall."

"Yeah, so I know damn right well, if I can get up and go out there and work a regular 9 to 5, you can get your self together. I just don't understand how you could be around someone like Brother Kaleem and still end up on crack."

Reba was silent, as if she was struggling to find the

right words to convey a powerful truth to her brother, and then she said softly, "We all fall down."

"True," Lil' Greg agreed. "But don't you think it's time for you to get back up?"

"I can't leave Willie by himself."

"You're still lookin' for excuses. If Willie wants to get himself together I'm here for him too. But if you really wanna know the truth, I think he's a bad influence on you. That nigga don't mean you no good, Reba. He just wants to keep you dependent on that shit so you'll help support his habit. His ass ain't slick."

"Just let me talk to him. If he doesn't want to quit, then I'll leave him and I'll go with you."

"Is that a promise?"

"Cross my heart and hope to die," she answered.

Neither one of them had the slightest idea that before the night was over that something would happen that would change their lives forever.

■■■■■■■■■■■■■■■■■■■■■■■■■■■■■■■■■■■■■■■■■■■■■■■■■■■■■■■■■

**A**ngela gave birth to a healthy, eight-pound, one-ounce bouncing baby boy. After talking it over with Larry, they decided to name him Larry Jr. Three weeks later she took him to see his father in prison. Larry took one look at his son and was as proud as he could be.

"Angie, I promise to be a good father. When I get outta here baby, I'm leaving the dope business for good."

Angela couldn't have been happier. "I'm glad to hear that," she said, handing the baby over to Larry. "I've always known that you're capable of doing so much more than simply wasting your God given talents on some criminal enterprise."

Glancing down at his son, Larry was filled with mixed emotions. He didn't have a father growing up, so he didn't really know how to be one, but he sure was willing to try.

*Wow, look at this little man, right here. I love you son, I love you with all my heart.* He couldn't take his eyes off the baby. At that moment, he wished he was free, home, safe with his family. He couldn't stop thinking how blessed he was, even locked away in jail, he was blessed. He had a beautiful, devoted and intelligent wife. He had a beautiful, healthy, baby boy and the perfect plan just waiting for him to set in motion.

"You know honey," Angela said, interrupting his thoughts. "There's this girl who just recently enrolled in one of my classes who comes from a background similar to yours. In fact, she claims to know you or at least, she says her brother knows you."

"Oh yeah? What's her name?"

"Reba Abernathy," Angela answered. "A few months ago her boyfriend, this guy named Willie Jefferson, shot and killed her mother during a house break-in. Reba's brother, the one whom she says knows you, caught up with the guy and really did him in. He's in jail now for torture and murder."

"The only Abernathy I know is Gregory Abernathy," he exclaimed, hoping it wasn't him. He had always liked and respected the young warrior because of his loyalty to BJ.

"Yes, that's his name," Angela said, ending all doubts.

"What, are you serious?"

"Yeah, that's what the girl told me."

"Look," Larry said. "I want you to find out who his attorney is and let me know. And Angie, make sure you send him a couple of dollars. Let him know if there's anythin' else we can do for him, to get in contact with you."

Angela smiled at her man with pride, then said softly, "You know something? That's why I love you so much. You have a heart made out of gold."

Leaning over, Larry gave her a quick peck on the lips then glanced down at his son, who was staring back at him with a look of awareness that was uncanny for an infant his age. Larry winked at him and could have sworn the baby winked back.

"Thanks, Angie. I needed to hear you say that. I love

you too, girl."

He knew it wasn't going to be easy to pull off what he had in mind, but with hard work and determination, it could be done. But first, he had to get out of prison.

# CHAPTER THIRTY-TWO

The road was slick with sleet and ice as the black Caddy rolled down I-96 and headed east. Inside, Thad kept his eyes on Jasmine as she expertly navigated through traffic while keeping up a steady stream of conversation with the love of her life, who had just been released on parole.

She could barely contain her excitement. "Oh, Thad, you just don't know how glad I am that you're outta that place."

"I'm glad too, baby. I'm glad too."

"Have you talked to BJ yet?"

"Yeah, we kicked it, we're supposed to be hookin' up tonight."

"Oh, no, I had plans for us," Jasmine said disappointedly.

"Don't worry baby. I'll be back in enough time for us to be together. It's just somethin' we have to take care of right away. I'll be back before you know it."

Jasmine glanced over at him, trying to read his true intentions. Thad turned his head and stared absently out the window.

"Do you believe it's been five years?" she asked.

"It don't really feel like it," he responded. It was amazing, how time past by so quickly. It seemed just like yesterday that he and BJ were shackled on their way to the penitentiary.

He thought about Lil' Greg. *They locked my man up for*

199

*life, fucking white people always locking somebody the fuck up.* What a raw deal he got. They gave him a life sentence for killing Willie, his sister's boyfriend, who murdered his mother for seven dollars and twenty-two cents to buy some funky crack. *I would have killed that motherfucker too,* he thought grimly. But now that he and BJ were back out on the streets, everything would be okay. BJ had already gotten in touch with Lil' Greg's appellate attorney and gave him twenty-five thousand dollars for the promise to have Lil' Greg back in court for a new trial in less than six months, at which time he'd arrange to have him freed on appeal bond.

Forty minutes later, Jasmine was pulling up in front of BJ's house on Outer Drive.

"Want me to wait?" she asked.

"Nah," Thad replied. "I'll have BJ drop me back off at home as soon as we're through with our business. I won't be long baby. I promise."

Leaning over, Jasmine threw her arms around his neck and kissed him in the mouth.

"Okay, baby. Don't be too long. I've been waiting on that dick for five long years. You owe me."

"Don't even trip. I got a five-year hard on in my pants and it's full of love juice. We might make two sets of twins tonight. I'll see ya later," he said, then leaned over and kissed her before getting out of the car.

He stood there watching as the car pulled off. Once it had disappeared from sight, he walked up to the door. BJ answered on the first ring. When he opened the door and saw Thad, he smiled broadly and clasped his hand.

"Glad to see you made it. You're right on time. Dirty Red called about fifteen minutes ago. He followed Raymond to this gambling spot on the East Side. Both of 'em are still there." They met Dirty Red when they were in the penitentary, and decided to let him hook up with them once they were back on the streets.

"You talkin' about Poppa Folk's spot?" Thad asked.

"Yeah, his old ass's still gettin' paid."

"I see Dirty Red's been on his job since he came home," said Thad climbing into BJ's Audi.

"So far he's taken care of everythin' I've asked him to. Looks like he might work out, but you can never tell. Right now I think it's best if we keep him on a need to know only basis."

"Damn right," Thad agreed, thinking about Bay Bay's betrayal. "From now on I ain't takin' no unnecessary chances. If I even think a cat's about to go bad, I'm sending him to thirteen-mile road and you know what's there."

Twenty minutes later, they were parked outside Poppa Folk's gambling joint, watching the high rollers come and go, jumping in and out of their expensive cars wrapped in furs and diamonds. Sitting there in the dark with the lights turned off, BJ and Thad silently observed the proceedings with great interest, noting all the newcomers who had come up in their absence.

BJ lit up a joint and took a deep drag.

"Wanna catch this?"

"Nah," Thad replied. "You know I don't get high."

BJ shrugged. "That's on you dawg. This is some bomb shit right here."

An hour later, Raymond exited the joint with a good-looking, well-dressed female at his side. Inside the Audi, Thad and BJ became instantly alert. Before they could make a move, Dirty Red eased up behind the couple and got the drop on them.

"Don't move nigga," he barked. "Get your hands up where I can see 'em. You too bitch."

Caught off guard, Raymond stuttered, "Wh-wh-what up dawg?"

"Just keep stepping toward that black Audi," Dirty Red said. "Don't make me blow your back out."

As they neared the Audi, Thad got out of the passenger's side and grinned like the devil himself.

"Well, well, whadda we have here now? If it ain't Mr. Big Shot himself. Hello Cross Artist, how does it feel seein' your benefactor?"

"Thad! When did you get out?" said a shocked and surprised Raymond.

"Like you really give a damn. Turn that ass around and get up against the car," he ordered before patting him down for weapons. He found a .357 magnum in Raymond's waistband. "Get in the car."

As Dirty Red pushed the drugdealer, into the back seat he climbed in behind him. Leaning down, Thad stuck his head in the window and stared at BJ. "Is this the girl?" he asked, indicating the woman who was with Raymond.

BJ nodded. "Yeah, that's her."

Thad straightened back up and looked at the woman who was standing there. "Here you go," he said, reaching into his pocket and removing a roll of bills. "You didn't see nothing and you don't know nothing, right?"

"You ain't gotta worry about that. Your boy, BJ, will tell you I ain't no rat. I been in the game all my life."

"Just beat it."

They took Raymond to a small apartment on the West Side and stripped him naked before tying him up.

"How bad you wanna live?" Thad asked him, enjoying the look of fear spreading across the man's face. Raymond was trembling like a dog shitting cinnamon seeds.

"If you want me to beg I will. I don't wanna die man. Please don't kill me, Thad."

Without warning, Thad suddenly lashed out with his .45, catching Raymond flush on the jaw, knocking him backward to the floor.

"Shut the fuck up!" he shouted, foaming at the mouth like a wild dog.

Just then, BJ returned with a Polaroid camera and stood there posing like he was a professional photographer.

"Okay, here's the deal," Thad said, at the same time unzipping his fly. "You can suck this big black dick and walk outta here alive, or you can be brave and go out like a man. So you're faced with a choice; what means more to you, your

202

pride or your life?"

Blood streaming out of his mouth, Raymond groaned. He realized his jaw was probably broken. "You know I wanna live," he mumbled. "But please man, don't force me to do no sick shit like that!"

"I ain't forcin' you to do a damn thin'. It's your call. You played me like a bitch when I was in the joint; now I'ma play you like one."

Lil' Greg was supposed to get Thad's cut on their deal, but Raymond said that he paid Thad twice what he felt he owed him and stopped paying.

On his hands and knees, Raymond began crawling toward Thad. "Please, Thad man," he begged. "I know I fucked up, but I'll make it right. I swear!"

BJ eased up behind him and kicked him square up in his ass as hard as he could. Raymond collapsed and laid prone at Thad's feet. He was sobbing and choking on his own mucus and blood. Thad pressed the barrel of the gun to Raymond's temple and racked the slide.

"What you gon' do, nigga?"

Reaching up, Raymond grabbed hold of Thad's penis and placed it inside his mouth and BJ began snapping pictures with the camera. They asked for a $50,000 ransom and after a few calls, Dirty Red picked the money up. Twenty four hours later, he was a released hostage, but the damage was already done, photographs of Raymond sucking Thad's dick were plastered all over every hot spot in the city. Everyone knew and there was no where for Raymond to hide. He was through in Detroit. No matter what he did, he would never be able to erase the shameful images and humiliation. A week later he left town, a broken and destroyed shell of a man.

# CHAPTER THIRTY-THREE

When Thad laid eyes on his ten-year-old son he couldn't believe how much the boy had grown. Thad would never be able to deny that he had indeed fathered him. The boy looked just like him, only a smaller version. It was hard for Thad to even look at him. Every time he did, he saw an image of himself and personally, Thad stopped liking himself a long time ago.

Meanwhile, Jasmine sensed that something was wrong. It all started the first night when he came home and they made love. It was merely going through the motions of sex, nothing like making love to a person. She could feel his stiff, cold body pretending to be there, but he really wasn't. It was as if he just couldn't relax. She asked him repeatedly, but he always responded that everything was everything. However, she knew it wasn't, she knew better. Nothing was right, nothing was balanced and she was at her wits end with Thad. She tried talking to him, but it didn't work. Finally, he told her that he thought it be a good idea if she would get her tubes tied.

"Are you nuts? I'm not tying my tubes. I want more children, Thad. Don't you?"

Thad was in his own deep, dark, evil world. Sometimes, he'd look at her with the coldest of stares. So cold, that she didn't even recognize him sometime. So cold, that he scared her. It seemed as if their relationship took a nose dive after Thad came home and Jasmine was determined to figure out why. She thought she could change him back into the Thad he was before he went away. But, Thad had his mind made up and he had already sworn on a stack of bibles there would be no more children brought into this world by his semen. In his heart of hearts, he had finally come to grips with the inescapable notion that he was a cold, uncaring beast, who didn't care if he lived or died. There was a hollow emptiness in his soul that could never be filled, a thirst that could never be quenched. Poor Thad had crossed the threshold between sanity and insanity and knew it was impossible to come back to his old self. Too much had happened. And the piper would have to pay for it. He vowed there'd be a lot of crying and a lot of moaning as he sent body after body to the graveyard.

■■■■■■■■■■■■■■■■■■■■■■■■■■■■■■■■■■■■■■■■■■■■■■■■■■■■■■■■■■

"**C**ollect call from Larry Westin," said the voice recording. "To accept this call, press five. To stop this person from calling in the future, please press seven."

Angela quickly pressed five, then waited for the recorded message to go off. After a few seconds, Larry's deep, velvety voice came over the line. It was a sound that each time she heard it, a calm, soothing effect came over her and she knew she was safe and secure from the cares of the world.

"Hello, sweetheart," he spoke into the phone.

Angela's whole demeanor lit up. "Hi, lover," she beamed. "I'm so glad you called. Just to hear your voice makes my entire day. How are you doing?"

"Fine, lil' mama, just fine. How's my son?"

"You mean, *our son*?" She corrected him good-naturedly.

Larry laughed. "Okay baby. Sho' you right. So, how is the little fellow?"

"He's fine, looks just like you. By the way, did you go to the parole board yesterday?"

205

"Yeah, I went," he let his voice trail off.

"Well, what happened?" Angela asked impatiently.

Larry allowed the suspense to build up before he spoke. "I'll be home in thirty days!"

"No, honey, that's great!" Angela gushed. She was full of jubilation. "Oh darling, I've prayed for this day. Now we can be together forever and nobody can come between us. What do you want to do on our first night together?"

"Before you plan anything," Larry said. "Thad and BJ are throwin' me a comin' home party. We'll wear his and her matching outfits and knock 'em dead."

"I was hoping we'd spend our first night together alone," she said trying her best not to sound disappointed.

"Cheer up, baby. We won't stay long. Just make a showing to show our respect, then it'll be you and me and the baby'll make three. Okay?"

"No, Larry, it's not okay. I really thought you were done with those people. I was hoping that you'd leave that part of your life where it belongs. In the past or better yet, leave it right there in the prison."

"Aw, baby, it's not like I'm going to be hanging out with them cats on a regular basis. I just need to make a showing outta respect. You already got my promise that I'll never sell drugs again, all of that is a thing of the past. Don't you believe me?"

"It's not that, I just don't feel you should be associating with those type of guys anymore."

"I know where you're comin' from, and like I said, you don't have to worry about it. Okay? It's just one night." Changing the subject, Larry quickly added, "Angie, I want you to send Lil' Greg another money order. Once I'm out, I'll look into getting him another attorney. No matter what he did, he don't deserve to do the rest of his life in the penitentiary for taking out that punk who killed his mama. That is absolutely crazy."

"Yeah, you're right, but he did take the life of another human being. He broke the law and now he's paying the penalty."

Larry had to bite his tongue. He didn't want to spoil the good news of coming home, but Angela's comments really upset him and made him realize that no matter how long she was away from law enforcement, in her heart, she would always be a cop, and he knew he had better keep it mind.

One week later, the same woman BJ had used to lure Raymond into a trap, was used to maneuver Big Black, a notorious drug lord, into a small, out-of-the-way motel in downtown Detroit. Waiting in the closet, holding their breath, were Thad and BJ. They waited right until they heard the oversize drug dealer caught up in the passion of lovemaking before making their move.

Tiptoeing out of the closet, they snapped the lights on and there was Big Black, butt-naked lying on top of the decoy who was just as naked as he was. Big Black heard the tippy toes of his intruders and rolled off the woman, reaching for his strap, but before he could get his fingers wrapped around his gun, the girl reached down between his legs and grabbed his balls in a firm grip and squeezed with all her might. Big Black screamed like a white woman in a cheap horror movie and Thad was on him like a flash of lightning.

A few minutes later, Big Black was lying spread-eagled on his stomach, tied to the bed. His eyes were wide-open in fear as he watched helplessly, while the woman began strapping on a huge black dildo, then slowly positioned herself over his naked body. When she penetrated him, flashes of light went off as BJ went to work with his Polaroid camera, taking pictures from every conceivable angle. This time, instead of having Thad rape their helpless victim, they thought it more interesting if a woman did it instead.

"Smile for the camera," Thad joked, enjoying the look of humiliation on the drug dealer's face. Before the night was over, he would fork over a hundred grand and promise to pay the same amount every month to keep the revealing photographs from hitting the streets.

So far, the plan to rob and blackmail drug dealers to

keep them from going to the cops, was working picture perfect. In the street life, all a playa had was his reputation. Once that was destroyed, he was through in the game. Nobody respected a man who took it up the ass under any circumstances. It didn't matter if he somehow got revenge; the image of him being fucked in the butt would never leave the mind of his fellow hustlas. So the victims of BJ and Thad's cruel game of blackmail and torture continued to pay and keep their mouths shut tight, and BJ and Thad continued to grow rich and powerful.

# CHAPTER THIRTY-FOUR

Lil' Greg's coming home party was the talk of the town. After being released on appeal bond, thanks to the combined efforts of BJ and Larry, Lil' Greg eagerly awaited his new trial with hopes of winning an acquittal this time around.

The party was held at the old Twenty Grand Ballroom on Detroit's West Side. Everybody and their brother was there. Rayfil, who had hooked up with this Colombian beauty, was there showing off his newfound wealth. It was rumored that he now had a new connect with the Colombians and was rolling in dough, pushing cheap cocaine by the barrels.

Thad and BJ were there, along with Dirty Red and the rest of their grave-digging crew, even Chi Chi was there. After being judged incompetent to stand trial for the murder of her step-father, she had made a miraculous recovery and had since been released to the custody of her mother. It was doubted that she would ever stand trial, especially after it came out through subsequent investigations, that her murdered step-father had been raping her since she was just a child. The prosecutor, a female attorney known to be compassionate toward rape victims, simply swept the entire matter under the rug. So, dressed in her favorite color, red, Chi Chi was more beautiful than BJ remembered her. Next to Angela, she was the most beautiful woman there.

209

As the party got into full blast, Larry called a meeting in the adjourning motel and invited all the top drug boys that moved 100 keys or more per month. Most of those invited were being extorted by Thad and BJ, unfortunately for them. Larry smiled on the inside and looked around the room.

"Gentlemen, I've called all of you here to discuss some very important business with you. If any word of what's said here tonight gets outta this room, whoever is responsible, will pay with his life. I hope that's perfectly understood, cause if it ain't, you need to get up and get out of here before another word is spoken."

No one said anything, so he continued.

"First of all, you all know Rayfil here." Heads around the room nodded. "He wants to have a word with you, so pay attention to what he has to say. Go 'head Ray."

Rayfil nodded, enjoying the spotlight. Shit, it was about time. After all the years he had to spend monkey'n around in the streets of Detroit, he had finally arrived. *That's right ya'll motherfuckers, you heard the man, pay attention god damn it.* He couldn't help it, after all the begging, scraping, and borrowing, Rayfil had done to get to where he was, he deserved his spotlight and was gonna make sure no one stealed his thunder.

"Check this out," he said, his bald head shiny with perspiration. "Most of you been coppin' from the guys in New York, mainly, Don Ferrano, who happens to be a good friend of mine. But friend or not, the days of the mafia rule is over. The Italians had their run; now it's our time to shine. Some of you may know that I got a boss connect with the Colombians. But, what you don't know, is that I'm ready to do my own thang. Through my woman, I got my own poppy field and I also got my own farmers in South America growin' cocoa leaves. What this means for you is that I'm in a position to give all of you a helluva price. From now on, you cop from me instead of the Italian boys in New York. And if any of you got a problem wit' that, then the rest of us will know we're dealing with a modern day Uncle Tom and will

210

act accordingly. Feel me? Now, King Larry wanna say something."

Larry moved right in where Rayfil left off.

"Rayfil's right. It's time brothas started doing something on our own. We've been allowing others to play us like errand boys too damn long. Now it's time for us to step out on center stage. And I'll tell you something else. All of y'all know that my wife is an ex-federal agent. Well, through her, I got a boss connect that guarantees safe delivery on all dope shipments coming from South America, so we can't never lose. Keep the game straight and the game will keep you straight. Put shit in the game and I'll put a bullet in your fuckin' head. Got it? Now, let's get money y'all."

As to be expected, all the men at the meeting were impressed, sensing a big pay day ahead. Even Rayfil couldn't have been more pleased. Things were moving faster than he had expected, and he was more than ready for the war that was sure to come from the Italians, who definitely wouldn't be too pleased about being cut from the food chain.

But what Rayfil and the others didn't know, was that Larry's connect didn't really exist. Not even Thad and BJ had a clue as to what was going on with Larry's secret plan. Truth was, Angela wasn't helping that nigga do no crimes. She didn't want him out there. All that talk was just that, part of an elaborate scheme Larry had concocted in his head. The way he pictured it, he was sure to win. He felt bad not being able to confide in BJ or Thad, but game recognized game and if they didn't it would just be too bad for them.

As the evening progressed, BJ sat with Chi Chi and talked quietly. A lot of time had passed since he had last seen her and a lot of time had passed since she walked out on everything they shared for King Larry.

"Would you like a ride home?" BJ offered.

Chi Chi just looked at him wondering if it was nothing more than an offer to knock her in the head a few times for what she had done to him.

"I'm not mad, I'm not gonna hurt you. I just thought

you might need a ride," said BJ assuringly.

"You sure," she joked.

On the way to drop Chi Chi off, BJ couldn't help but to pry into the past. Honestly, he still loved her. He knew he had to be the biggest sucker, he knew it and his ego wouldn't allow him to admit it to anyone but himself. There would be no way Thad, Larry and no one else would ever know his true feelings for Chi Chi, not even her. But at the same time, he wished for what they had before he went to prison. He was still back there in the old days.

"I'm sorry I hurt you, BJ, I am. I should have never crossed you, I know it now. You see Larry married and all," she said as if BJ was dumb.

*Yeah, but you still fuckin' him,* he couldn't help but to think. *You still fuckin' him and you can keep on for all I care. All I want to know is everything you can tell me about that nigga and his wife, Angela. You should know plenty, you should know it all.*

212

# CHAPTER THIRTY-FIVE

**S**ince her kidnapping, Chi Chi hadn't been the same. The fire and naked aggressiveness that had blazed her path through life had slowly been replaced with a more cautious, realistic approach. BJ didn't know want to make of the new Chi Chi, but she damn sure wasn't the woman he had left behind. He didn't know who the hell she was. He could tell the Chi Chi he knew was somewhere inside her, he just never knew if he'd ever see her again. Still, he felt no pity for her or what had happened to her. How could he, she ran off with King Larry after he got knocked. *Bitch, please, you're 411, information, nothing more.* Shit, you wouldn't think that was what BJ was walking around thinking, he was playing the love struck role to a tee. Even Chi Chi didn't know any better. Niggas in the street was laughing, his family was laughing and all his friends were laughing, of course they were all doing it behind his back, but he knew. He knew how they was all calling him a fool. *But, that's okay. Call me whatever you want to call me*, he thought to himself. What no one knew was that he was merely using her to orchestrate his opera, the name of it was called revenge and BJ had every intention of having his day, all dogs do.

As for Chi Chi, she was bent over backwards trying to please him, willing to do anything for him, especially in bed. She didn't mind either, it was a small price to pay for her redemption.

■■■■■■■■■■■■■■■■■■■■■■■■■■■■■■■■■■■■■■■■■■■■■■■■■■■■■■■■■■

"**S**on, it's in a woman's nature to be dominated. But if the man in the relationship is weak and submissive to the female, then she will automatically reverse the natural order and assume control."

Larry recalled his mother telling him this when he was still a pimply faced teenager. There had been a lot of things that had changed in his life, but never his mother's words.

Angela began asserting her will and independence as a woman; Larry didn't care. But when she took things to another level and started trying to call the shots, he had to draw the line or at least try to. So, when she started poppin' her shit about his friends, Larry figured now was a good time to gain back some of that manly control.

"I thought it was all about me and you tonight."

She snuggled up closer, kissing him on the cheek.

"It is about us, darling. That's why I'm concerned about the company you keep. I don't want anything to interfere with our happy home. I really don't think I could stand being apart from you again. Not when we have the perfect opportunity to build heaven right here on earth. I'm not here to fight with you, Larry, but there are certain things only a woman can see. You have to trust me."

"I do trust you. Everything you say is appreciated and received in the same spirit that it is given. But you have to understand that if we are able to discover that heaven you spoke of, then hey, you can't try to dictate who my friends are or try to control me. I don't wanna dominate you either. You have a say-so in this relationship too. It's all about achieving the proper balance baby."

*This nigga must not be clear.*

"Larry, look, there's something about Thad and BJ that gives me the creeps. It's not something I can put my finger on; it's just a feeling I get deep down in my soul and I'm seldom wrong about these kinds of things. I just don't want to have to say, *I told you so,* somewhere down the road. Sweetheart, you simply have too much to lose."

"I understand, baby. I would be a straight up fool to outright ignore what you're tellin' me. Trust me, I hear what you sayin'."

Angela reached over and embraced him, pressing her face next to his. She wanted him to feel what she was feeling so he would know beyond the shadow of a doubt, that what they had was real and worth fighting for.

"Darling," she whispered breathlessly. "I trust you with my life. We're a single unit, and the root word of unity is unit. This means we have to be on one accord. I know you'll always guide us down the right path, veering neither to the left or right, but staying on the straight and narrow path. Just promise you'll always be here for your son and you won't do anything to jeapordize that."

"I promise. I promise."

■■■■■■■■■■■■■■■■■■■■■■■■■■■■■■■■■■■■■■■■■■■■■■■■■■■■■■■■■■■■

Lil' Greg sat in the silence of his darkened apartment listening to the sound of the wind outside his window. He heard his mother's name whispering in the breeze as he stared at her picture on the wall. *She had so much faith in Jesus, so much love for the Lord.*

"Where were you when she needed you?" he screamed. "Where were you when Willie crept in her room and raped and murdered her? What kind of God are you?"

*You should have taken Reba, not mommy,* he couldn't help but to think how much fault Reba was to blame. Had she not been so blindly and crackly in love with Willie, his mother would still be there. *Now, they want to lock me up for the rest of my life? All because of fucking Reba's dumb ass and crack head Willie. They can't find me guilty this time. They just can't. What the fuck am I going to do?*

"*Awww baby, don't worry, just put it all in the Lord's hands, it will all work out,*" said the picture back to him.

"Fuck, might as well, I done tried everything else," he joked with his mother.

# CHAPTER THIRTY-SIX

Larry had just left Broadway Men's Fashion Store when he was accosted in the parking lot by three white men wearing dark business suits.

"Hello King Larry," one of them said. "There's someone in that car over there who would like to speak with you." He pointed to a black limousine parked right next to Larry's beige Rolls Royce.

Without hesitation Larry reached for his strap.

"That won't be necessary," the same guy assured him. "Believe me, if we wanted you dead, we would've hit you as soon as you stepped outta the store. C'mon follow me," he ordered before heading in the direction of the limo.

Boxed in on all sides with no options, Larry decided to play along. As he followed the men back to the car, the back window slid down. Inside, sitting in the backseat was Tony Ferrano, who flashed a quick smile

"Hello, my friend. Long time no see, get in. Let's kick the game around."

A little hesitant, Larry bent down and climbed inside what could be his coffin. He knew he had no options and he also knew he'd have to deal with Tony one way or the other. As the door slammed shut behind him, Larry looked at Tony.

"Hey, Tony, when you get in town?"

217

"Just yesterday. I wanted you to know I could find you anytime I wanted to."

"Oh yeah, that sounds good, but what you need to be findin' me for? We ain't got no beef between us, do we?"

"This is what I came to find out. By the way, had I known you were comin' home, I would've rolled out the red carpet."

"I appreciate that, but the fellows gave me a party."

"So I hear," Tony replied. "Matter-of-fact, a little birdie told me that you and Rayfil plan on doing your own thing and cut old Tony out of the picture completely. I don't consider that very friend-like. Do you?"

Larry knew that it was now or never. If he was ever going to cut his ties with the boys from New York, then he had to do it now. Otherwise he'd be under their wings until the cows came home, and that wasn't a part of his plans.

"Look, Tony," he said determinedly. "I got no beef wit' you, and you shouldn't have any with me. When we did business I always gave you every penny. I was never one nickel short. I got popped, went to trial, did my time, and hey, I kept my mouth shut. In other words, I know how to carry my own weight and I don't crack under pressure."

"I know that," Tony replied. "That's why I still got respect for you, despite what I been hearing."

Larry's facial expression didn't change.

"Whadda ya been hearing?"

Tony removed one of his trademark Cuban cigars. "You don't mind do you?" he asked.

Larry shook his head no.

Holding up the cigar to his nose, Tony inhaled deeply taking in aroma before placing the cigar in his mouth.

"I always say, there's nothin' like a good cigar when you have to make a difficult decision," he stated, glancing over at Larry, who took out his gold cigarette lighter, flicked it, then held the flame to the tip of Tony's cigar.

"Here you are, old pal. Enjoy your smoke," Larry said.

Tony smiled. "You know I'm deeply concerned," said

Tony blowing cigar smoke in Larry's direction.

"Concerned?" asked Larry playing dumb.

"Economics, old pal. And when somebody threatens to interfere with mine, I take it very seriously. Word is that you and Rayfil have been instructing guys not to buy from me anymore. Any truth to that?"

"Look," Larry said seriously. "I don't care what you been told. Whoever you're talking about can keep copping from you if they wanna. That's their choice. I can't stop no body from doing business with you."

Tony puffed his cigar, then blew a cloud of smoke in Larry's face. "That ain't what some of 'em been tellin' me and the boys," he said angrily. "I hear you and Rayfil are squeezin' 'em to buy from you guys exclusively."

Larry waved away the smoke and said politely, "I don't know what you've been told." He wasn't at all surprised that someone told Tony what had been said at the meeting, probably word for word. But he couldn't help but to wonder who it was. Suddenly, Tony sat up straight on the plush interior of the limousine.

"Look, Larry, I'ma keep it straight wit' ya since for the most part you been straight wit' me. I don't blame you guys for wanting to go for yourselves, and you got every right to do so. But if you try to keep someone from coppin' from me, you got a problem. Capise?"

Larry looked him directly in his cold blue eyes.

"I guess this is where we draw the line then, old pal."

"I guess so. You can go now. Just remember what I told ya."

As Larry climbed back out of the limousine, he half expected to feel a bullet slamming into his back. Once he was out the death trap he breathed a whole lot easier, and as he watched the limosine pull out the parking lot, his body still in tact, he really exhaled. Out the corner of his eye he saw a black Volvo pull out into traffic, he dropped his white handkerchief on the ground as the car rolled by him. Inside, sitting on the passenger's side was Dirty Red. The ex-con grinned shrewdly at Larry then turned away, focusing his eyes and attention on the limousine up ahead.

Larry had been expecting Tony to show up sooner or later. As an extra precaution, he had instructed Dirty Red and Winky to watch his back by trailing him everywhere he went. If and when Tony showed up and Larry dropped his handkerchief on the ground it would be the signal to smoke Tony and whoever was with him. As the limousine cruised down Woodward Avenue, it made a left onto Jefferson Avenue and kept rolling. That's when the black Volvo appeared at its left side. The barrel of an AK-47 peeked out of the passenger's window and a two-inch flame of fire, shattered the peace and tranquility of the midday atmosphere. The driver of the limousine was hit first. The side of his face ripped in half as huge AK-47 slugs penetrated his left cheek and eye socket. With no driver, the limosine was out of control, jumping the curb and rolling down the sidewalk before crashing into a traffic light pole.

Shaken by the impact, the men inside the limo tried to pull themselves out, but Dirty Red got out of the Volvo, walked up to the men trapped inside the limo and one by one murdered them leaving Tony for last who was trying to hide behind one of the open car doors. He never saw Dirty Red approaching him from behind. He was too busy trying to get his gun from his holster. Dirty Red pointed the gun to the back of Tony's head and killed him execution style for an open public to witness.

Everyone in plain eye sight, screamed, panicked and ran for cover. Calmly Dirty Red checked everyone to make sure they were all dead, then he ran over to the Volvo hopped inside and closed the door as the Volvo sped down Jefferson making before disappearing in broad day light.

# CHAPTERTHIRTY-SEVEN

"**D**amn you!" Chi Chi screamed at the top of her voice.

BJ stood there squinting at her through blood shot eyes from too many drinks and too much partying. He had lipstick on his collar and the scent of sex all over him. It was 7:00 in the morning and he had been out all night partying and only god knows what else. Chi Chi, unable to sleep, sat up all night and waited for him to come home.

"I'm tired of your shit, BJ. I knew it was a mistake comin' back here with you. I should have known better."

"Bitch, is you crazy? You done fucked my man, left me while I was in the joint, and got the nerve to stand in my face talking about a fucking mistake. Bitch you the mistake. You motherfucker," said BJ ready to knock her block off her head. "Man, you can't be serious. You so disrespectful, you should be thanking me for not kickin' your ass all over this motherfucker. Now get the fuck outta my face."

"Are you crazy or am I. Get outta your face? I'll get outta your face alright. I'm getting the fuck outta here. I knew this shit was a mistake."

"Where you think you going?" he asked as he laughed at her.

"Don't you worry about it, away from here."

He began to laugh at her as the Henessey filled his mind with crazy thoughts of violence and rage. He could see himself striking her down repeatedly until her body no longer

221

moved.

"Bitch, you ain't goin' nowhere."

"The hell I ain't," Chi Chi said. "Who gon' stop me? Surely not your drunk ass."

Spinning on her tiny heels, she stomped off in the direction of their bedroom.

"Hey, hey, don't walk away from me!" he shouted, all the while bobbing and weaving like a punch-drunk boxer.

After knocking over a lamp and a picture frame that sat on an end table next to a loveseat sofa, he finally caught up to her. She didn't even see him coming, and before she realized it, he had flipped the script and turned into Mike Tyson, punching her all over her body. Anywhere his drunken fists would land. All she could do was cover up her head and her chest. By the time he stopped, she had black and blue markings from her face to her thighs. Her entire body was back and blue. It was the first time he had ever laid hands on her, and if she had anything to do with it, it would be the last.

She lay on the floor sobbing and moaning softly, refusing to cry out loud, refusing him the glory. She wouldn't give him the satisfaction of seeing her break down. She had too much pride for that to ever happen.

"See what you made me do?" he asked, his chest heaving up and down as he tried to catch his breath. "Huh, see, you see what you did?"

She didn't respond, just continued to lay there and watch him, ready for another attack. She wanted to be prepared this time. If he thought she intended to lie there like a battered dog too afraid to fight back, he was badly mistaken. To his credit, he simply turned and walked away.

Chi Chi pulled herself to her feet and stumbled over to the gold-framed mirror hanging over the mantelpiece. Her eyes were puffy and in the morning they'd both be black and blue. She couldn't believe he snapped on her like that. BJ accepted her back, he knew exactly what he was dealing with. *What the fuck is wrong with him? He really done went too far now. He shoulda never took me back. He'll regret the day he put his hands on me. Payback is a bitch, and her name is Chi Chi.*

■■■■■■■■■■■■■■■■■■■■■■■■■■■■■■■■■■■■■■■■■■■■■■■■■■■■■■■■

**G**lancing both ways before leading Rayfil into the sunlight, two big bodyguards watched the sounds on the street carefully. Tony, his driver and his bodyguards's assassination, was the talk of the town. Nothing that spectacular went down in Detroit since the YGS had been dismantled.

Detective McQueen was sure he knew the reason behind the recent wave of murders. It didn't take a genius to figure out that ever since BJ and his crew had been released from prison, bodies had been turning up left and right. A special task force had been assembled to bring those responsible before the bar of justice. McQueen made a bet that the trail of bodies would lead eventually straight to BJ and Thad's doorsteps.

By the time Rayfil and his bodyguards reached the Mercedes, he was feeling real spiffy. Finally he had come up. In no time at all, the entire city would be his. Only one man stood in his way of having total control. Larry Westin. *If I didn't need his connections,* Rayfil thought bitterly, *I would close his eyes.*

Once he and his men were safely inside the bullet proof car, they all relaxed. The driver inserted his key into the ignition and turned it. It was the last thing he ever did. The car exploded into a huge fireball, pieces of flying glass and red hot metal were sent in all directions. The glass windows of several nearby shops shattered from the deadly impact as people inside hit the floor. Rayfil and all the men with him were killed instantly.

A block away, parked at the curb was a black Chrysler New Yorker. Inside sat two Italian guys, both of them wearing black leather jackets and wraparound shades. Neither one of them spoke to the other, but one was checking out the scene of the carnage through high-powered binoculars. Pleased with the results, he turned to his partner and nodded. The other man started the engine up and slowly pulled off down the street, making sure he drove by the smoldering hunk of twisted metal with the charred bodies inside.

The war had begun.

# CHAPTERTHIRTY-EIGHT

"Lil Thad, I want you to meet your cousin, Kamal."

The young boy who looked just like his father, held out his hand. His cousin, Kamal, starred at him with his one good eye, while the missing one was covered with a black pirate's patch.

"Uncle Thad, he looks just like you," said Kamal like everybody else who saw Lil' Thad.

"Yeah he does," Thad admitted, looking at his son with pride. "I want y'all to stick together, because all you got is each other. Don't ever forget that."

"I got Mama too," Lil Thad said, not knowing he was irritating his old man.

"Yeah, but I ain't talking about her, I'm talking about you and your cousin. I want the two of ya'll to stick together," Thad explained. "You understand Kamal?"

"Yes, Uncle," Kamal replied, images of his sister and mother being coldly gunned down inside the Northland Shopping Mall, still fresh inside his mind.

"Uncle Thad, when you going to teach me and Lil' Thad how to shoot? You promised you were going to teach us."

"I know," Thad said, grinning from ear to ear. "All things in due time. Ain't no hurry. Right now your uncle got it held down. All I want you and your cousin to be doing at

225

this particular time is going to school and getting somethin inside your head. It's easy being a warrior, but you gotta know how to think, because ain't nothing exactly as it first appears. Not even me. You have to learn how to look beneath the surface. Let me ask you boys somethin'. Are diamonds and gold found on the surface or deep down inside the earth?"

Lil Thad appeared confused, but Kamal quickly replied, "In the ground."

"You're right. That's a lesson to be learned, if you know what to look for."

"Dad, I wanna go see Mama," Lil Thad said, looking like he was bored.

"Okay lil' man. Hold your horses."

But even as he spoke the words, he was busy thinking that he couldn't wait for Lil' Thad to get a little older. Messing around with Jasmine, his son was sure to be a sissy. God forbid, he definitely had to get him away from her skirt tails and quick.

"We're on the way home now," he said. "But first I gotta drop Kamal off. Then you'll go see mommy, you think you can hold on that long?"

Lil Thad nodded, then turned up his nose and began to cry.

■■■■■■■■■■■■■■■■■■■■■■■■■■■■■■■■■■■■■■■■■■■■■■■■■■■■■■

"**W**hat's the number one killer of black males?" Kaleem asked sitting in his conference room of the cultural center.

Lil' Greg thought for a moment and suddenly blurted out, "AIDS".

"You're almost right, but the number one killer of black males is black males. We gotta hurry up and do something to change these statistics. Otherwise we ain't got a fighting chance. The crackers are already committing genocide against us by throwing us into concentration camps disguised as prisons, where they keep us until we're old and gray, then release us knowing that we're to old to do anything, especially reproduce. They got these brothers in these penitentiaries gunnin' each other and slavin' for corporate America. I tell you, young brothers, we got our work cut out if we wanna survive these white folks' plan to do us in. And we can't lay back waitin' on the minister to save us. He has his hands full as it is. It's time for us to step up and give that brother a helping hand. What I need to know from you is this: Can I depend on you when the going gets tough?"

Lil' Greg glanced at the man speaking to him as if he were his son, and realized just how much Kaleem had become a father to him.

"Brotha Kaleem, you can count on me," he said, and meant every word. "I trust and love you like you were my own father."

Kaleem grinned widely. "Good!" he exclaimed. "I'm so glad to know that I can count on you. Your sister is in the next room and she badly needs to talk to you. Her guilt and your silence is eating her up like cancer, and if it keeps spreading it'll be too late. At this point you are the wise surgeon who's able to remove the cancerous growth and make her whole again. Now go. Your patient awaits you."

Realizing that he had allowed himself to be trapped, all Lil' Greg could do was smile.

"Brotha Kaleem, I'm not ready to talk to Reba. I'm not."

"I know, but it's time, my brotha, it's time."

Kaleem looked at the young man who had become a part of his life and felt a strange range of mixed emotions. In his wisdom he knew that Lil' Greg had reached the crossroads of his life. His entire future now depended on the decisions he was going to have to make in the next few days. Would he go to the left or would he go to the right? Only time would tell.

# CHAPTERTHIRTY-NINE

"**L**arry, please be careful," Angela moaned, the expression in her eyes setting off alarms of suspicion in his mind.

"What's up Angie? Something troubling you?" he asked.

Strolling across the room, Angela sat down next to him on the beige suede sofa and stared at him.

"I still know a few people in law enforcement. From what I've been told, a special task force has been created to send you and your buddies back to prison. This time they plan on throwing away the key. But I guess none of that matters to you since you're clean, right?"

A look of impatience came across Larry's face as the full weight of what she had said, sunk into his mind.

"Look baby, the most they'll catch me with is a pistol. Other than that, I'm totally legitimate and so are all of my business establishments."

"Listen how you sound. That's all it takes, right, just tell me anything. Why do you have to carry around a gun if you're no longer involved in anything illegal? Especially, when you know the police have a bull's-eye painted on your back?"

Sighing deeply, he sought to make her understand his position. "Angie, baby, you know I handle large sums of cash, right? Well, this makes me, you, and our son, prime targets. I gotta have a heater at all times. How else am I supposed to protect us?"

"With your mind."

He laughed at her like she was a silly little girl. "I don't know what world you've been living in, but the real world don't work like that. I don't mean to be rude, but baby these niggas out here is hungry and they comin' with a pistol pointin' at your head. You gotta be ready, you gotta be ready to dance. You know, Ang, I'm on some different kinda shit. You work your end and let me work mine. We'll meet up at the crossroad and tie it together. Okay?"

She looked at him deeply, studying the expression on his face while wondering how to make him understand what she was feeling. "Alright sweetheart. Just promise me one thing."

He returned her stare. "I'm listening."

"Promise me you'll only carry a gun when it's absolutely necessary. Can you do that for me?"

He smiled. "Alright baby. You win. I'll only strap up when somethin' is on the floor. Now come here and give me some of that sugar."

She smiled and it was like a thousand beams of sunlight flooded the room. As she melted into his arms, he embraced her and kissed her long and deep.

"You got good sugar baby. Give me more."

She laughed and playfully pulled away. "You're silly."

Locking his strong arms around her so she couldn't get away, he looked deeply into her green eyes.

"Angie, there's nothing in the world I wouldn't do for you. And no matter what happens, remember that I love you more than anything else in this whole wide world. Always remember that."

"I will, Larry. I will."

• • • • • • • • • • • • • • • • • • • • • • • • • • • • • • • • • • • • • • • • • • • • • • • •

The next night Larry met Thad and BJ at this

secluded, out-of-the-way bar on the corner of Woodward and Milwaukee. They found a table near the back and ordered cold beers and pizza.

"Looks like Rayfil got caught with his drawers down," Larry said by way of making conversation.

"Yeah, it didn't take long for Tony's people to strike back," BJ replied. "I guess it's their way of saying they still in the game."

"From here on out we gotta start moving more cautiously," Larry said matter-of-factly.

"Look here, man," Thad said impatiently. "All we gotta do is take Vito's punk ass out and the rest of them bitch ass motherfuckers will fold shop, ain't that many of 'em in the first place, and they getting by on their past reputation. But I don't give a fuck about 'em!"

"Thad's right. There never have been more than ten or fifteen made members here in the city, but they move as one body of well-disciplined soldiers who know how to follow orders and stick together. See that's where they been winning. But if we can somehow tap Vito's ass, it'll send a crystal clear message that we ain't fucking around wit' 'em."

"How we gon' do that?" BJ questioned. "Vito probably got all kinda security wrapped around his ass now."

"Listen, I may have a way. I gotta think about it."

Both Thad and BJ glanced at each other with curious expressions. "Wassup?" BJ asked.

"It's too soon to tell right now," Larry answered. "When I get all the details worked out in my head, I'll put y'all up on it. Until then my advice is to lay low and chill out. Ain't no sense in letting them faggots catch us wit' our guard down."

"Okay, I'll tell you what. Let's get back together tomorrow night at eight. We'll hook up at LaPlaya's Lounge. Is that cool?" BJ asked.

"Yeah, that's cool."

Thad agreed, then all three men clicked their beer mugs together in a toast filled with conspiracies of death and destruction.

# CHAPTER FORTY

July, 2000.

Sitting alone inside the plush LaPlaya's Lounge, Larry Westin glanced quickly around at his surroundings, then at the front door. Outside, he could see the summer sun fading fast beyond a reddish orange horizon.

The few people inside the bar were in a jovial mood as they kicked the game around and waited for the regulars to fill up the room so the games could begin.

Larry tried to relax, but something about the entire setup just didn't sit right with him.

He couldn't explain it; he just had a strange feeling that made him uneasy. He knew he should have never left his piece at the crib, regardless of Angela's warning. It went totally against his principles as a pretty-pimpin' gangsta.

Maybe, he told himself for the second time since entering the bar, he should just get right up and split. He could hit Thad and BJ up later on and explain why he decided to leave instead of hanging around for them like they planned. They would probably be drugged, so they wouldn't know what's going on, but so the fuck what? He was still the boss.

Not that he didn't respect the two men or value their

231

opinion; the fact remained that he alone had the final say-so and whether they agreed with his decisions or not, he was calling the shots. If they didn't like it, then they knew what they could do about it.

Leaders in their own right, both Thad and BJ had crews of their own, but they decided to play subservient roles to Larry out of respect. He was the undisputed boss even though there had never been any kind of formal vote designating him as such. It was more or less an unwritten, unspoken, mutual agreement.

Glancing down at his diamond-covered Patek Phillippe, Larry saw that it was approaching 8:00 p.m. Soon, the spot would be coming alive with the sights and sounds of Detroit's colorful black underworld.

Gangstas and playas draped in designer threads and flashy jewelry, would be pulling up in expensive cars, ready to spend money and talk shit. These symbols of success, gave them status and power. As to be expected, many people lost their lives – and took the lives of others – in the pursuit of this material wealth.

He was so caught up in his thoughts, that Larry never saw the two men enter the bar carrying 9 millimeter pistols. The people nearest the exit saw what was about to go down and almost ran each other over, trying to get out of the way.

As the gunmen closed in, Larry was sorry he didn't leave when he had the chance. *Only God can save me now*, he thought wildly.

But God didn't save him and neither did anyone else. As the first shots rang out, those left inside the bar scattered like cockroaches. Amid the yelling and confusion, the shooters took care of their business and made good their escape. Not a single soul attempted to help Larry. He was left lying on the cold, marble floor, his life and bodily fluids slowly leaking out, forming a huge pool of thick, dark red blood beneath him.

Lying there helpless, Larry thought about the good life and asked himself if the ride had been worth it. In his

232

wildest imagination, he never thought he would live like a king, only to be shot down like a dog and left to die among strangers. His plan had been to go out in style.

He could hear approaching footsteps and wondered if his assassins were coming back to deliver the coup de grace. If so, it would be an act of mercy on their part to spare him the final indignity of suffering before he died.

Out of nowhere, greedy hands appeared, snatching and grabbing. He could feel his jewelry being removed from his fingers, wrists, and from around his neck. But the last thing he remembered before the darkness took over, was his pants pockets being ripped off, as the crowd of human vultures robbed him without remorse or shame.

Outside, cruising slowly by, was a steel gray Cadillac. Behind the steering wheel was BJ. Sitting right next to him was his right-hand man, Thad Jones. They had been sent to make sure all went according to plan.

**R**ayfil's funeral was a sight to behold. All the major playas in and around Detroit, Chicago, Philadelphia, and New York all turned out to pay their final respects. Their appearance confirmed Rayfil's status in the underworld.

His wife, the beautiful young Colombian he had copped then married, was full of grief, dressed in black, weeping and dabbing at her heavily made-up eyes with a silk hankie. He had taken her out of poverty and turned her into one of the most desirable women in the city of Detroit. At that very moment several top-notch playas were hawking her every move, waiting for an opportunity to shoot their best shot. After all, Rayfil was dead. After the proper period of mourning she would be good to go, or so they hoped.

Swanson's funeral home was famous in the black community. And todat Swanson's was filled to the capacity. The room where Rayfil was laid out in regal display was filled with a crowd of well-dressed mourners, each of them wrapped up in their own private thoughts. To most, Rayfil

had been a man of great principles, principles that he had
stood for and ultimately died for. But, there were a few
people there who believed that the dead man had gotten just
what he deserved and they were only there to gloat over his
dead body.

BJ and Thad, both dressed in black were seated near
the family in the second row of pews. Out of no where a loud
door slam and a sudden commotion could be heard out in
the hallway. Two white guys pushed their way into the
crowded room and marched up the center of the aisle
carrying AK-47s. The startled mourners immediately got up
to get out of the white men's way. When they reached Rayfil's
casket, they suddenly took aim and began firing, sending a
spray of bullets into the dead man's body and a wave of fear
throughout the room. Everybody and their momma was
trying to get out of Swanson's. They were there to see Rayfil,
not join him. In the ensuing madness, BJ and Thad calmly
observed the entire proceedings with a look of amusement.
They didn't even bother to leave their seats, run for cover or
duck down. And why should they, when they orchestrated
every movement that was going down?

They were the ones who had set both Rayfil and Larry
up. They didn't consider themselves cross artists; they
thought of themselves as great opportunists. Why take an
unnecessary chance going to war with the Italians, when
they could use them to get rid of their competition? It was
down right genius.

After the gunmen were through shooting up Rayfil's
corpse, one of them calmly walked up to the casket and drew
back his right leg, then kicked the expensive, silk-lined box
to the floor where it landed with a resounding crash, sending
Rayfil's corpse sprawling all over the place. Laughing now,
both gunmen turned back around and walked out of the
funeral home, nodding at Thad and BJ on their way out the
door. But they were in for a big surprise. Unfortunately for
them, federal agents were outside on assignment taking
photographs of all the drug dealers that showed up to say

good bye to Rayfil. Those two guys didn't make it around the corner before a swat team had them surrounded.

# CHAPTER FORTY-ONE

**W**hen BJ dropped his man, Thad, off at his house, he was on top of the world. Nothing could touch him now. After Don Vito had contacted him a week ago and made him an offer he couldn't refuse, he had in turn sold Thad on the idea and the cross was in. Both Rayfil and Larry would be sacrificial lambs in exchange for unlimited access to Sicily's poppy fields and Don Vito's downtown connections that virtually guaranteed them riches beyond their wildest imagination, as well as protection from the law.

As he drove through the streets of Detroit in his new Caddy, he was full of jubilation. Not even the thought of arguing with Chi Chi when he got home, could interfere with his joyous mood. *As a matter-of-fact,* he told himself, *I might even take her out on the town to help me celebrate before I kick her jazzy ass out my house and send her back to the mud where I found her. Nobody crosses me and gets away with it.*

As he pulled up in the driveway of his house on Outer Drive, the thought entered his mind that it was time to buy a new crib. *Maybe I should move out to Southfield where Larry used to live. That way I can be next to Angela, with her fine ass. Mmm hmm, wouldn't that be something, me and Angie girl. That's right Larry you reap what you sow and I'm going*

236

*after your bitch. Nigga, when I'm done, I'll have your son calling me daddy. Aww don't start rolling over now. You did Chi Chi, right? What's good for the goose, is good for the gander.*

Leaping out of the car, he bounced up the stairs to the front door of the red brick house and was about to stick his keys in the lock when it was flung open. Chi Chi stood there with fire in her eyes.

"C'mon in, Mr. Big Shot," she stated sarcastically. "I been waiting on your slick ass."

"Yeah, I bet you have. Now get the fuck out my way bitch and get dressed. We're goin' out tonight. We're gon' get our party on."

Chi Chi shook her head. "It's too late." The tone in her voice made him take a closer look at her. She was holding something in her hand. Upon closer examination he saw that it was a .38 snug nose revolver.

"What the fuck you doing? Put that away. Are you crazy?" he asked.

"Hell yeah I'm crazy, nigga. Did you forget that? You shouldna put your hands on me, BJ."

He lunged forward, trying to knock the gun out of her hand. It went off once, then twice more, and BJ found himself falling backward, clutching his stomach. Glancing down he saw his shirt soaked in blood.

"Bitch, you shot me," he uttered in shock.

She shot him twice more, spinning him around as he tried to get away. He felt himself sliding downward to the floor. He lay there gasping for breath, eyes wide-open, staring at Chi Chi.

She walked up to him and aimed the gun at his head and pulled the trigger but nothing happened. The gun was empty.

"Call 911," he whispered. "If you call now I can still make it, baby. I know you didn't mean to shoot me."

Ignoring him, Chi Chi turned away and went outside and sat on the porch in one of the rocking chairs.

237

Having heard the shots, their next-door neighbor called the police. Fifteen minutes later a blue and white squad car arrived and found Chi Chi still sitting on the porch with her head between her legs. She was rocking back and forth humming, "Hush little baby, don't say a word. Mama gon' buy you a mockin' bird. And if that mockin' bird don't sing, Mama gon' buy you a diamond ring and if that diamond ring don't shi...."

"Just take it easy, ma'am," said an officer who approached her and gently took the gun out of her hand. "How many people are in the house, ma'am?"

By this time, a crowd of nosy people had gathered out in front of the house trying to see what was going on.

The first officer stood guard over Chi Chi while the other one entered the house, gun in hand, eyes darting from side to side. The first sight to catch his eyes was BJ lying on the floor in front of the fireplace.

"George! I got a gunshot victim, man down, man down."

The officer slowly walked over to BJ, lifted his arm and checked for a pulse, nothing.

BJ was dead.

■■■■■■■■■■■■■■■■■■■■■■■■■■■■■■■■■■■■■■■■■■■■■■■■■■■■■■

**M**cQueen was furious.

"Whadda ya mean you can't find him?" he questioned sharply. The four uniformed cops standing around his desk gave him a sheepish look. "I don't care if you have to go door-to-door; I want Thaddeus Jones found, arrested, and brought to my office within the next twenty-four hours!" McQueen shouted. "Otherwise, there's going to be some heads rolling around here. Now get to work!"

The four officers bumped into each other as they scrambled to clear the room. At that moment they wanted to be as far away from McQueen as possible. If they didn't find Thaddeus Jones, it would be someone's ass, and no one wanted it to be theirs.

One hour later, blue and white police cars flooded the streets of Detroit searching for the fugitive. Thad's mug shot was being flashed across the television screen every hour on the hour as one of the biggest manhunts in Detroit's history rapidly unfolded. Jasmine, her mind in a blind panic, gathered Lil' Thad and went to her mother's house to lay low until the heat blew over.

"Mama, why are the police lookin' for Dad?" Lil Thad asked. "Did he do somethin' wrong?"

Jasmine looked at her son. She simply said, "It's in the hands of God. Now go on and play, son."

"But I don't wanna play wit' those kids. I want my daddy!"

Jasmine looked down at him and knew she was looking at little Thaddeus Demon Jones, Jr. All the time and effort she was putting in to make sure her son didn't turn out like his father now appeared to be a waste of time and energy. It certainly didn't help when the police showed up at their door with an arrest warrant for Thad. He was charged with running a criminal enterprise and violations of the RICO Act. The white officers stormed through their home looking for Thad and Lil Thad suddenly became hysterical, demanding that they leave his house and leave his father alone.

"Do white people think they're God?" he asked his mother out of no where. Jasmine had no answer for her son.

239

# CHAPTERFORTY-TWO

The rain fell relentlessly from the bluish black sky, chasing away the night insects along with the dirt and grime covering the nearly deserted city streets. Taking the backstreets, Thad drove in silence, observing everything and everybody. Every time a car pulled beside him, he glanced away, afraid he'd be recognized. Dressed in a dark blue windbreaker and a black tracksuit, he was ready, ready for whatever came his way.

He pulled over to a pay phone on a lonely side street and called Winky.

"Hey man, what's happening?" Winky asked.

"Man, shit is crazy right now. I can't sleep, can't eat, I'm fucked up."

"Hey, listen, if you want your shit, you need to come get it now. I'm getting the fuck outta here, man. I think I'ma go on over to Canada and chill out till this shit dies down. If you know what I know, you'll get the fuck outta town too."

Thad listened real closely to Winky. He couldn't be trusted, no one could at that point. *What the fuck am I going to do? Damn, I wish I had never given this nigga my dough to hold for me. Fuck!*

"Where you at now?" Thad asked.

"Where do you think? At the crib. I'll wait 'til you show. Don't be too long, my nigga."

"I'll check ya out in about fifteen minutes," Thad replied, knowing he was taking a big risk. Winky couldn't be trusted. Especially now that the organization was in shambles and everybody seemed to be going for themselves, snatching and grabbing what little they could. But as things stood, Thad really didn't have much of a choice. He had given Winky ten grand to hold for him a week earlier and now that he was on the run, he needed it. He patted the .45 beneath his windbreaker reassuringly and resolved that Winky would be the first to die if he was up to some bullshit. Then he remembered Melvin and how they tricked him into swalling the balloon full of poison when they were locked down. *What if Winky's got revenge on his mind. Yeah, anything could go down, this guy could definitely be a set up.*

As Thad pulled up in front of Winky's pad, he parked at the curb and decided to keep the engine running. He didn't plan on being inside any longer than what was necessary. Checking to make sure his bulletproof vest was in place, he removed the .45 from under his jacket and got out of the car. Walking up to the gated front door, he knocked and waited as he heard footsteps on the other side. Suddenly Winky opened the door and the two stood toe to toe.

"C'mon in, nigga," he greeted. "You got the whole city on fire. Hurry up and get what you came for so I can split." Opening the door, he stood to the side so that Thad could squeeze by him. As Thad moved inside, Winky saw he was strapped.

"Damn, nigga, you got the guns out on me and shit,"

As soon as he said that, Thad realized he had walked into a trap. Out the corner of his eye he saw Winky diving toward the floor as the staccato sound of automatic gunfire erupted all around him. Plain clothes and uniformed officers had been planted inside the house and were firing their guns at him. Thad was hit so many times he was knocked backwards and out the door. He felt himself falling and continued to return fire, hoping with all his heart that he had hit Winky with his first shot.

The next thing Thad remembered was staring up at the black sky, lying flat on his back unable to move.

Miraculously, he managed to turn over on his stomach and drag himself down the steps. He was in a lot of pain despite his body armor. He realized that some of the hot lead must have penetrated his vest. He could feel the warm blood dripping down his leg and he could feel the shots he had taken in his legs. Still, he managed to make it to the front gate where he collapsed, gasping for breath.

Appearing in the doorway, several officers followed him with their guns drawn on his fallen form. None of them could believe he had made it that far.

"Drop your weapon!" McQueen shouted. He had made it his business to be among the arresting officers. He wanted to see the look in Thad's eyes when the handcuffs were clamped around his wrists.

Thad was in pain and had trouble breathing, but ignored the order, and pointed his gun right between McQueen's eyes. Before he'd ever fire his weapon, raising it would be the last thing he'd ever do in this lifetime. Eight armed officers opened fire from all different angles, this time killing him as bullet after bullet penetrated his skull.

"That was one crazy nigger," said one of the white officers standing around Thad's body.

Gazing down, all McQueen saw was another dead black man. *That could be my son lying there*, he thought sullenly. Suddenly he was tired of the whole scene, the killings, the stink of dead bodies, and the faceless mothers crying over a murdered son or husband.

"I've told you before to watch your mouth, Dombroski," McQueen barked at the white officer who had made the remark. "How would you like to be back on the block with those same crazy niggers? It could be arranged fairly easy. I got you off the street; I can put you back there again. And don't you forget it."

The white officer's face turned red.

"Sir, I sincerely apologize. I didn't mean anything negative. I was just using the word like the rappers, sir."

"You really must think I'm Willie Lump Lump!" he said

out loud, "Don't play on my intelligence." Turning to the other officers standing around gawking over their fresh kill, he said harshly, "Call the coroner. Have him bring a body bag. The rest of you clean up this mess and make sure you preserve the scene."

Inside the house writhing on the bare floor, Winky bitched and moaned and could be heard outside by the officers and McQueen.

"Call the muthafuckin' ambulance! That muthafucka shot me in the ass. Sho' me some love goddamnit! You can at least act like you appreciate me helping you that crazy nigga off the streets!"

This burly black detective who despised informers, yet needed them, looked contemptuously at Winky and said sarcastically, "Sounds more to me like you were trying to get him off your Judas ass."

Winky lay there seething, imagining what he was going to do with the reward money.

■■■■■■■■■■■■■■■■■■■■■■■■■■■■■■■■■■■■■■■■■■■■■■■■■■■■■■■■■

**A**ccompanied by Lil Thad and Kamal, Jasmine entered the Kabaz Black Jewel Cultural Center and found three empty seats near the back of the otherwise crowded room where the Melanics held their weekly meetings. Desperate, Jasmine was determined to keep the streets from devouring Lil' Thad and Kamal like they did her late husband. The Melanics were her last hope.

It was a warm, humid evening made even worse by the sweating bodies packed tightly inside the aged building. Several overhead fans twirled rapidly, but they were only circulating hot air. Standing in front of the gathered crowd, Kaleem held a microphone in his right hand as he spoke from the heart. Every now and then he dabbed at his brown face with a white handkerchief. Standing to his immediate left decked out in traditional Melanic gear, Lil' Greg looked sharp and handsome in his black uniform, black combat boots, and black beret. Once he had been inducted into the fold, Kaleem personally requested that he be made a part of his personal security team. To Kaleem's right was the ever faithful Kambui, the man Kaleem trusted with his life. They had been together through thick and thin and never came up short. Kambui was a good man to have by your side when shit got thick. Trained in the martial arts and an expert marksman, Kambui stood ready to kill on demand if it was for the struggle.

"One week ago," Kaleem was saying, "This city erupted in open warfare between black gangstas and the Italian mob. The Italians want to continue running illegal activities in the black communities and now blacks have challenged them for control. They feel the blacks should shape and control their own destiny, whether it be good or bad. I'm not going to stand judgment one way or another, but I do feel there has to be a better way for us to come up!"

"Amen, son!" said an elderly black man.

Kaleem continued. "Even when blacks engage in criminal pursuits, all they seem to do with the money is show off. Then once they're broke, the feds move in and lock them up for the rest of their lives. So their offspring are faced with the same bleak future their parents were confronted with and the cycle continues. It's time to get off this vicious merry-go-round. It's time to create a lasting legacy for our children and for those coming behind us.

"In Jewish communities, as soon as a boy turns thirteen he has a bar mitzvah. This is a ceremony where he is taken before his family and community members and given financial support to get started in a business of his own choosing. He is also blessed with moral and spiritual guidance so that he can develop a political agenda commensurate with that of his own people. The entire community shares in the responsibility of preparing him for the world. Our ancestors in Africa had a saying for this. Who knows what it is?"

One heavyset woman sweating profusely, fanned herself and struggled to get to her feet.

244

"I know what it is," she said.

"Go 'head and tell us then," Kaleem quietly urged her.

Looking around the room, the woman cleared her throat.

"It takes an entire village to raise a child," the lady said before sitting back down.

"Thank you, sista. We have got to start protecting ourselves and each other far better than what we have been doing, because if we don't, we're gonna look around and ain't nobody gonna be left."

# CHAPTER FORTY-THREE

**E**ighteen months later.

The black couple, along with their two-year-old toddler who was busy building a sand castle, laid back on the sandy beach soaking up the warm Caribbean sun. The temperature was a balmy eighty-five degrees and the sky over head was clear blue, tinged with big, fluffy, white, clouds that looked like cotton candy. The beautiful Atlantic Ocean stretched for miles around as far as the eyes could see.

The woman, wearing a red string bikini, shielded her eyes from the blazing sun rays with a pair of Gucci shades and a wide, big-brimmed straw hat. Lying next to her with his eyes glued on his son, the black man rose to a sitting position and glanced lovingly at his companion.

"Would you like something from the concession stand?" he asked. "I've got to stretch my legs before they cramp up on me." With the help of a walking cane, he rose awkwardly to his feet and steadied himself.

The woman looked up at him with a smile on her lips. "No, darling, I'm fine. You be careful and hurry back."

He smiled back and began walking over to the bar with a pronounced limp. Old bullet wounds marred his upper body, but other than that, and the fact that he walked with a limp, he couldn't have felt better.

As Larry limped across the warm sand, he inhaled the tropical air and thought about how lucky he was to be alive. After spending months in the hospital fighting for his life, he went into rehabilitation and there rapidly recovered. He had been shot multiple times and no one believed he'd survive, let alone every walk again.

He looked out at the clear blue crystal water. *What a wonderful life,* he thought to himself. He never in a million years thought he'd be here, let alone looking at the bluest water he'd ever seen in his life. *You guys should be here to see this.* He couldn't help but to think of Thad and BJ. Who the hell would have thought Chi Chi would have murdered BJ. *She'll be locked up in that crazy asylum for the rest of her life?* But, Thad, boy oh boy, he was something else. *I always knew you'd go out in a blaze, my brotha.*

Knowing that the Mafia would still be out for revenge if they found out he had survived their assassination attempt, Larry decided to fake his own death and leave the states for a few years. The only other person besides his doctor who knew he was still alive was Kaleem, and Larry wasn't worried about him revealing his secret. As he glanced back at Angela, she smiled again and blew him a kiss. Larry could only thank God and good fortune for the happiness he had found. He had faked his death and somehow managed to escape the vengeance of his enemies.

"Hey, old head."

"What's happening, young blood?"

"Mak'n, just mak'n."

Larry thought for a slight second, *Pac,* and then turned back around to find that the young man had seemingly disappeared into thin air. *I know that wasn't him... can't be...naw...no way.* He turned back around to the bartender.

"Pina Colada."

Along the sandy beach of the island of St. Croix, Larry could hear the faint sounds of the island music and a soft voice singing in the island breeze.

*Yeah, I'm mak'n, just mak'n.*

*The End*

# IN STORES NOW

TRUE TO THE GAME

B-MORE CAREFUL

THE ADVENTURES OF GHETTO SAM

DUTCH I

TRIANGLE OF SINS

TELL ME YOUR NAME

DUTCH II

DEADLY REIGNS

RECTANGLE OF SINS

DOUBLE DOSE

DEADLY REIGNS II

ANGEL

*Teri Woods Publishing Presents, Predators*

# COMING SOON

## DEADLY REIGNS III

## CIRCLE OF SINS

## FOR GANGSTERS ONLY

## SECRETS

## CONFIDENTIAL INFORMANTS

## ANGEL II

## ORDER FORM
### TERI WOODS PUBLISHING
P.O. BOX 20069
NEW YORK, NY 10001
(212) 252-8445
www.teriwoodspublishing.com

| | |
|---|---|
| PREDATORS | $14.95 |
| Shipping /Handling (Via U.S. Priority Mail) | 4.05 |
| TOTAL | $19.00 |

## PURCHASER INFORMATION

Name: _____

Reg. #: _____
(Applies if incarcerated)

Address:_____

_____

City: _____ State: ____

Zip Code: _____

## HOW MANY BOOKS?   _____

For orders being shipped directly to inmates the costs are as follows:

| | |
|---|---|
| PREDATORS : | $ 11.21 |
| Shipping and Handling: | $ 4.05 |
| TOTAL : | $15.26 |

True to the Game, B-More Careful, Dutch, Deadly Reigns, Dutch II, Triangle of Sins, Rectangle of Sins, Tell Me Your Name, The Adventures of Ghetto Sam, Double Dose, Deadly Reigns II, Angel, and Predators are all the same price.

**ORDER FORM**
TERI WOODS PUBLISHING
P.O. BOX 20069
NEW YORK, NY 10001
(212) 252-8445
www.teriwoodspublishing.com

| | |
|---|---|
| PREDATORS | $14.95 |
| | |
| Shipping /Handling (Via U.S. Priority Mail) | 4.05 |
| TOTAL | $19.00 |

**PURCHASER INFORMATION**

Name: _____

Reg. #: _____
(Applies if incarcerated)

Address:_____

_____

City: _____ State: ___

Zip Code: _____

**HOW MANY BOOKS?** _____

For orders being shipped directly to inmates the costs are as follows:

| | |
|---|---|
| PREDATORS : | $ 11.21 |
| Shipping and Handling: | $ 4.05 |
| TOTAL : | $15.26 |

True to the Game, B-More Careful, Dutch, Deadly Reigns, Dutch II, Triangle of Sins, Rectangle of Sins, Tell Me Your Name, The Adventures of Ghetto Sam, Double Dose, Deadly Reigns II, Angel, and Predators are all the same price.

**ORDER FORM**
TERI WOODS PUBLISHING
P.O. BOX 20069
NEW YORK, NY 10001
(212) 252-8445
www.teriwoodspublishing.com

| | |
|---|---|
| PREDATORS | $14.95 |
| Shipping /Handling (Via U.S. Priority Mail) | 4.05 |
| TOTAL | $19.00 |

## PURCHASER INFORMATION

Name: _____

Reg. #: _____
(Applies if incarcerated)

Address:_____

_____

City: _____ State: ___

Zip Code: _____

**HOW MANY BOOKS?** _____

For orders being shipped directly to inmates the costs are as follows:

| | |
|---|---|
| PREDATORS : | $ 11.21 |
| Shipping and Handling: | $ 4.05 |
| TOTAL : | $15.26 |

True to the Game, B-More Careful, Dutch, Deadly Reigns, Dutch II, Triangle of Sins, Rectangle of Sins, Tell Me Your Name, The Adventures of Ghetto Sam, Double Dose, Deadly Reigns II, Angel, and Predators are all the same price.

**ORDER FORM**
TERI WOODS PUBLISHING
P.O. BOX 20069
NEW YORK, NY 10001
(212) 252-8445
www.teriwoodspublishing.com

| | |
|---|---|
| PREDATORS | $14.95 |
| | |
| Shipping /Handling (Via U.S. Priority Mail) | 4.05 |
| TOTAL | $19.00 |

## PURCHASER INFORMATION

Name: _____

Reg. #: _____
(Applies if incarcerated)

Address:_____

_____

City: _____ State: ___

Zip Code: _____

**HOW MANY BOOKS?** _____

For orders being shipped directly to inmates the costs are as follows:

| | |
|---|---|
| PREDATORS : | $ 11.21 |
| Shipping and Handling: | $ 4.05 |
| TOTAL : | $15.26 |

True to the Game, B-More Careful, Dutch, Deadly Reigns, Dutch II, Triangle of Sins, Rectangle of Sins, Tell Me Your Name, The Adventures of Ghetto Sam, Double Dose, Deadly Reigns II, Angel, and Predators are all the same price.